Choosing Sophie

By Leslie Carroll

Choosing Sophie

Leslie Carroll

AVON

An Imprint of HarperCollins*Publishers*

CHOOSING SOPHIE. Copyright © 2008 by Leslie Carroll. All rights reserved. Printed in the United States of America. No part of this book may be used or reproduced in any manner whatsoever without written permission except in the case of brief quotations embodied in critical articles and reviews. For information address HarperCollins Publishers, 10 East 53rd Street, New York, NY 10022.

HarperCollins books may be purchased for educational, business, or sales promotional use. For information please write: Special Markets Department, HarperCollins Publishers, 10 East 53rd Street, New York, NY 10022.

FIRST EDITION

Designed by Elizabeth M. Glover

Library of Congress Cataloging-in-Publication Data
Carroll, Leslie Sara.
    Choosing Sophie / Leslie Carroll. — 1st ed.
       p. cm.
    ISBN 978-0-06-087137-6 (pbk.)
    I. Title.
PS3603.A77458C48   2008
813'.6—dc22   2007034818

08 09 10 11 12 OV/RRD 10 9 8 7 6 5 4 3 2 1

For my late uncle Adam Carroll,

who always promised to take me to a Mets game and never got to do it.

"My knight in shining armor," I purred gratefully, as Tom stepped onto the balcony and placed a steaming mug of coffee in front of me. "Where would I be without my morning fix?" I teased, reaching up to run my hand through his hair.

"The coffee or the *New York Times* online?" Tom leaned over and pressed his lips to the top of my head. "*Mmmm* . . . you smell good. Must be all this Colorado sunshine." He kneaded my shoulders and took a deep breath, filling his lungs with the sweet mountain air. "I can never get enough of this," he said, gesturing to the wide world beyond as if he owned the place. "If this is 'God's country,' as they say, it's almost enough to make a man a true believer."

I kissed his hand and rested my cheek against it. The view of the mountains was indeed spectacular. In Tom's chalet-style house I felt like a modern-day Heidi. "The longer I stay here, the greater the urge to yodel," I kidded, turning back to my laptop.

"What could be better to look at than *this*?" Tom glanced over my shoulder at the laptop and frowned at the screen. "A garbage strike, another rapper shot in front of a nightclub, re-cord-breaking heat—this is as close as I ever want to be to your precious New York City." He shuddered dramatically, faking a visceral adverse reaction that he knows always gets my goat.

"Hey—no picking on my hometown!" I squeezed Tom's hand. "I thought you didn't mind it so much when you lived there."

"As a grad student. With an exit visa. Two years of business school and I knew I was coming back to the slopes. There are no decent places to ski in your state."

I took a sip of coffee, savoring its warmth as it coursed down my throat. Tom had brewed it just the way I like it—strong enough to stand a spoon in. "Oh, c'mon!" I gently bit his knuckles.

"Ow!"

"I told you not to insult New York. We've got great mountains! What about the Catskills? And the Adirondacks? This coffee is perfect, by the way." I tilted my head to beam at him. "So, I guess I'll keep you, after all." I twisted my engagement ring with my left thumb so the diamond would catch the morning light. "Yeah," I sighed happily. "You're a keeper. Even if you dis my city all the time. After all, it's so hard to get a great cup of coffee these days."

Tom took my left hand in his. His skin felt warm against mine. "The *Catskills*? Those aren't mountains. Those are *hills. These*," he said, gesturing expansively toward the incomparable vista of the jagged Ten Mile Range, "*these* are mountains."

The sky was impossibly blue. "Della Robbia blue" as Blanche Dubois would have called it. A color found in early Renaissance ceramics and the Colorado sky. Another perfect day in Paradise.

I turned back to the computer screen, where a *Times* headline announced the indictment of a city council member. "You don't really hate New York that much, do you?" For some reason, I found Tom's over-the-top distaste for the city more amusing than annoying; it was writ so large that I found it hard to take seriously.

"It's a nice place to visit."

"What about as a place to get married?"

"I thought we were going to get married here?"

"But all my friends are in New York. Except for your family, I don't know anyone here but you." And we'd only known each other since February. I'd treated myself to a ski vacation over Presidents' Day weekend, or whatever the calendars call it these days. Tom was conducting a clinic at Breckenridge that was really designed to introduce potential customers to Elliott and Sons equipment—the company that's been owned by his family for four generations. Nowadays, there are Elliott daughters in the business, but the name remains a Victorian-era throwback. By the end of the holiday weekend Elliott and Sons had taken my credit card number in exchange for a state-of-the-art pair of boots and bindings, new skis, and poles—and I'd given my heart to the CEO.

Sometimes you just know.

"We'll fly your guests out here, Ollie," Tom offered.

"You're not *that* rich!" I teased. "Nor am I. And you know I hate it when you call me Ollie. Shades of a dragon puppet from a long-gone TV show. Besides, no one else does."

"Which is why *I* do. I figure the husband-to-be ought to get some special privileges or something."

I placed his hand on my breast. "You already do."

"Yay!" Tom's jubilant exclamation came out like a soft peal of music. He grinned. "I'm so glad you want to be Mrs. Tom Elliott of Breckenridge, Colorado."

"*Mmm* . . . aren't *you* an old-fashioned guy?" I nuzzled his knuckles. "Actually, I'll still be Ms. Olivia deMarley, late of New York for most of her years, and Las Vegas for several, by way of Massachusetts for three of them." I guided his hand over the mountainous landscape of my chest. "But I'm still looking forward to marrying Number One Son of Elliott and Sons ski company and manufactorium."

"Is *manufactorium* a word?"

"It is now." I laughed and craned my neck to meet Tom's lips as he bent toward me. "You're the only man I've ever even *considered* marrying."

Come to think of it, I haven't had too many offers over the years. Burlesque dancers don't tend to be the kind of women a guy brings home to meet his mother. They hear what you do and figure it means you're a stripper. I've spent half a lifetime explaining the difference in order to justify my existence to people who don't deserve the disclaimer. But the truth is that most of my relationships tanked long before the subject of marriage (doing it, as opposed to avoiding it) was on the table.

"The only man?" Tom asked. "Really?" I nodded my head. "You never told me that before." He lifted my mane of hair and kissed the back of my neck. He could do that for days and I'd never tire of it. "The only one, huh? And why is that?"

"Skiing for compliments, I see." I turned toward him and snaked my hand between the buttons of his shirt, my fingers finding a slightly raised scar—the result of an unfortunate collision with a tree root—as I caressed his abdomen. "Because I love your crooked smile. And your curly hair. And the fact that you never curse, where I sound like a fucking stevedore sometimes. And because you give me earth-shattering orgasms, which I'd like to think is something I'll get to enjoy for the rest of my life. And because we totally trust each other and always have. But mostly. . . ? Because you make me laugh."

"Gee, I didn't know I was that funny looking." Tom went back inside the house and emerged a few moments later, shrugging on his knapsack. "All right, my love." He leaned down and kissed me fully on the lips. "I'm off to work."

"I can't wait to see you later," I murmured.

Almost absentmindedly I clicked on the link to the *Times* obits. "Give each of your sisters a hug for me. And tell Luke he still owes me five dollars from that Trivial Pursuit match we had last month."

"My brother's not in on Fridays. But if I see Dad, I'll tell him to make good on Number Two Son's losses."

I reached for Tom's hand and squeezed it affectionately. "Nah—I can't take money from Papa Bear." I glanced back at the computer screen and literally felt the color drain from my cheeks.

"Ollie, honey—are you okay?"

"Uh . . . no . . . actually . . . I don't think." My head felt as though someone had just unscrewed it and, untethered, it was floating skyward of its own accord, leaving my body a hollow, gaping, useless thing, like a lamp stripped of its bulb.

"It's a very strange feeling to discover that you're an orphan by reading about it on the obituary page," I muttered, the words tumbling out of my mouth into the mug of hot coffee, where they melted into the dark liquid.

I have a morbid habit of checking the *New York Times* obits online every morning; it's what comes of having been a professional dancer for several years and losing too many friends to disease.

And there it was in black-and-white, with a decades-old portrait in shades of gray. Tom stood behind me and read the headline: AUGUST DEMARLEY, SELF-MADE BILLIONAIRE, *82.* I found myself rooted to the chair, too stunned to move; Tom placed his arms around my shoulders and pressed my body against his midsection, holding me protectively. "Rats, Ollie. I'm so sorry."

Numb and tearless, I read the article. Deep inside, I'd hoped for a bit more illuminating detail. Like *August deMarley, self-made billionaire, stubborn bastard, and rotten, absentee father*. The obit spent a few paragraphs on how he built up his business, gobbling smaller competitors like Pac-Man. "It's really a terrible photo they used. It has to be thirty years old," I said quietly.

I hadn't seen my dad in over two decades, not since I decided to chuck my trust fund and become a dancer, a rich girl's rebel experiment in living like a "real" person. But of course I went a bit too far for Dad's taste. With Dad, everything was a double-edged sword. In accordance with his no-handouts philosophy, I was expected to obtain my college tuition the old-fashioned way: I had to earn it—from freshman orientation week all the way through to commencement. And once I'd achieved that, I'd gain access to the trust.

But one Saturday, for a lark, I took a special master class offered through the dance department with the burlesque queen Sherry Britton, and I was hooked. I bought my own boa and never looked back.

Putting myself through Harvard by performing in pasties, however artistic, wasn't exactly what he'd hoped I had in mind as an after-school job. I'm sure he would have been happier if I'd cleaned toilets or flipped patties at Bartley's Burger Cottage.

So, August deMarley vowed that if his daughter was willing to cavalierly shed an Ivy League education to fan dance and twirl her tassels, not only would she never get another penny from him, but she'd never hear from him again. And he'd stuck to it, the bastard. The irony is not lost on me that I never gained his trust.

He even knew why I'd dropped out. And evidently didn't care.

Before I turned twenty-one, I ripped the Virginia Woolf and

Superman II posters from my dorm room walls, said ciao to my three suite mates, and headed for Las Vegas, where you could still make a damn fine living in burlesque; where some folks understood that there was more titillation and allure in what was artfully kept *on*. By that time, my mom was gone, too—long gone; but in her case there was no hope of reconciliation unless you held a séance. Mom was the only one who had a way with old Augie; she could extend a Shalimar-scented arm, and with a manicured hand that always had the magic touch (when it wasn't gripping a cigarette holder), gently reach for Dad's knee, or sleeve, as if to say "Stop. Reconsider." Lung cancer took Lilith deMarley just when I needed her most, just when my legs seemed to grow six inches longer overnight, hurtling me toward a precipitous six feet—ever been four inches taller than your prom date?—and my burgeoning bosom, horribly out of control—ever been four inches taller than your prom date?—began to resemble a grade B sci-fi movie: the boobs that ate the Bronx. Riverdale, to be more geographically specific. To be most precise, the private tree-lined enclave of sprawling Arts and Crafts homes known as Fieldston.

Augie deMarley was the quintessence of the up-by-the-bootstraps businessman. If you've poured a can of deMarley High-Performance Ultra-Viscosity Motor Oil into your engine, you've put oleo on our family table. I was in kindergarten the first time I heard the phrase "I don't raise spoiled brats." Then came the "learn-the-value-of-a-dollar" speech that I'd been compelled to listen to so often I could recite it in my sleep. And once or twice I probably did.

I read on as Tom stood by, a silent presence ready to offer moral support, Kleenex, and as many hugs as I needed. "'*A dozen years ago, he indulged a childhood fantasy by purchasing a controlling interest in the Bronx Cheers, a minor league baseball franchise, building a brand-new stadium, deMarley Field, on City Island. The Cheers became deMarley's greatest love in his golden years, although, to his dismay, it always performed near the bottom of the pack, never even making it to the playoffs. Of the owner's zeal, manager Dusty Fredericks recalled, "The boss used to yell at the kids a lot, but at the end of the season, no matter how lousy we played, he would come into the clubhouse with a grin on his face like it was the Fourth of July. 'Just wait'll next year!' he always said, like he was revving up the troops. He could be a real pain in the patoot, but he loved that team like they were his own kids.""*

I tried to chuckle, but it stuck in my throat. *Like his own kids,* I thought. *Yeah, right. If this Dusty guy only knew.* The obit ended with the sentence, *deMarley is survived by his only child, Olivia, a former burlesque queen who performed nationally as Venus deMarley. Ms. deMarley currently resides in Manhattan.*

I guess he had no idea that, having just gotten engaged to the CEO of a Colorado-based sports equipment company, I'd put my Manhattan duplex on the market and winged it out West. But Dad had evidently known where I'd been for the past several years. Or someone close to him did, because my number is unlisted. And I'm not sure how I feel about that. Every year I sent him cards for his birthday and Christmas . . . even Father's Day . . . and they always came back stamped RETURN TO SENDER. So if the bastard knew where to reach me, and never did anything about it . . . son of a bitch! With a spiteful click of my mouse, I minimized the obit on my computer screen.

Then I cried all over my keyboard.

"I bet if someone were to hold a symposium on a mountaintop in Montana for everyone who spent their lives trying to please their parents and failing at it miserably, there'd be no one left in the rest of the contiguous forty-eight states, and an awfully deep crater in Big Sky Country. I've always admired your closeness to your family," I sniffled.

Tom knelt beside my chair and dabbed at my tears with one of the navy bandannas he uses for a handkerchief. "Are you going east for the funeral?"

I took the bandanna and finished the job. "If there is one. I guess I'd better do some sleuthing and find out. I *should* go. It would feel wrong not to."

I jumped at the sound of a disembodied jangle.

"Your pocket is ringing," observed Tom.

I reached into the Navajo cardigan and answered the phone. Realizing I was in no shape to concentrate on memorizing anything, I waved to Tom for a notepad so I could jot down the information, while the caller—Dad's lawyer, Casper Gaines— did most of the talking. I held up my end of the conversation by managing a few subdued "*uh-hunh*s" and "*mm-hmm*s."

"There's not going to be a formal funeral," I said, flipping the phone closed. "Just a memorial service on Sunday."

"Do you want me to go with you?" Tom softly stroked my hair. "I'll even buy a suit."

I shook my head and glanced up at him. "Papa Bear would be very disappointed if you were to miss the annual staff retreat. Besides, considering the way things were—or weren't—between old Augie and me, I think it's probably better anyway if I go it alone. It's only for a weekend. I'll catch a flight back on Monday."

He was trying very hard not to look relieved. "You sure?"

"Yeah," I sighed, still unable to muster a feeling I would characterize as grief. "And you're kind and sweet to want to be there for me—with me." I managed a weak smile. "But given the way you feel about New York, you'd probably have an even more miserable time than I will."

Within five minutes I'd booked a flight.

Tom perched on the edge of our bed as silent as a cat and watched me struggle with what to pack. If the little black dress and Ferragamo pumps I'd brought out to Colorado wouldn't cut it, somewhere in my closet in New York was a suitable outfit. It had been a while since I needed to don a dress and heels. I hadn't worn much more than jeans and boots in the six weeks I'd been living with Tom in Breckenridge.

Tom drove me to the airport in the (IMO) unnecessarily capacious Expedition I always refer to as his Ford Mastodon. "I'll miss you," he whispered in between good-bye kisses.

"I'll miss you, too. Sorry I made you late to work," I murmured, tasting his post-breakfast Snickers bar on his tongue. I patted my purse. "I'll just have to make do with cuddling your photo for the next couple of nights." I glanced toward the security checkpoint. The TSA attendant was glaring at me with an air of exasperated impatience. I surmised that she didn't have a sensitive and handsome fiancé to comfort her on the demise of her dear old dad. "I guess I should go, sweetheart. Enjoy the retreat. Don't eat too much junk food."

We kissed once more. Tom cradled my face in his hands. I could see my reflection in his hazel eyes. "And you enjoy the—well, no, I suppose that would be wildly inappropriate. See you Monday, my love."

I drank in his body—tall and fit in his fleece jacket, the boyish blue backpack, the curls that flopped over his forehead and refused all attempts at taming, his sweet, off-center smile—and mouthed the words "I can't wait."

✐

"It's a big day, Marty. At least you could dress like a man." Marty deMarley's wife, Linda, was smoothing a pair of twenty-eight-dollar pantyhose over her freshly waxed legs. "Take off the stupid jersey and put on a suit, for Chrissakes. The lightweight navy pinstripe. At least you look like a grown-up in that one."

Who is this harpie and why did I marry her? Marty wondered, yanking the Bronx Cheers shirt over his head and folding it reverentially before placing it in a dresser drawer. "I thought," he said, trying very hard to pitch his voice in a tone that his wife wouldn't consider whining, "that I would honor Uncle Augie by wearing the team jersey."

Linda emitted an exasperated sigh. "Not to a funeral. Have a little respect."

"I thought that's what I *was* having."

She gave a little snort. It was a personal habit of hers that Marty detested. In fact it set his teeth on edge. "No class, Marty. No class," Linda scolded, without a trace of irony. "You can have all the money in the universe, and still have no class." Marty was a wealthy Chihuahua of a bond trader, who more than anything had wanted to become an athlete. But given a naturally scrawny build that all the Wheaties in the world couldn't improve upon, and his complete lack of hand-eye coordination, Marty couldn't have followed his bliss with a divining rod. And once upon a time, about ten years ago, he'd considered himself very lucky to have married the tanned, toned, highlighted and lipo'ed Linda Buddinsky. She had all the elegance of a racehorse, was always the best-dressed among their set, and took care of her body the way their gardener Emmanuel tended to their prize orchid collection.

What Linda got out of it was the opportunity to change her surname to something that screamed WASP breeding, a generous allowance, and a man she could push around like a wheelbarrow. Neither one of them had wanted children, which suited Linda just fine because half the time Marty behaved like more than enough of a child for her to handle.

"You never know who you're liable to run into," Linda continued to carp. "Your uncle Augie was quite the philanthropist.

The mayor could be there . . . Donald Trump. The press. People know about this event; it's been in the papers. You need to prepare yourself for the spotlight."

"For God's sake, Linda, it's a *memorial service*, not a ticker-tape parade." Marty took the freshly pressed blue suit from his closet. He was still upset about his wife's nixing of the baseball jersey. "I have to dress like this every day," he muttered.

Linda chose to ignore him, turning her attention to Rosebud, her Yorkie, which she carried everywhere in her monogrammed Prada bowling bag. "*You* never give me any trouble," she cooed to the dog's liquid brown eyes and wet nose. She opened a drawer filled with carefully organized accessories and removed a black satin bow, murmuring inanities as she affixed it to a topknot of hair.

"You . . . you aren't bringing her to Campbell's . . . are you?" Marty asked his wife.

Linda's expression managed to blend both pout and sneer. "She calms my nerves. You know how I get at funerals."

"It's not a funeral, it's a memorial. There won't be a body. Just a bunch of people making nice speeches," Marty insisted. "And under the circumstances, I think it's inappropriate to bring the dog. Can't you leave her home just once?"

"She has a delicate constitution. You know she throws up when we leave her alone for too long." Linda meticulously folded her black pashmina, and used it to carefully line the inside of the Prada bag. "Are *you* going to clean up the mess?"

⚾

The limos lined Madison Avenue outside the Frank E. Campbell funeral home. Frankly, I was surprised that so many people had turned out to say good-bye to Augie deMiser. I didn't know any of them, though the folks from the Bronx Cheers organization wore lapel pins with the team logo, a biplane dropping a baseball. I always hated the logo, but I guess someone thought it was clever, since the image suggests the venerated New York Yankees—affectionately known as the Bronx Bombers. Actually, it was pretty funny when the players burst into "Take Me Out to the Ball Game" and tossed boxes of Cracker Jack to the mourners sitting oh-so-respectfully amid Campbell's staid, faux¯eighteenth-century decor.

"You ever wonder why they're called Cracker Jacks when there's no crackers in them?" whispered my cousin Marty to his wife, Linda.

"No, Marty," I haven't," she hissed back. "Now look respectful."

There were several "civilians" in attendance, including a tall young woman who nervously played with her brown ponytail and hung by the wall looking distinctly uncomfortable. After a second glance at her, I briefly wondered whether Dad had committed a little indiscretion somewhere along the way, but I wasn't in the mood to chitchat, let alone condole, so I didn't approach her—or anyone else for that matter. I was there out of obligation, not out of love—or even curiosity.

The *Times* obit had mentioned Dad's philanthropy, so I suppose a lot of beneficiaries decided to pay their last respects. In our household, charity didn't begin at home, so it pleased me that at least someone—several someones by my head count of dark suits—had derived more than a clean engine from de-Marley Motor Oil.

"Were you invited to the distribution, Livy?" Linda de-Marley, my cousin-in-law, whispered jealously. We'd never particularly seen eye to eye, especially since hers tended to be right at my chest level. At forty-three, Linda was perfectly toned, though entirely lacking when it came to curves. My cousin Marty, however, had a bit of a beer gut, despite his resemblance otherwise to the ninety-pound weakling in the old

Charles Atlas ads. Linda always reminded me of a whip with a human face. Not just because of her too-rich-and-too-thinness, but because at any moment, she looked like she might crack and unleash a helluva sting.

The "distribution" meant the reading of Dad's will, and to my surprise, I had in fact been invited. Casper "Cap" Gaines, Dad's lawyer—whose nickname had been deliberately bestowed—had e-mailed me about the 2:00 p.m. postmemorial appointment in his office. I wondered what sort of a gathering it would turn out to be.

I'd expected to be no more than a spectator at that shindig, asked to attend out of courtesy, given that I was Dad's only child. So I tried not to express any astonishment when a black leather chair was pulled out for me in a most gentlemanly fashion by Cap Gaines. His conference table was about the size of a football field, dominating a multiwindowed room high over Wall Street with an enviable three-way vista. The August heat visibly shimmered off the rivers. Even through the summer haze, you could see all the way east to Coney Island, catch the Statue of Liberty in mid-wave to the south, and glance north to glimpse the House that Ruth built. *These are* my *Rocky Mountains*, I thought, my lips curling into a faint smile, which I quickly suppressed by covering my mouth with the back of my hand. I slid into the chair and slipped off my slingbacks, hoping no one would notice. As it was, in my four-inch heels I'd towered over everyone at the memorial service. Though my height had been somewhat intimidating, truth told, it masked the incredible insecurity I'd felt—worried I'd seem such a phony—that after all these years The Daughter only showed up once her difficult dad was safely resting for all eternity in a brass urn.

There was my cousin Marty, who had changed into his Bronx Cheers shirt, wearing the custom-made number 0, which I found rather amusing, since it pretty much summed up my opinion of him.

My keenest memory of Marty is when he tried to feel me up outside the wood shed during a family reunion somewhere on Martha's Vineyard, back when we were teens. I wondered if he still had a crush on me.

As far as I know, Marty has no legal interest in the ball club, but plenty of it from a personal one. His eager expression had all the look of the heir-apparent about it. Linda sat beside him, in an elegant black ensemble dominated by a wide-brimmed hat better suited to Royal Ascot than a minor league ballpark. She flipped through the current issue of *Town and Country* as she waited for the proceedings to commence. Among the suits were Peter Argent and Dick Fernando, who introduced themselves as the limited partners of the Bronx Cheers, the Cheers' General Manager, Barry Weed—whom I immediately nicknamed "Mr. Slick"—and the team's manager, Dusty Fredericks. Dusty had scrounged up a herringbone tweed sport-coat and a knitted tie for the occasion. Clearly, he was a guy who didn't own much in the way of civvies. Though the conference room was chilly as an igloo, he must have sweltered out on the pavement. Baseball players, managers, and coaches look so different to me when they're in mufti—almost like grown-ups.

The tall young woman I'd spotted at the funeral home was there, too. I noticed she'd taken a chair on the sidelines.

"Well, I think we all know what we're here for," Cap Gaines said. His voice had a certain heaviness to it, and his eyelids were red-rimmed and swollen. Had he been crying for my father? All these people seemed to know a different man than I had. They murmured among themselves and didn't bother to speak to me, though I caught some sidelong glances, mostly at my chest or my bare legs or my mane of flame-red hair. I'd left it long and loose, since the tasteful chignon-thing wasn't my style, anyway, and it had seemed hypocritical to dress in deep mourning for a man who for years considered me dead to him; it was a part I wasn't suited to play.

Cousin Marty stopped glad-handing the Cheers investors when Linda tugged conspicuously on his team jersey.

We began with another moment of silence for my dad, led by Cap, and then the lawyer got down to business.

"Now, in case any of you are operating under a misapprehension, this is theater this afternoon. What I mean by that is that this is an *informal* reading of August deMarley's will, after which time it will be offered for probate. In front of each of you is a Consent to Probate form, which I am requesting you to sign before you leave the room today."

There was a shifting in seats and a scratching of pens. The lawyer waited for everyone to return their undivided attention.

"Most of this is pretty straightforward," Cap said. "The bulk of his fortune goes to philanthropic bequests that don't concern any of you; furniture and personal effects donated to charity to raise additional funds for the Bronx Cheers community outreach programs." He waited for a reaction, and receiving nothing but grim-lipped silence, pressed on. "To his nephew, Martin deMarley and his wife Linda Buddinsky deMarley, he left the 1999 Leroy Neiman painting of Cheers center fielder Carlos Esquivel sliding into home plate. The artwork has been appraised at half a million dollars."

Linda looked smug. I could almost smell her gears grinding as she wondered what she could get for it at auction. She had as much interest in baseball as she had in a tailgate party at a NASCAR rally. Marty, on the other hand, looked disappointed. "That's it? I mean, that's all I get?"

Actually, he got more than that. He got a sharp elbow in the ribs from Linda. "*Shhsst!* Marty!"

"I'm not entirely sure what *we're* here for." Peter Argent glanced over at Dick Fernando, who nodded in agreement. Argent checked his watch. "I've got a 4:00 p.m. uptown."

"August deMarley's will is very specific about the future of the Bronx Cheers," Cap replied. "He loved the team more than anyone, but he was also fully aware that they'd been called the 'Jeers' more often than not in the past few seasons. Face it, guys, the team batting average has been well under the Mendoza line, and their fielding's been compared to Charlie Brown's skills on a good day."

Dusty Fredericks looked grimmer than anyone. I felt sorry for the guy. I know squat about managing a ball club, but maybe he was hamstrung by some executive decisions. I looked over at Dick and Peter, who appeared unfazed somehow by the attorney's reminder of how pathetically their team had been performing. You didn't have to be a total sports fanatic—just listen to a few games on TV—to know that a reference to the "Mendoza line," named for the legendarily lousy hitter Mario Mendoza, was not a compliment!

"Augie's final wishes were that some changes should be made." Now the suits squirmed visibly. "But his stipulation came with caveats." Everyone hung on Cap's words. As a trial attorney, Cap Gaines knew how to build the drama. "According to his will, August deMarley left the controlling interest of the Bronx Cheers solely to his only surviving issue, his daughter, Olivia—"

The collective gasp sounded like the deflating immolation of the *Hindenburg*.

"Provided she—and this is the exact wording of his will—'closes the circle.'"

The silence was deafening. After several stunned moments, I

said, "Pardon my French, but what the fuck does *that* mean?"

"It means your uncle Augie was a raving nut job, Marty!" Linda exclaimed.

"Venus deMarley—the stripper—owns the Bronx Cheers?" Peter Argent's face couldn't have been redder, his body language more apoplectic. I was certain he would burst.

"Former stripper, I believe," muttered Dusty. "Not that it makes any difference."

"It was burlesque," I said, sick of hauling out the explanation. "Not stripping. There's actually quite a distinction." I began to enumerate the differences, but my clarification didn't matter. No one had paid attention to a word of it.

Dick Fernando couldn't have looked more flabbergasted. Speaking as though I wasn't in the room, he said, "She may have been very good at what she did—I think I still have one of her old calendars somewhere. But I never in a million years imagined that a pinup would be calling the shots here! I'm with Linda. I don't believe Augie was of sound mind when he made his will. He must have had dementia!"

Cousin Marty exploded. Bouncing out of his chair he shouted, "Excuse me—with all due respect—Venus—I mean Livy—knows shit about baseball! Why didn't he give *her* the fucking painting for her fancy duplex, and give *me* the fucking team?!"

"Apparently your uncle had his reasons," Cap said smoothly. "Damned if I know what they were, though. I'm a lawyer, not a mind reader."

And me? I was in shock. "I—I just got engaged . . . to a man with a family business in Colorado . . . and I'm in the process of moving out there to live with him." This drew Linda's attention to the sparkling cushion-cut diamond on my left hand. "I've put my 'fancy duplex' up for sale, Marty." Shit—what a mess! After I hit the big four-oh, lightning struck and I met the greatest guy in the world, a man who wants to marry me despite what some people might view as my dubious past. So I once fan danced for a living! His family is as cool with it as the Colorado weather. The Elliotts couldn't give a rat's ass what people did, or do; it's who they are that's important to them. I couldn't ask for more in a man, or in a pride of in-laws. And now—when I have a terrifically happy love life?! What sort of woo-woo stipulation is "close the circle," and what am I supposed to do about it? Does this mean I have to stay in New York? I'm not even sure I *want* to inherit his silly baseball team. This is a curveball I certainly never anticipated. I feel like Cap Gaines just dumped a garbage can filled with ice-cold Gatorade over my head while I'm wearing a silk dress and suede heels.

"And if I somehow decode my dad's esoteric stipulation and then do something about it, when would I get the team?" *What the hell am I going to do with a baseball team?* Actually, glancing around the table at the Cheers' unsuccessful current management, I thought about what to break, but I hadn't a clue how to fix it afterward.

Cap waved his hand for silence. "I also have in my possession a sealed letter which is not to be opened until six months after Mr. deMarley's death. According to the decedent's instructions and explanations, the letter explains what he meant by the phrase 'close the circle.'"

"Is this b.s. legally binding?" Barry Weed, the GM, wanted to know.

Cap Gaines nodded. "Grant it, I'll be damned if I know what he meant when he wrote 'close the circle,' but August deMarley did. He was of sound mind and body when he signed this will. If you gentlemen want my free legal advice, I'd caution you against contesting it. And as the attorney for the estate, I will be representing Ms. deMarley in any legal action that might be brought against her as a result of the will's contents." Cap smiled like a crocodile. "You may have a few issues with your new boss, the lovely Ms. deMarley, but I don't think you boys want to play hardball with *me*. In addition—" the attorney smiled again. "In addition, there is a paragraph contained in this will which states that anyone who contests the will loses what was left to them in it. And there's nothing unusual or irregular about *that* language, gentlemen."

"Jesus! Why did we all rush to sign those consent forms *before* he read the will?!" exclaimed Dick Argent.

"Lemmings! We acted like lemmings!" added Barry Weed. "Fernando signed his, and then we all followed suit!"

My legs felt like jelly even though I was sitting down. *Whoa.* Gaines had given me a helluva lot to consider. At least I could eliminate money from the equation. I'd invested my earnings well and didn't need a job. I danced my tootsies off (and a few other parts as well) for years and had a nice nest egg to show for it. After all, I'd always assumed my only legacy from Dad was self-reliance. What did I need this crazy bargain for? Three-fourths of a business degree from Harvard, natural-born rhythm, and years of dance lessons, plus a killer body, had always been all the tools I needed in my personal arsenal. My life was my own. And I'd just committed to sharing it with an amazing, kind, generous, and loving man. Now I was about to owe it to a dead father. It might have been Shakespearean, had the Bard given a fig for minor league baseball.

The dark-haired young woman eyed me curiously, and I couldn't keep my mouth shut any longer. My voice was gentle, even if my words weren't especially sweet. "Excuse me—I've met everyone in the room but you, and you seem to be soaking up every word we're saying like some sort of sponge. Did you know my father? I mean—okay, this may sound rude, but hell,

I can't keep it to myself anymore—damn it, you *look* like him. Would you mind introducing yourself?"

Cap Gaines lifted his hand. "This young lady e-mailed me after she read your father's obituary. Sent a wild pitch my way, so to speak. It seems she's quite adept at Internet searches. Her interest in today's proceedings is not monetary; it's purely personal." The lawyer looked at Weed and Fredericks, Argent and Fernando. "Gentlemen, would you give us a moment, please?"

The men rose to leave; Cap Gaines waited until the sound-proof glass door had shut behind them with a sharp click. The bright room felt suddenly claustrophobic. I was certain Cap was about to tell me that the young woman was Augie's late-in-life by-blow, preserving her dignity by sharing this infor-mation with me privately, well outside of the Cheers guys' earshot.

"Ms. deMarley, I would like to introduce you to Sophie Ashe. Ms. Ashe has reason to believe that she is your daughter."

My jaw hit the floor, followed by a series of uncontrollable sobs that burst from my gut like a volcanic explosion. There certainly had been a Sophie. She was the reason I'd left Harvard. A fling with a former Red Sox infielder, whom I'd met while I was dancing in Waltham, led to an unplanned pregnancy. In an agonizing decision, I'd dropped out of school and then opted for adoption. The player very publicly went back to his wife, after he got suspended from the team for—frequently—attending a local burlesque revue. Not his finest hour. Or mine.

Seeing Sophie, who must be twenty years old now, renewed the torrent of emotions, and there was nothing I could do but stand there, still barefoot—Gaines had caught me so off guard that I hadn't time to shove my feet into my slingbacks—repeatedly blubbering "Oh my God, Sophie."

I threw my arms around her and held her close. In her flats, Sophie was about two inches shorter than me. I stroked her silky dark hair, thinking she'd inherited that from her father.

When I finally disengaged from our embrace, I noticed that Sophie's eyes, though moist, were devoid of tears. Now I realized why I'd thought of Dad when I looked at her: she had his eyes.

My gut told me no DNA test was necessary. I didn't doubt for a minute that she was mine.

⊘

In all these years, I've never tried to find my daughter; it was the deal I'd made with the devil, so to speak, when I let her go. I'd been her age at the time, rebellious and clueless and estranged from my only surviving parent. Under those circumstances, she never would have had the life I'd wanted to give her. On the other hand, I'd never really wanted to remain anonymous forever. And now that Sophie had managed to track me down, I didn't want to let her go. We had so much catching up to do, so much to learn about each other. After the distribution, I insisted that she come back to my apartment and I bombarded her en route with a stream of questions that scarcely left the poor kid with a chance to catch her breath.

At the subway, I wouldn't let her swipe her own MetroCard; *let Mommy take care of it*, I was thinking. She was a lovely young woman. I wanted to shout out to everyone in the subway car: "Hey, this is my long-lost daughter!" Yet Sophie's perpetually ambivalent expression pricked at my heart. It put me in mind of a somewhat curious puppy who gives every impression of wanting you to take her home, but when you actually pick her up and cuddle her, she starts to go all gun-shy.

"Sit across from me so I can get a better look at you," I told her. She had my long legs, but not my narrow waistline, and certainly not the boobs. She did have broad shoulders, though, like her father had. I have no idea where he is, by the way. He hung up his glove years ago, and for all I know he's selling real estate in Phoenix. I gazed at Sophie and continued my inventory of her features: my cheekbones, *her* dad's jawline, *my* dad's eyes, and, alas, Augie's eyebrows, too. So much for nature. But what about nurture? What had the Ashes passed along to her? Who *was* this stranger who had sprung from my loins half a lifetime ago?

We stepped out of the subway on West Twenty-third Street and walked along Eighth Avenue. The sidewalk cafés were doing a brisk business. "There's a super ice cream place just up the block, if you want to stop in—I feel like I should take you for ice cream—all those Mom-daughter things we never did." She gave me that ambivalent face again. "Well . . . it's never too late . . . is it?" I asked hesitantly.

Sophie shrugged. "I can't." Followed by an apologetic look. "I'm a vegan." And when I didn't seem to get it, she gave a little sigh that seemed to indicate that I was either very clueless or totally pathetic. "No dairy products."

"Oh." I felt disappointed. A bit rejected, even though I rarely indulged in desserts. "Sorry. I mean not sorry you're a vegan— I'm sure you're happy with your life choice—I mean sorry . . . well, you know what I meant." Turning west toward my duplex we passed a charming little bistro on a Chelsea side street that sold terrific homemade scones. "Can you drink tea?"

"Of course!" She caught my relieved sigh in mid-bounce. "But no caffeine."

I've raised a frickin' health nut, I thought, followed immediately by the reminder that in fact I hadn't. I'm not sure which of those notions bothered me more.

I chose an outdoor table offering maximum people-watching opportunities in case our first-ever conversation turned a little tense and I craved the safety of multiple distractions. People who don't know me well have mentioned that I emit an aura of supreme confidence. Maybe it's my height that fools them. And I confess that part of it is deliberate. It's my armor. Why should strangers see the seams and glimpse my vulnerabilities? But if they had X-ray vision, they'd see my nerve endings tying themselves into an intricate macramé. At the moment they'd made enough knots for a good-sized hammock. My heart beat within my chest the same way it did when I sensed that a beau was about to call it a day. I wondered what Sophie was thinking. After all, she'd gone to a good deal of time and effort to find me. Was she as nervous? Those eyes—that feature she so clearly shared with her grandfather—I couldn't read them. I could never read Dad's either, except in the most extreme cases, where they conveyed displeasure and disappointment in 72-point type.

Neither of us knew what to say. The waitress finally flipped her cell phone closed and decided to get back to work, truculently dropping the menus in front of us. Still, Sophie and I were both relieved at the chance to focus on something benign.

"What's good?" she asked me.

"I always get an iced chai in weather like this." As if on cue, a bead of perspiration trickled down my cleavage. Another good reason to move to the Rockies. I wasn't going to miss this climate. I've always hated the heat. Las Vegas made me miserable. Indoors it was faux frigid and outside it was being thrust into a giant Easy-Bake oven. "Chai okay for you?"

Sophie shook her head. "Caffeine. And milk products. I think I'll have one of the tisanes."

"Oh—then *I'll* have that, too!" I said, thinking that ordering the same thing would be a nice little way to begin to bond. "How does the apricot infusion sound?"

She pointed to something else instead. "The mango-blueberry is better for you. Blueberries are high in antioxidants. I'm surprised you don't know that," she said brightly.

Who says I don't know about antioxidants? Maybe I just didn't feel like ingesting them this afternoon. Wait—who's the mother at this table?

We ordered Sophie's choice.

"How did you feel when you gave me up for adoption?" she suddenly blurted out, as if she was relieved to get the words out after so many years of storing them up.

She'd dealt me a body blow for which I was unprepared and undefended. Perhaps I expected the question—just not so soon. I felt winded, and it took me a few moments before I could breathe normally again. I tried not to cry when I told her it had been the hardest decision of my life. "And at the same time, I felt like I had no choice. I . . . I thought we'd both have a better shot at life . . . a better life, I mean . . . than if I was a single mom barely out of her teens. The wealth and privilege I'd been raised with was never going to be part of the equation, Soph. Maybe I could have somehow managed my final year in college with an infant in tow, but . . . " My eyes stung with tears. "The me who was me twenty years ago just wasn't equipped to handle motherhood. I'd gotten in way over my head—that much, at least, I knew—and if I was going to drown, I didn't want to drag you under, too."

"Did you ever think about me?" Sophie asked, her expression still unreadable.

I reached for her hand. "All the time," I told her. It was the truth. But I'd always force myself to let the moods pass, figuring what actually *was*, was the way things were supposed to be.

She'd allowed me to touch her, but her physical passivity stung. Still, I suppose I might have acted the same way if I'd been in Sophie's shoes. "Any regrets?" she asked me.

"Sometimes. Of course I wondered what our lives might have been like if . . . if I'd kept you." I tried to smile. "It helps to imagine that you've had more opportunities than I could have given you."

"I guess it's not black and white," Sophie said. "It's always helped *me* to imagine that it was."

I folded my hands in my lap, giving Sophie her space. I

realized I needed it, too, though my instinct was to learn everything about my daughter as quickly as possible. Instead, I gazed at the stranger seated across from me, looking for signs of myself.

"In case you're wondering, I found you through the Adoption Information Registry—four months ago—but I was too freaked to do anything about it. Then I saw your name in Augie's obit and figured it was karma. I was supposed to meet you now. I looked up my biological father, too," said Sophie, after the iced infusions arrived. Her brown eyes betrayed no emotion beyond mild curiosity. "He used to be a baseball player."

I nodded. "He played for the Red Sox. Did you speak to him? I haven't spoken to him since you were in utero." Funny how I hardly remembered anything about him but the way his hair felt when I ran my fingers through it, and the faint scent of his Brut aftershave. "Sadly, I couldn't even tell you how his voice sounded."

Sophie shook her head. "I sent him a card in June for Father's Day, but he didn't reply."

I nodded grimly. "I know the feeling." Truth told, I was only politely intrigued about the whereabouts of Rodney the Red Sock, but it dispelled some of my anxiety about discussing Sophie and me instead. "What's your bio-dad doing with himself these days?"

"Selling time-shares in Taos. Why are you smiling?"

I shrugged it off. "Nothing." *Score one for me on a lucky supposition. Taos . . . Arizona . . . close enough.*

Then I sucked down a gulp of healthy iced tisane, froze my nerves, and bit the bullet. "So tell me about yourself—I want to know everything—who are you? I mean—I haven't seen you since I said good-bye to you at the hospital. I don't suppose you'd remember that." Funny, I remember it like it was yesterday. I was surprised, yet pleased, that the Ashes hadn't changed the name I'd given her. "Sophie" means "wisdom." When I'd put her up for adoption I hoped she'd grow up to be wiser than her mother had been when she'd conceived her.

Sophie bit her lip, looking vulnerable for the first time since I'd seen her. Even at Dad's memorial service she'd seemed an enigma. I looked into her eyes, but she glanced away and began to fiddle with her straw. I noticed she had the same three freckles on the right side of her nose as I do. I always cover mine with foundation.

"You . . . you kind of intimidate me," Sophie said when she finally found her words.

"Me?" Honestly, I was thinking it was more like the other way around. She seemed so grounded.

Sophie's laugh was exceptionally welcome. "Yes, you! You're—well, you're gorgeous. You're glamorous—even in mourning. Your hair—your figure, too—is like something out of a guy's fantasy comic book. I'm such a frump!"

I grabbed her hands. "No, you're absolutely not, and don't ever let me hear you say that about yourself again. We have different builds, that's all."

"Yeah, I'm probably built more like Rodney."

"Not quite."

Sophie shrugged. "At least the athletic physique is good for something. I'm at Clarendon College in Westchester on a softball scholarship. Well, a partial one. It's all good, though. My parents pay only half what it would have cost to send me otherwise."

I tried not to react at her mention of the word *parents*. Maybe Sophie didn't mean it cruelly—I'm sure she didn't—but it hammered home the fact that although I was my daughter's mother, I'd never been her parent.

"What's your major?"

"Communications; I want to be a sports broadcaster."

I swallowed my pride along with another gulp of tea. "So, tell me about them—the Ashes. Are they good to you?"

Sophie beamed. "They're wonderful. Very . . . normal . . . I guess, is the best way to describe them. I'm their only kid, so they kind of spoiled me. Joy is a calligrapher and has a high-end stationery store in our town, and Glenn is a high school coach. He was *my* softball coach at Larchmont High, actually. And he coached our little league team, too, when I was a kid. He used to be a talent scout for the major leagues. Ever heard of him?"

I shook my head. My two baseball connections have been acquired through blood in the one instance and through semen in the other, and I wasn't about to point that out.

I sucked down the last of my tea and flagged down the waitress for another round. "Well . . . Joy and Glenn seem to have done a very good job." I fought the stab of envy that threatened to puncture my efforts at maintaining a pleasant expression.

Sophie picked at her napkin. "I think you'd like them—Oli—I don't know what to call you, actually."

I took one deep breath, then another. "Tom—my fiancé—calls me Ollie. And my girlfriends call me 'V,' But you . . . you can call me Mom," I said softly.

I spied just the tiniest beginnings of a tear in the lower-right corner of Sophie's left eye. "But you're not my mom. Except . . . "

Ouch. "Except?"

"Except . . . except, well . . . literally, I guess. Biologically."

I reached for her hands again. "Any time you want to give it a try . . . see how it feels on your tongue . . . well . . . I wouldn't mind it."

Sophie swallowed hard. "Okay," she nodded. But she didn't say it. I had a feeling it would have been pretty neat to have heard, "Okay—Mom."

Rachel Bronstein, my real estate broker, looked like she was about to have a coronary at the prospect of kissing good-bye such a great commission. "You're taking it off the market?" she exclaimed, her South African accent popping into her aghast vowel sounds. "You do realize that the peak is past, darling. We're teetering on the top of a slippery slope. Ever since 2005, prices have been dropping at a rate of six percent a year. The longer you wait, the less it will be worth."

And the less you'll make on the deal, I thought.

"I wanted to sell the apartment because I'm planning to have a wedding, not to make a killing."

"You're not getting married?"

"I didn't say that." But I hadn't told Tom the news yet. That after meeting my daughter, I'd suddenly considered changing my plans about selling my home and rushing back to Colorado on the next flight. Now I wanted to stay in New York for a bit to get to know her. Who knows when I'd ever have the same opportunity? Then again, I could say the same about marrying Tom. Oh God, this was not easy. I'd call Tom and ask if he might be able to come east for a few weeks. On the other hand, I really coveted the chance for time alone with Sophie. Throwing a fiancé into the mix, especially one who hated everything about New York, would complicate things even further. *She and I* needed to get to know each other first. Otherwise, it wasn't fair to any of us.

"Right, then, what do you want me to tell the McNichols?" The bells on the hem of Rachel's peasant skirt jangled with agitation.

"Tell them I'd like to cancel the deal. Their down-payment check hasn't been deposited, so no harm, no foul."

Rachel scowled at me as though I'd snatched the last crumb of food from the hands of a starving woman.

"Don't worry. When I decide to sell again, I'll call you." I figured I owed her that much. She'd made herself available at all hours to show the apartment in my absence, knowing how eager I'd been to move out and move on, uninterested in straddling the country—with one foot, and half my wardrobe, in each of two cities.

I'd taken care of the easy stuff first. I'd make the last flight back to Denver in the evening, but I wasn't looking forward to the conversation on the way home from the airport.

"Everything go all right?"

I'd phoned Tom when I got to New York, just to tell him I'd landed safe and sound, and had called him again before Augie's memorial service to tell him how much I missed him and couldn't wait to get home—having thoroughly wrapped my brain around the concept of his home being mine from now on—but so much had happened since then. Where to begin?

I was pretty silent on the ride to Breckenridge, afraid that what I'd tell him might surprise him so much, he'd lose control of the wheel. And when we undressed for bed and our bodies began to melt into each other, the sensation of his warm skin against mine the ultimate comfort food, I wondered whether I should take his hand and sit up and say, "I met my long-lost daughter this weekend. You know—Sophie—the child I gave up for adoption when I was still pretty much of a kid myself. Not only that, my father's will has this crazy clause in it where he's making me the controlling owner of his minor league baseball team as long as I 'close the circle,' whatever that means."

Which is where I began, but not until the morning light seeped past the drawn shades. Not until after we'd made love, such gentle and exhilarating love, that I never wanted to stop.

Tom's mouth went dry when I sprung the news. He leaped out of bed for a glass of water. "Well . . ." he said, and then he said nothing at all.

"Well what?" I asked quietly. "Where's *your* head at?"

"Sure you can take a few weeks with Sophie. Bring her out here, too, if you want. There's plenty of room and I'd love to get to know her. After all, she'll be family." He sat on the bed, cross-legged, with the covers pulled protectively around him, south of the waistline.

"What about that 'circle' line?"

"My gut reaction is that your dad wanted to reconnect with you; to end the family cold war. But since it's too late to do that now, unless you hire an equally woo-wooey person to conduct a séance, you're off the hook."

"But then I don't get the Cheers."

Tom looked at me earnestly. Lovingly. Do you *want* the Cheers?"

It was too much to think of right now. "The truth?"

Tom nodded. "Always. For better or worse."

"I don't know," I sighed wearily. "I honestly don't know. And yet it's what old Augie wanted for me. Though, come to think of it, I've spent a lifetime rebelling against what Augie wanted for me."

"What do you want for yourself?" Tom asked me, drawing me close for a cuddle.

"You."

"You got me." He held me for what felt like several minutes, long enough for our breathing to find a unison that brought a smile to my lips. Neither of us said a word.

"I—I want to get to know Sophie. I've been given an as-tounding opportunity. I never expected her to find me—or even imagined that she'd want to. Thing is . . . I don't know how much time I need. It's not exactly a thing you can put a limit on—to catch up on two lifetimes of experiences and then *poof*, disappear again."

Tom stared down at the sheets. "And where do I fit into all this? Where do *we*—you and I—fit in?"

I scooted beside him and slid my arm around his shoulder. "You could come east with me and we'll live in the duplex for a while. I know you want to get married out here, but we haven't set a wedding date yet, anyway. Lots of couples are engaged for a year or longer—sometimes lots longer—before they finally do the deed."

Tom frowned. "'Do the deed?' You make it sound sort of nasty. Something dirty-ish."

"Oh, c'mon." I kissed his cheek. "It's a figure of speech. I didn't mean anything by it. Not anything 'dirty-ish,' certainly."

"But what about the baseball team?" Tom asked. "First of all, though I'm no lawyer, that wacko clause in your father's will may not be ironclad. It's probably vague enough to be contestable by anyone with a mind to—especially anyone who wants the Cheers a whole lot more than you do—and is willing to litigate."

"Augie's lawyer cautioned everyone against contesting the will."

Tom rolled his eyes. "Oh, please. I know you're not remotely naïve. A lawyer's warning doesn't mean beans, my love. If someone wants to sue you, no matter how frivolous it seems—and in your case they might actually *have* a case—they'll slap you with a summons. Hey, a competitor once dragged my dad into court over a stripe down the center of one of the Elliott snowboard designs. He claimed he thought of it first."

"That's nuts! You can't copyright a stripe!"

My fiancé chuckled ruefully. "But he tried. And it cost my dad a lot of time and money to defend the lawsuit." His fingers brushed an errant lock of hair off my brow. "But supposing you do decode the clause and 'close the circle.' Then you own the Bronx Cheers. Minor League ball is played all summer."

"Fall weddings are lovely," I said hopefully.

"So what's in your head, Ollie? To split your time between there and here? The Cheers are a New York team. Owning it will require you to spend more time out East than you think. It won't just be summers that will demand your participation. There's spring training . . . there's. . ." Tom buried his face in his hands as I knelt beside him on the mattress, cradling him in my arms. "This isn't what I signed on for. I can't take off an entire year to live in New York with you. Even if I loved it out there, my business is here and it's not something I can run from a desk across the country, or telecommute to. What we do and how we do it—it's manufacturing, design and research, product testing and development. It's hands-on. I'm the CEO. That's not something I can—or want to—hand back to Dad or down to Luke." He could scarcely look me in the eye. "Ollie, I consider myself a pretty evolved man, but I don't want a part-time wife."

"I thought you loved me," I said, feeling foolish even as I said the words.

"Of course I do. And I don't doubt for a minute that you love me, too. But sometimes the rest of life rears its ugly head, and you have to deal with it, instead of lopping off that head and sticking it in the sand."

My gut seized up. I wasn't liking where this was going. "So what are you saying, sweetheart?" I reached for his hand.

"I guess I'm saying . . . maybe . . . maybe we should . . . oh, rats."

"What?" I asked, terrified to hear the answer.

"Maybe . . . I don't know . . . put things on hold for a while."

"I thought you don't want to put things on hold. I thought

that's what this discussion is all about." My voice barely rose above a whisper. It was the hardest conversation of my life so far. I felt as though everything I'd ever wanted had turned to sand and was slipping through my fingers onto the sheets. One quick *whoosh* of the comforter, and my dreams would be gone for good.

"I don't want to wait . . . and I don't want *not* to wait, either," Tom murmured.

"Huh? You're losing me."

He looked up, his eyes wet with tears. "Maybe I am," he said, taking the phrase literally. "None of the solutions seem to work for me. They're all compromises I just don't want to live with." He sighed into his cupped hands. "This wasn't what I signed on for."

"But sometimes shit happens," I said.

"*Stuff* happens. I know it does. But that doesn't mean I have to like it." He glanced over at me, and with the most painful reluctance admitted, "Ollie, you're the best thing that ever happened to me . . . and at the same time, I guess we're not a good fit. Not right now, anyway."

"What about later?" Silent, hopeful tears coursed down my cheeks.

"We each have too much going on right now in other parts of our lives, things we can't give up, or put aside—and don't want to, or aren't in a position to. Just because two people want to get married, it isn't—*poof!*—always so easy. Life gets in the way of love sometimes."

Through my tears I looked down at my engagement ring. It seemed to wink at me from a rheumy haze, as though it was sitting just underwater. A sob caught in my throat as I wriggled it off my finger. "I think what you're saying is that it doesn't make sense to think about planning a life together right now.

So I don't feel right about keeping this, since I don't expect you'll want me to keep wearing it."

"No, I guess I don't," he murmured, looking away from me so I wouldn't see him cry. "You're right."

"I'll pack up all my stuff and try to get a flight back to New York today. What I can't carry, I'll just ship." I felt sick, numb, heartbroken. Augie's demise hadn't hit me nearly as hard. *This—this* was a death.

At the airport, Tom left me at the curbside check-in. "I really want to keep in touch," I told him.

His hands remained at ten and two on the wheel, as if he were gripping his emotions for dear life. "I do, too," he agreed.

I wondered if we really would.

⚾

"Sue my own cousin?" Marty deMarley was intrigued. "I've been looking for a way to sock it to Livy ever since I was nine years old," he said, the thought of revenge as sweet as the fistful of M&M's he'd just popped into his mouth. "Aw, shit, I forgot to wish on the green ones. Anyway, you heard Uncle Augie's lawyer. In his own WASPy way he basically said 'fuhgeddahboutit.'"

Linda deMarley threw her hands up in disgust. "Get real, Marty. Gaines said that to scare everyone. In my experience, there's no such word as *no*." After three glasses of champagne, her nightly cocktail of choice, the alcohol had begun to slur her speech. She tipped the bottle into her glass again. "You know what *I* like about all thiss?" she asked, gulping down the champagne.

"No, Linda, what do you like?"

"The quesstion was rhetorical, Marty." Noticing a chip in her manicure, she frowned, as if to blame her index finger. "What *I* like is that the language in Augie's will iss so vague that a lawsuit is sustainable. I'm going to call my brother-in-law. Maybe Sherman can file a proceeding in Surrogate's Court, to declare the will invalid. So, we forfeit a hideous oil painting we never wanted to own anyway. When a partner from Wachtel Lipton slaps Ms. Va-Va-Venuss with a summonss, Casper Gaines will be outgunned and outmanned." Linda clapped her hands. "It's deliciouss. Gaines'll be paperworked to death with interrogatories demanding Augie's medical records, mental health reports." Her eyes grew moist with vengeance.

"Come here, pookie." Marty motioned to Linda to sit on his lap as he reclined in his mitt-shaped leather lounger. "*Ooh—ohh*, watch the knees. You know I have weak knees."

"As long as it's not your resolve." She nuzzled his neck and darted her tongue in and out of his slightly fuzzy ear, a gesture that repulsed her, but never failed to turn her husband into malleable mush.

Marty moaned as his gaze met Linda's. "Ohh, Linda, I love it that you want to nail Venus's ass to the wall as much as I do. You're such a supportive wife. And she's not even your blood cousin; *you* don't even have a *reason* to despise her."

"Oh, Marty," Linda murmured, gazing longingly at the coffee table, where she had left her half-full glass of champagne. "If you only knew."

✐

So what do you think? Can my repulsive cousin Marty or any of the sleazy misogynists in the Cheers' front office challenge old Augie's will?" I asked my friend Tessa. Tessa is my former college roommate, and she had just completed her freshman term in Congress. We were killing a bottle of wine in my apartment while her husband, Jamie Doyle, was taking a turn behind the bar at the Irish pub that bears his name.

Tessa laughed. "How should I know? I was a speechwriter, not a lawyer, V." She refreshed her glass and rested on her elbow. For some reason, whenever we visit each other's homes we always wind up sitting on the floor, probably a twenty-year holdover from the days when the carpet was more comfy than the saggy-seated sofa in our suite.

I gazed gloomily into my wineglass.

"Hey, where'd you go, V?" Tessa waved her hand in front of my face. "You spaced out on me for a moment. Apart from the will-related stuff and Sophie—which is a big enough deal in and of itself—is everything okay?" She rearranged her limbs and sat beside me, our backs against the couch, our knees pulled up toward our chests. "How is Tom taking all this?"

I hadn't told Tessa. "Not as well as I would have hoped," I began. "Not too well at all, in fact." Teardrops splashed into my wineglass as I shared the ugly details of our breakup. "About seventeen times a day I ask myself whether I haven't gone and done the stupidest thing in my present life by choosing to stay here indefinitely and get to know Sophie. I had everything I'd always wanted, always dreamed of, only to agree to slam on the brakes and call the whole damn thing a day. I keep telling myself I should have fought harder. On the other hand, he said the whole Sophie-Cheers situation wasn't what he'd bargained for, so unless I opted out of all that, what good would fighting to have held onto Tom have done, anyway?" I swirled the wine in my glass and stared at it. "I'll miss Tom's family as much as I'll miss him. How many women can say that about their potential in-laws? I was so fucking lucky—and I chucked it and let him go. What do you think of old Augie's directive from the Great Beyond? Do you think I know how to run a minor league baseball team?" I asked glumly.

"As opposed to a major league team?" Tessa playfully jabbed me in the ribs. "I'm just kidding. C'mon, I've never known someone so capable and determined. I know you can do anything you turn your mind to."

"Sports?"

"If need be."

"Need be."

We laughed.

"Your dad didn't say you were supposed to *manage* the team, just *own* most of it. Make sound economic decisions; be sure you've hired the right people to get the job done. You just have to know about running a business, managing myriad male egos—"

"Maybe more like *massaging* myriad male egos. They're deceptively fragile items, you know."

"V, you've already devoted almost half your life to the care and feeding of male egos. Dancing, and running those strip clubs in Vegas—"

I tossed a peanut at her. "You always say that!" I wasn't a stripper—I've been a showgirl and I've been a burlesque dancer. I ran nightclubs, not strip joints." I launched into my distinction litany, exasperated to have to explain it to my best friend, of all people.

Tessa threw up her hands. "Okay, okay, I'm sorry if I insulted you. My point was just that you know how to handle the testosterone-fueled male of the species. C'mon?! If I were a betting man—"

I burst out laughing. "Neither of which you are."

"But if I were a gambler and I were a man, I would lay odds that you'd do such an alarmingly swell job that you'd knock their sweat socks off. Hey, pal . . . in the twenty-two years I've known you, I've never seen you look disheartened. Don't take this the wrong way, but I don't think of you as being vulnerable."

"Hah!"

"You always seem so together."

"The operative word in that sentence is *seem*. And, as I said a minute ago—*sports*? Tess, I never in a zillion years thought I'd be in a position to run Dad's precious Bronx Cheers."

"So? I never in a zillion years thought I'd be appointed to the Congressional Subcommittee on Prevention of Nuclear and Biological Attack. Go with the flow, girlfriend. Chin up! Maybe Tom will be smart enough to want you back, and agree to put the wedding plans on hold until you've both got everything sorted out."

I took a swig of wine. "That kind of thing happens in fairy tales and movies of the week, T."

Tessa refused to admit I was probably right. She leaned over and gave me a hug. "V, you're going to knock the ball right out of the park!"

I was out at my yoga class when Sophie called a few days later. She left an excited message on my voice mail saying she'd like me to come up to Larchmont for Sunday brunch . . . to meet the Ashes.

Oh God. I wasn't sure I was ready for this. Part of me had been dying to see the people who raised my daughter. But she was _their_ daughter, too. Even more so. They were her real parents. I'd only been the womb. So far, anyway. I'd brought her into the world and bought her a glass of tea. Big whoop, compared to sheltering, feeding, clothing, educating, and loving her for the first twenty years of her life. What would they think of me?

I was in an absolute tizzy. Over the phone, Tessa counseled me to calm down. I know she realized this was impossible, but someone had to try to keep me sane. "Look, V, you can't be who you're not. Don't even try. Did I ever tell you how amusing I find it that inside that glamazon body of yours is a pea-sized kernel of self-esteem?"

"Very amusing. Ha-ha," I said sarcastically. "And with a father like mine, ever wonder why? It's the biggest crock of horseshit that attractive people are never insecure. I read an article once where Michelle Pfeiffer—who in my humble opinion is one of the most beautiful women in the world—said she thinks she looks like a duck. Well, there are plenty of mornings when I look in the mirror and see a giraffe that swallowed a dromedary."

"I think you mean a camel. Dromedaries only have one hump. And in the immortal words of Cher—who *I* think is one of the most beautiful women in the world, massive plastic surgery aside—'Snap out of it!'"

"Oh, T, I wish you could script me something," I groaned, only half kidding, "so I don't make an utter fool of myself in front of the Ashes. Dancers are accustomed to communicating with their bodies, not with words."

"I'm not going to tell you you're blowing this all out of proportion, because meeting Sophie's real parents is undeniably huge," Tessa said pragmatically. "But I know you'll be fine, even if you don't believe me."

Just then the doorman buzzed my intercom. "Oops—I'd better get that; I'm expecting a grocery delivery, and I need both hands to unpack the boxes. Will you be home later, T? I may need another pep talk."

"Sure. What do I have to do for the rest of the day but read a five-hundred-and-seventy-six-page bill to protect the Blue Point oyster?" Tessa said sardonically. "Just kidding. Not about the bill, though. The proposed legislation is real. But you know I'm always here for you!"

I hung up the phone and lifted the receiver on the intercom.

"Are you expecting someone?" Larry asked.

"Yes—I am," I told the doorman. "Send them up."

A few minutes later my bell rang. I opened the door and saw a slender, well-groomed man who looked as though he might be some sort of performer. The kind you see around my Chelsea neighborhood all the time.

"Are you Olivia deMarley?" he asked me.

"Ye-es," I said, hesitatingly. "But you're not Fresh Direct."

"'Fraid not," he replied. "But I do have a delivery for you."
He opened his canvas messenger bag and removed a thick tri-
folded document, which he then stuffed into my hand. Before
I could get a good look at the papers, he'd scampered for the
fire stairs. I had a sinking feeling I'd just been ambushed. Still
standing, stunned, in my doorway, I unfolded the document,
and as I flipped through the pages I felt my gut plummeting
to the parquet. Cousin Marty and Linda were suing me—to
contest my father's will.

I don't remember which I did first—called Tessa again with
the bad news or downed a double scotch. Maybe I threw up. I
know I did all three of those things in fairly rapid succession.

And then I phoned Cap Gaines to tell him Marty had called
his bluff.

⑦

I'm sure I made quite the picture when I rang the Ashes' doorbell the following day. I'd gotten no sleep, my eyes looked
like they'd been made up by a raccoon, and I was having a
killer bad hair day. Fabulous first impression. Having caught a
glimpse of myself in daylight via my rearview mirror, I pulled
over into a gas station on the Hutchison River Parkway and
dashed into their grotty ladies room, where I'd tried to mask
the dark circles with more cover-up and tame my mop of frizzy
red tangles. My nerves remained frazzled, however, and there
was no cure for that that wouldn't have gotten me busted for
a DUI.

I turned onto East Garden Street and stashed my MapQuest
directions in the glove compartment. The Ashes lived at the
end of a cul-de-sac in a lovely stuccoed Tudor with a fieldstone
porte cochere. Elegant but unpretentious. A good start. So this

is where my—our—daughter grew up. I stood outside and admired the house, with its modest sloping lawn planted on either side with hedgerows and borders of tiger lilies. Someone was a very attentive gardener. I inhaled several cleansing breaths of air. It was only twenty miles or so north of Manhattan, but it sure smelled good up here.

Well . . .

And yet of course I was vastly curious to meet the people who had raised my little girl. Their little girl, too, I guess.

The Mother meets the Parents. Yikes!

I took another deep breath and used the large brass door knocker—a lion's head—to announce my arrival. There was a scurrying of footsteps just inside—from both two- and four-legged creatures, and the door was flung open.

"Well hello!" the Ashes chorused, enormous smiles plastered on their faces. Their golden retriever's nose immediately made a beeline for my crotch. *How embarrassing is that?*

Sophie took me by the hands, after scolding the dog, and pulled me into the foyer. "I'm so glad you came!" she said. Though she, too, seemed very upbeat, I could see in her eyes that she was as nervous as I was. Thank God for a kindred spirit.

"Livy—I want you to meet my mom and dad—this is Glenn. And this is Joy."

Her parents both reached to shake my hand at the same time, and laughed nervously over the synchronicity. My first reaction was that they were shorter than I'd imagined them. Sophie towered over Joy, a petite brunette with a pert pageboy. I pegged her at about five years my senior. Glenn was in his mid-fifties, about five-ten, with a sturdy athletic build. Clearly confident in his masculinity, he sported a Clarendon Kumquats baseball cap.

"Welcome—welcome to Larchmont," Glenn said, pumping

my hand. He had to glance up to look me in the eye. "We're very proud of our little seaside village. We may not be as grand as New York City, of course, but did you know that Lou Gehrig lived here?"

"Baseball. All you ever think of is baseball," Joy jested, an uncomfortable kernel of truth concealed behind her laugh.

"*And* softball!" Sophie chimed in. She turned to me and grinned. "I'm a Daddy's Girl!"

"That you are, sweetie," Joy said musically. "Hon, would you put those tapes away, please." Joy gestured to a stack of videocassettes strewn across the coffee table in their den. "He and Sophie were watching some of her game tapes last night; Glenn has every softball game she ever played on VHS." She gestured to an expansive pseudo-colonial entertainment center, its cabinets flanked by carved mahogany pilasters. There must be hundreds of cassettes in there."

"Don't exaggerate, Mom. Dozens. Not hundreds."

"Well, several dozen are a couple of hundred, and that's hundreds," Joy replied cheerfully.

They all seemed so normal, with their GAP jeans and shrine to Sophie—and then there were all the trophies and laminated plaques that adorned the fieldstone mantelpiece—and their chirpy dispositions that felt utterly genuine. What a freak they must have thought I was—I who'd spent my adult lifetime under the hot lights wearing little else but spangles and sequins and feathers, I who knew nothing of Little League and PTA meetings and senior proms and tussles over curfews.

"Come, Olivia, let me give you the nickel tour," Joy said. "Oh, hon, weren't you going to serve Bloody Marys?"

"*Whoops!*" Glenn jumped to his feet. "C'mon, kiddo," he said to Sophie, "come out and help me pick the secret ingredient." He winked at me. "We use fresh tomatoes. Joy's just a wizard in the garden. Give her anything, she can make it grow."

Glenn and Sophie headed outside, while Joy beckoned to me to follow her, proudly showing me their kitchen first—a room so vast you could have shot a cooking show in there. I've seen entire apartments in Manhattan that were smaller. "This is Glenn's domain. He's the chef around here. He's right that I can grow just about anything; but I'm not very good at doing anything with it once it's picked, whether it's a tomato, a peach, a petunia, or a pound of beef." She laughed nervously. "*We* like it," she said, as if she assumed I didn't. "It's homey, don't you think?"

"It's beautiful," I said truthfully. "I'm not the greatest cook myself, but I'd kill for a kitchen with this much space."

"*This* is really *my* sphere," Joy said, leading me into a mullion-windowed solarium. Dominated by a drafting table, the room was filled with high-end art supplies, including a couple of standing easels. A set of expensive calligraphy nibs rested beside an inkwell.

"So I understand you . . . danced." Joy's voice expressed curiosity, though her eyes conveyed value judgment.

"Yes, I did. I found it to be a tremendous lesson in anthropology," I replied.

"I'm not sure I follow you."

"The male of the species—ours, I mean—is a fascinating animal."

"I wouldn't know," Joy said. "Glenn and I were high school sweethearts." She lowered her voice to a conspiratorial whisper. "He was my first. And only." Her smile was the one of a woman who was truly happy. Though I envied Joy her joy, I found that I couldn't dislike her.

Joy broke the awkward silence, changing the subject. "I don't know if Sophie told you that I run my own business. I like to tell people that I write for a living." She chuckled at her own pun. "They usually think I'm an author or a journalist, and then—oh, I'm like George Washington and the cherry tree; I cannot tell a lie—I admit that I *hand*write. I'm a calligrapher. Wedding invitations, ketubahs—you know, when Jewish people get married, they have these fancy wedding contracts—it's very lovely . . . and lucrative." Joy giggled like a schoolgirl, and I glimpsed the young girl Glenn must have been smitten with twenty-five years earlier. There was something still vaguely childlike about her; something somehow unfinished. Suddenly, I wanted to protect her. Both she and Sophie seemed to lack the armor so necessary to guard against predators.

"You know I wasn't sure how I felt about it when Sophie told me she'd met you." Joy's forced cheer had evanesced; her expression was one of dead seriousness. "When she told me she wanted to find you, of course I couldn't say no. All the books tell you it's a bad idea to dissuade an adoptee—I mean now that she's really an adult. If she'd wanted to find you when she was ten, I can't say I would have encouraged it. But she's over eighteen, and she needs to do what she needs to do, I guess. Sophie's very strong willed. I guess she gets that from Glenn."

Or me, I was thinking.

There was a rap on the open door. "Hey-ho, anybody home?" Glenn poked his head in the room. "Bloody Marys for all who are over twenty-one."

"Hey, no fair!" Sophie protested. "It's a special occasion."

"And you're still under the legal drinking age," I said, but immediately zipped my lip when I realized I probably should have let her parents deal with her request for a cocktail.

Sophie pouted. "It's only vegetable juice—with a little Tabasco."

"And a lot of vodka," Glenn said. "And the answer is still no."

"God, you guys—you're really embarrassing me in front of

Livy. It's not like I drink or anything. I just wanted one because, I mean, how often do all your parents have brunch together for the first time?"

I was ready to relent at this argument, but Joy's disapproving face checked my inclination.

"It's still a no, slugger," she said.

I never quite thought of calling Sophie "slugger." Still, I hadn't been around when she first developed a passion for America's pastime, so maybe she didn't mind it.

"I hate it when you guys call me *slugger*." Sophie extricated herself from Glenn's embrace and hugged Joy. "But I guess old habits die hard."

"It's hard to teach your father new tricks," Joy said apologetically.

Sophie grinned. "It was *you* who said it, Mom."

Joy shrugged. "So I'm an old dog, too." She looked over at me. "We all are, I guess."

I plastered a smile between my cheeks. "You won't find an ally in *me*, I'm afraid."

"Well, you dress so youthfully, I'm sure the other mourners at August deMarley's memorial mistook you two for sisters."

This was not intended to be a compliment. Sophie and I exchanged a look.

"So, what's for brunch?" she asked, pouncing on the words.

"Your dad's making omelets. I hope you eat eggs," Joy said to me. "I'm sorry, I just assumed."

"*I* don't eat eggs, Mom," Sophie said, a note of disgust creeping into her voice. "But no one asked *me*."

"Sweetheart, you barely eat *anything* breakfasty," Joy replied good-naturedly. "There's some fresh fruit in the fridge, Ms. Vegan."

"W-when did you tell Sophie she was adopted?" I asked,

looking at my napkin, afraid to make any direct eye contact.

"When she was seven," Glenn said as Sophie emerged from the refrigerator with a banana.

"She had an assignment for school. Second grade. To make a family tree," Joy added. And I remember debating with myself as we worked on it whether to tell her that she could add a couple more branches—more than that, really, if you included the parents of her birthparents, too. But I bit the bullet and I told her. Soph, do you remember what your reaction was?"

Our daughter chuckled as she peeled her banana. "Yeah, I asked you, 'Does that mean I get twice as many birthday presents?'"

"God bless whom- or whatever—God, I guess—that she was such a well-adjusted kid," Glenn said. "You know, we read a lot about the behavioral, I dunno, psychoses, of adoptees, but Sophie didn't seem to manifest any of what we read, Joy and I. The books say that as children adoptees often apologize for everything all the time—"

"Yeah, and I never apologize for anything!" Sophie exclaimed, grinning from ear to ear.

"Well, Glenn, you and Joy can count your blessings for that," I quipped, adding, "as Erich Segal said, 'Love means never having to say you're sorry.'"

Glenn began to whip up omelets with Joy's homegrown tomatoes, scallions, and green peppers. "We're sorry to hear about your father's death, Olivia."

"Thank you. And call me Livy—please. Olivia always sounds so formal."

"Is your mother still alive . . . Livy?" Joy asked. I guess she hadn't read the obit.

I shook my head. "No. She passed away a long time ago. I'm an orphan," I said, the concept really sinking in as I sat around the large trestle table with this happy family of Ashes. I fiddled with my Bloody Mary glass so that I wouldn't have to make eye contact. I didn't want them to see me trying not to cry. "And my dad and I weren't close for years, either. I never stopped trying to reach out to him, and he evidently knew where I was, but I guess he had his reasons for not reaching back. Did Sophie tell you about the crazy clause in his will—closing the circle? My fiancé—well, my fiancé that was—seemed to think it was about patching things up between us, but that couldn't be it, since he died without even trying."

"Because it wasn't about you and him," Sophie said, lining up the blueberries on her plate as though she were directing a marching band. "It's about you and *me*."

Glenn almost flipped an omelet onto the floor. "It's what?"

"I think Grampa knew it was too late to fix things between you guys. Too much bad blood, or whatever. Maybe he was too proud. Heck, you knew him; I didn't, so this is just my guess, but I would bet a gazillion dollars I'm right. He knew you gave me up for adoption, and I bet that if he was secretly keeping tabs on you all these years that he also knew we'd never met."

"Then why didn't he just say, 'Olivia inherits the controlling interest in my minor league ball club once she meets her daughter'?"

"Because he was one of those eccentric billionaires?" Sophie posited.

"Besides, Cap Gaines told me you'd looked him up when you saw old Augie's obituary in the paper. And you couldn't have known about the clause in the will."

"Synchronicity," Sophie answered immediately. "Or karma. Or something." Glenn handed me my plate, and before I tucked into my omelet I reached for the salt shaker and tossed a tiny bit over my left shoulder.

"Ohmigod—did you see that, Mom, Dad? What Livy did

with the salt?! Ohmigod, I've done that all my life, and I always got shit for it. 'Don't make me take out the DustBuster,' Mom always says." Sophie did a perfect imitation of Joy; tensile steel under a falsely benign exterior of sunny smiles.

"We always wonder where she picked that up," Glenn said. "I mean we never do that salt—superstitious—thing."

"I always thought she learned it at a friend's house or something. I'd tell her that it's a crime to waste food when people are starving all over half the globe, but she's always done that thing with the salt."

Weird, I thought. *Or maybe not. Is it possible one can unwittingly "inherit" that sort of thing?*

"Anyway, dudes, I am totally convinced that 'close the circle' means that Livy and I are supposed to bond. I guess he couldn't know it would ever happen, but he was an old man who had never really bothered to know his own daughter, and he really hoped that she would not end up the same way as him! See, guys, this is like the kind of stuff we used to do in my psych class sometimes. We'd, like, take a newspaper article about some people and psychoanalyze why they might have done what they did—like the kid who killed his own grandmother for drug money."

"Well, that's a waste of time, slugger," Glenn said. "You just said it yourself. He wanted money for drugs."

"Yeah, but he could have murdered *someone else's* granny for the money if he was that desperate for a fix. Why put fifty stab wounds in the woman who raised you and gave you all the love you never got from anyone else?"

"I empathize," Joy murmured.

Somehow I didn't think we were meant to respond to that comment.

"Anyways, Grampa got lucky because I did track down Livy."

"But maybe he *did* never expect that to happen," I suggested. "Maybe it was like one of those impossible-to-ever-occur events like they have in fairy tales, and it was his way of more or less *preventing* me from ever inheriting the Cheers."

Sophie shook her head. "That makes zero sense, Livy. You probably never even thought about owning the Cheers, am I right?" I nodded my assent. "So it's not like you were the one who already had a lot of shares in the team and thought you'd get it when he died. Like dorky Marty deMarley and his horrible wife. Besides, don't you know that all the impossible-to-ever-occur events in fairy tales *always* happen?"

"I have a difficult time believing that my father the hard-nosed businessman invoked a concept out of Hans Christian Andersen or the Brothers Grimm in something so important as his last will and testament."

"Maybe that was something you never knew about him. His Joseph Campbell side," Sophie argued.

"You've been watching too much PBS, slugger," Glenn teased.

"There's no such thing as too much PBS," Joy said tartly.

"I agree. But I think most people, the sort who aren't conversant in Joseph Campbell's work in comparative mythology, would concur that the phrase 'close the circle' is pretty damn vague. And legally contestable." My highball glass slipped out of my hand, spilling Bloody Mary all over the tablecloth. "Oh God, I'm so sorry." I leaped from my chair. "Where do you keep the sponges?"

"Livy, are you okay?" Sophie asked.

"Uh . . . yes . . . actually, no . . . not right now . . . I'm not. I'll be okay in a . . . just let me . . ." *Oh shit*. The Ashes were probably thinking I'd had too much to drink.

Do I mention Cousin Marty's lawsuit? Oh, why ruin their brunch?

"It was serendipity," Sophie said, looking at me. Concerned. "So I was thinking that I could move in with Livy!"

Everyone over twenty-one yelped "What?!"

Sophie deliberately ignored the collective expression of shock. "Yeah—I mean, here we are and I'm like all grown up now, and this is my chance to finally get to know her. I mean, we get to get to know each other, y'know? And I've always wanted to move into Manhattan. So now I could, like, be her roommate."

Glenn was the first to recover what might be called composure. "First of all, slugger, you're not quite grown up all the way; you still have a year of college left, and you're not twenty-one."

"Plenty of kids move out when they're eighteen."

"But—but you don't know Olivia—Livy's—situation. She could be living with someone already, or her apartment might not be conducive to sharing it—New York apartments can be very small, you know. Did you think of what Livy might be feeling? Or what she might be thinking about this proposal of yours?"

"I don't think you've thought things through, honey," Joy interjected softly. "Besides, I don't think your dad and I are ready to let you go just yet. Did you think about how this might land with *us*?"

Sophie reddened. "Well, yeah. Kind of. I guess I thought you'd be cooler with it. At least that you wouldn't totally freak. I mean, I've been here for twenty years and now's my chance to get to know my birth mom, finally."

"Twenty years; damn right, twenty years!" Glenn said, beginning to lose his temper. "Look at your mother. You've made her cry."

"I'm not trying to be ungrateful or anything," Sophie said defensively. "I mean, I guess there's no way to do this without hurting somebody's feelings. I'm sorry. I guess I was really excited about the idea of closing the circle and everything, and maybe I didn't bring it up the right way."

"Well, *duh*," said Joy, wiping her tears with her napkin.

"Look. You're my mom and dad. I love you guys. That's not gonna change if I move in with Livy."

I reached over and covered Joy's hand with mine. "I think it's too much too soon," I said to Sophie. "I'm incredibly touched that you want to fling yourself into bonding with me—and believe me, I feel the same way—but there are other people's feelings to consider. Besides, you live not too far from Clarendon; commuting to classes from Manhattan for a whole year is going to get awful old very soon. To tell you the truth, Sophie, I'm not sure *I'm* ready for such a big thing as your moving in with me. I'm kind of used to living alone. And at some point, I was hoping to try to patch things up with my fiancé in Colorado. Why don't you finish college and then we can all sit down again and talk about your getting an apartment in Manhattan after graduation? "

"You don't get it. I want to live with *you*. We have to close the circle. And we have to do it now. I don't think the lawyer's warning scared your cousin Marty and Linda, and the Cheers dudes—Peter Argent and Dick Fernando and Barry Weed— and maybe even Dusty Fredericks—so much that they'd back off if they thought that the controlling interest in the Cheers was within their sights." Sophie chuckled. "I bet *nothing* scares Linda deMarley. If anything, it's the other way around. Imagine what she'd be like as a ball club owner: Marge Schott meets Nicole Ritchie."

I groaned. But she had my sense of humor. "That's my daughter."

She laughed heartily. "That I am—God help me."

Glenn and Joy exchanged an uncomfortable glance.

"And it's a little too late to avert a lawsuit." I drew in my breath and bit the bullet. "I hadn't wanted to spoil our brunch by sharing this . . .," and then I told the Ashes about the legal papers I had received.

"See! See!" Sophie exclaimed, jumping out of her chair. "I knew it! They'd all think the clause in the will was too vague and they'd all contest it. I bet you anything the other guys are going to sue you, too. They're going to gang up on you because they want the team. And they've all run it straight into the fucking toilet!"

"Sophie!" Joy's disapproval at our daughter's language was so palpable it practically jelled.

"But, slugger, just because *you* think closing the circle means bonding with your birth mother, what are the odds a judge is going to arrive at the same interpretation?" Glenn said.

"Because Mr. Gaines will make that the cornerstone of his defense," Sophie replied confidently. "I'm not wrong about this, you guys. I'm so totally right, I could—I don't know—I'm just so totally right about this. You have to trust me. Whatever we do, we can't let them get the Cheers. It's not what Grampa would have wanted. Dad, you don't want to see my favorite ball club go belly-up, do you? I just know Augie deMarley wanted Livy to have the team. So *we* have to do whatever it takes for her—and not them—to inherit it."

The Ashes exchanged glances and looked at me. It was Glenn who leveled a verdict. "Well—as long as Livy is comfortable with the arrangement, perhaps we can try your living together on a trial basis, pardon the pun."

And so it came to pass that the Ashes and I hammered out the details. Frankly, I had no idea how any of us were going to handle the situation from now on. The Ashes felt abandoned. I felt blindsided. And Sophie? I think Sophie was pretending really hard that we'd all get over it.

Tom tried to sound supportive when I told him about the new housing situation. I was keeping my side of our pledge to stay in touch, if only as friends. Of course, it's nearly impossible to do that when the break-up wounds are so raw, especially when you've scuttled marriage plans you both intended to honor. Every time I mentioned Sophie's name, I could almost hear the tinges of resentment in Tom's replies, as if he knew he *should* want me to get to know my daughter, but if injected with truth serum would have admitted that he would have been happier if she'd never found me—or at least didn't take me out of his life in the process. I tried the shoe on the other foot, and part of me couldn't blame him for his reaction. No man in the world is so Dudley Do-Right noble, so self-sacrificing, that he wouldn't harbor even a trace of bitterness or jealousy over what happened between us.

Brokenhearted, and questioning my own sanity, I spent every third second wishing and wondering how I could have held onto Tom and still have managed to bond full-time with Sophie—and battle my cousin's lawsuit.

Just before the fall semester began, Sophie loaded her clothes and prized possessions into her Camry and motored down to Chelsea. *Wait'll she learns about the joys of finding parking in Manhattan, and the garages that charge as much by the month as rental apartments*, I was thinking. I set her up in my downstairs bedroom. The idea of a duplex was the coolest, most glamorous thing in the world to her, though she didn't seem too crazy about my "house rules," such as when you finish with a plate, don't leave it sitting out; put it in the dishwasher. "Didn't you clean up after yourself up in Larchmont?" I asked her. She gave me a begrudging shrug.

I gave her a hand with her unpacking. She'd just sort of tossed everything into boxes. Not that she was a slob—she just evinced a haphazard and careless disrespect for her own stuff. "Well, it wasn't going very far," she rationalized.

I flipped through her hanging things. Jeans, jeans, sweats, jeans, cargo pants, cords, jeans. "Sweetie, where are your dresses?" After locating one dowdy peasant skirt that looked like she might have salvaged it from the Salvation Army, and then finding nothing but more jeans and khakis, I made a mental note to take the girl shopping. She was too lovely to hide her light under a bushel. "What do you wear on dates?"

She shrugged and looked at me with those dark, enigmatic eyes. "I don't really go on any."

I sat beside her on her bed. "Then what have you been doing for fun these past three years?" I asked softly.

She shrugged again, just as noncommittally. "I have friends. And I like to study. I dunno . . . wild parties and drinking and stuff like that . . . just doesn't appeal to me."

"I'm glad to hear it, but I'd still love to know that you're making the most of your college years."

"Don't worry. I have fun. I'm really into the softball team. We hang out a lot after practice. It's not like I do nothing but hit the books."

As long as she was happy, I was happy. She kind of put a period on the subject, so I let it go. How much mom-ness could I get away with? I still wasn't sure what to say and what to avoid. It was like tiptoeing through quicksand. Would I ever find the right balance?

⑦

Linda deMarley hung up the phone and broke out the champagne. "I hear there's trouble down in Chelsea," she said smugly. "Cheers, dear!"

Marty accepted one of the flutes and took a sip. "I know this brand is supposed to be good . . . but I just can't wrap my tongue around it. Have we got any beer?"

His wife gave an exasperated little snort. "How many times have I told you, champagne doesn't come in *brands*?" She removed the glass from his hand and placed it on their Chinese lacquered coffee table. "More for me, then. Especially at two hundred bucks a bottle." Linda located a Michelob in the fridge and gave it to her husband, who immediately complained that it was Lite.

"Think I like being married to Tubby the Tuba?" she shot back.

"Oh, give it a rest, Linda, my spare tire could barely hold up a bicycle."

"You're right, Marty; you're not that fat. Per se. But you'd be a toothpick in an inner tube if you didn't drink 'diet' beers." She sat beside him on their white leather sofa and stared at the space on the wall where the Leroy Neiman painting had so briefly hung.

Marty changed the subject. "I take it you heard something about my cousin and that kid of hers."

Linda grinned. "A little evidence for our lawsuit, perhaps. The Clarendon Clash's first string baseball pitcher Tommy Du-Pree is dating Carleen McLure, the girls' softball team pitcher, who is Sophie Ashe's best friend." She looked over at Marty. "You still with me, here?" He nodded unconvincingly. "Good. Barry Weed says DuPree is a hot prospect for the Cheers next season. Apparently all Clarendon's known for is turning out ballplayers." Linda dropped the other shoe. She could barely contain herself. "Barry told me that DuPree says that Carleen McLure says that Sophie and Livy fight over absolutely everything. Felix Ungar and Oscar Madison were more compatible as roommates." She took a satisfying sip of champagne. "Isn't that delicious?"

"The champagne? How would I know?"

"No, you scrawny moron—the *gossip*! They haven't even been living together for a month and already it looks like Livy's headed for disaster." Linda all but licked her lips. "Casper Gaines filed papers in response to my cousin Sherman's lawsuit. He claims that fakakta 'close the circle' phrase in your uncle's will means that Livy has to close the circle of her family's broken ties and bond with her biological daughter. That's what the eccentric old coot really wanted out of life—says the lawyer for the estate. So what happens if Livy says, 'Hey, Sophie, great to meet you, but it's time to tootle home to your other Mommy and Daddy, and don't be expecting anything more from me than a Christmas card?'"

"Dunno. I guess we get the Cheers. Hey—Lin? Can we make them hate each other? I mean, do you think there's anything we can do to be *sure* they'll never get along and wish they lived on separate continents or something?"

"That's one of the smartest things you've thought of since you proposed to me! I'll ask Sherman."

"Holy shit!" Marty practically jumped out of his chair— hard to do when it's a deeply scooped seat. He dashed into the bedroom and began rummaging through the closets. Several minutes later, he emerged with a mailing envelope, which he handed to Linda. "I can't believe I didn't remember this until just this second. We might not even need all this evidence, hon. I just found a prior will—that leaves everything to ME!"

He threw his arms around his wife and began to do an odd sort of off-kilter polka with a lot of gusto and absolutely no rhythm.

Linda reached for the kitchen counter as she spun past it, drained her glass, then Marty's, and poured herself another. She was clearly celebrating the idea of Livy's prospective failure. Not only that . . . she might even have sex tonight.

🖊

Sophie had been in classes for a month when Parents' Day rolled around. I'd been dreading the day ever since I'd seen it on the calendar; certain the Ashes would arrive brimming with nondysfunctional good cheer, while I would be a total bundle of nerves. I took an extra yoga class the day before, and even tried meditating, but all I could focus on as I endeavored to free my mind was the tension I was feeling about Parents' Day.

A stunning Indian summer day bathed the Clarendon campus in golden light. The air could not have smelled sweeter; the aroma of freshly mowed lawns hanging in the air as if to assure the world that spring training was just around the corner. Shortly after lunch the Ashes showed up at our appointed meeting place just inside the student union.

"How's my baby doll!" He enveloped Sophie in a bear hug.

I'm not very good at blending into the shadows, no matter how much my psyche wants to send me there. While Sophie and Glenn were embracing I strode across the room and extended my hand to Joy. "Good to see you again!" I bent down to give the sparrow of a woman a hug.

"Goodness, you *are* tall! Joy exclaimed. "I hadn't really noticed it that morning at brunch. I told you our slugger must get it from somewhere," she said over her shoulder to Glenn, who came over to say hello, pumping my hand with enthusiasm.

He turned back to Sophie. "So, kiddo, we never get to hear what's up with you anymore. Are you dating anyone this semester?"

"I've been focusing on my classes," she said.

"Well, don't forget, all work and no play makes Jill a dull girl," said Glenn unhelpfully. I was mortified for Sophie. From his relaxed manner and the warmly casual tone of his voice, undoubtedly he meant well, but it hadn't quite come out of his mouth that way.

"I always thought you were going to marry Wilson Peete," Joy sighed. She turned to me and said, "Wil was Sophie's high school sweetie." She sighed again, as though she had been more deeply disappointed by the breakup than Sophie had. "I'll never know what happened there. There's nothing like your first love. I wish it could have lasted forever for Sophie like it did for Glenn and me." Her comment made me want to ask about Sophie, who seemed to have a similar naïveté when it came to men. I'd been worried about her lack of social experience, and now it dawned on me that perhaps the apple hadn't fallen too far from the tree onto which it had been grafted.

"I got you guys great seats for the exhibition game," Sophie said. One thing that gave Clarendon an edge among northeastern schools in turning out pro ballplayers was the ability to practice year-round in Farina Arena, with its retractable dome, an endowment from the multitalented alumnus JoJo Farina, who in his professional heyday had been both a Pirate and a Patriot. In fact the Cheers used the arena for tryouts and training.

Pointing to Glenn, Sophie told me, "Dad taught me everything I know. About playing ball, anyway. And thanks to you, Mom, I have great handwriting," she added, looking at Joy.

Joy looked at me and chuckled uncomfortably. "Well, Sophie, hon, I certainly hope I taught you more than penmanship!"

I drew in my breath. "What do you say we get out of here and get some fresh air?"

Under a blue sky worthy of postcard immortality, the trees were a pageant of red and gold. Two by two, we strolled the leaf-strewn campus walks, Sophie ambling ahead with Glenn, and Joy probing me, in the nicest possible way, for my life story. Sophie had already told her that her biological father was a Red Sock.

"Yes, but I'm afraid we were a mismatched pair." A limp attempt at levity. We walked in silence, neither of us sure what to ask, afraid we might not want to hear the answer.

I watched Sophie and Glenn strolling on ahead of us. I was sure he could take care of himself. I hoped that beyond whatever batting tips and defensive fielding maneuvers he had passed along, that he was a good father to her. If he was anything less, I'd have to kill him.

"And you're engaged to a skier?"

"Was." Skier . . . ski manufacturer . . . well, Tom did ski, of course, but not professionally. Clarification required too much explaining, and whenever I thought of him, it was like picking at a scab on my heart. "He thought we'd better call it a day," I said ruefully. "We met on the slopes at Breckenridge last winter." My memory drifted to the private lessons he'd given me after the group demonstration had dispersed. I recalled our first kiss—by the ugliest, saddest little tree I'd ever seen, "a Charlie Brown Christmas tree," I'd called it; our goggles had clunked together and we laughed at how goofy the moment was, when it should have been dreamy and romantic. I remembered how warm his hands always were, no matter how cold it was outside. *Warm hands . . .* cold *heart?* No—I wouldn't let myself go there. Besides, it wasn't true. I wanted to blame Tom for not sticking with me—us—for not waiting. But there were so many other factors in the mix. He had a site-specific business he couldn't just up and leave for a year. He hated New York. I used to think sometimes that to Tom, New York = me: but if you hate the city, you hate the girl, because she has its vibe pulsing through her veins.

"Hey, Soph, wait up!" I turned around just as a sweat-drenched young woman in jogging clothes caught up with us. Her accent was faintly southern.

Sophie looked up. "Hey, Carleen!" She gave the girl a hug. "Dude, you need a shower. Carleen, meet my bio-mom!"

"Awesome! So you're here with Sophie for Parents' Day, Mrs. . . .?"

"Livy." I shook her hand.

"Livy used to be a burlesque dancer—you know, with the feather boas and stuff. And she was a Vegas showgirl, too."

"Dude—that is so awesome!" said Carleen, nodding her head so appreciatively that her blond ponytail flagellated her trapezius. "What do Glenn and Joy think of that?" she asked Sophie.

"I think they're keeping most of their opinions to themselves these days. Joy hasn't met too many people who aren't, like, suburban vanilla and collect Hummel figurines. Livy, Carleen McLure is the best softball pitcher in Kumquats history!" Sophie exclaimed.

"Brava, Carleen! Though I'm sorry for you girls that your team is named for a fuzzy fruit."

"Not as sorry as we are," muttered Carleen sourly. "The *guys* call us the Cum Twats."

"*Carleen's* on a *full* scholarship, so you know how awesome a player she is!"

Awesome. Everything is "awesome." I wonder what they would say if something were truly awesome.

"Ah gotta grab a shower. Ah'll see you in the locker room, if Ah don't see you before?" Carleen enveloped Sophie in another sweaty hug. "Great to meet you, Livy. Ah hope y'all can catch our games!"

"I won't miss a single one," I assured her.

"Awesome!"

When we reached Farina Arena, Sophie left us so she could change into her uniform for the Kumquats exhibition game— just five innings—against the Clash—a gender-bending twist on intramural play. Their pitching ace Tommy DuPree had been boasting for days about how he was going to mow the girls down.

Sophie had secured seats in the bleachers along the third base line, yet close enough to home plate that Glenn could watch his protégée-daughter at bat. The mid-autumn sun cast a vermillion glow over the field. As I dug into my purse for my sunglasses, I began to feel warm and fuzzy toward the Ashes. From what little I'd had the chance to observe, I felt safe in the knowledge that they'd been good to Sophie, loved and admired her, given her everything in their tool kit. As her mother, I couldn't have hoped for a better set of parents.

"Well look who's here!" exclaimed a familiar voice. I peered out from under my wide-brimmed hat to discover Linda de-Marley, outfitted to the teeth in cashmere and gold. "Mind if we join you?"

"Hello, Cousin Marty. Good to see you too, Linda," I added, though they were just about the last people on the planet I wanted to run into.

"Mind if we join you?" Marty reiterated.

He *had* to be kidding.

"We figured blood is thicker than lawyers. Get it?"

Good grief.

"Are you sure you're not here today to check on Tommy DuPree's arm? Don't look so shocked, Marty; I've heard he's a draft prospect for the Cheers. Or maybe you're also here to spy on me—see how good a mom I am to Sophie."

Just then the Clarendon marching band struck up the national anthem, drowning out Marty's sputtered denial, and the ball game began.

There had been a whole hullabaloo about the format of the game; after all, the Kumquats pitched underhand, while the Clash played hardball. And yet the point of the exhibition was to show off each team's prowess. Several proposals were floated, most of which had been soundly rejected out of hand. Both Carleen and Tommy were adamantly opposed to the dean's suggestion to have the girls pitch overhand to the fellas, while the guys pitched underhand to the women. Dean Squires thought it would level the playing field, so to speak, but all it did was piss off both teams and their respective coaches.

Then there was the not-so-brilliant idea to flip a coin to decide which pitching style to use for the entire five innings. The dean got flipped a birdie by both starting pitchers. Carleen had a few choice words for Mr. Squires that nearly got her ejected before the game even began.

The eventual compromise suited the pitchers, but had everyone else in an uproar: the men would have to hit the women's underhand pitches, and the Kumquats would be compelled to hit the Clash's overhand ones. Even Carleen, who was glad to be able to show off her stuff, was anxious about "hittin' one of Tommy's missiles." Actually, she threw harder and faster than he did; she just wasn't used to playing the boys' game. Things could get very interesting.

The Kumquats were up first; Sophie was batting cleanup. After the first three batters had come and gone, I turned away from Linda and grabbed Joy's arm. "It's Sophie!"

"Choke up on the bat, honey!" Glenn shouted. Turning to us, he leaned past his wife and said, "She needs to choke up on the bat. Otherwise she may never get a piece of his fastball, assuming he can find the strike zone."

"I don't think she can hear you," I told him. So he screamed louder. Sophie looked toward the stands. "Choke up on the bat!" we yelled. Somehow, she managed to hear us and adjusted her grip.

"Atta girl," muttered Glenn.

The count went to three balls, then Tommy DuPree threw two consecutive strikes. Glenn complained that the second strike should have been ball four. "The ump needs corrective lenses," he griped.

Marty pointed to Tommy DuPree. "See that kid on the mound. I hear he tops out at an eighty-nine-mile-an-hour fast ball. I'm telling ya, this kid's got a gun for an arm," he told Linda.

Glenn nudged Joy. "See that kid on the mound? They claim he's got a fast ball in the high eighties—the only way that would buy him a cup of coffee in the majors is if he could control it consistently. But he got lucky finding the strike zone on that first strike to Sophie, and the second one never should have been called in the first place. It's gonna be a couple of years before he's a legitimate prospect."

I soaked up the comments from either side, neither of which had heard the other's remarks. It was a valuable lesson in talent scouting. I'd almost forgotten that Glenn had experience in that aspect of the game—which made me take Cousin Marty's comments, as big a fan of the game as he was—with a healthy dose of salt.

Facing a full count, Sophie very deliberately choked up even more, but as soon as Tommy's arm came forward to deliver the pitch, she smoothly lowered her hands and swung at the fast ball right over the plate.

"Fake out!!" shouted Carleen.

The ball went sailing past the shortstop into the gap and landed in the outfield, where, as Glenn pointed out, the guys had been playing too deep. If Tommy DuPree had gift wrapped the pitch, Sophie couldn't have enjoyed it more. "That's my girl!" Glenn shouted above the roar. We were on our feet as Sophie rounded second with a stand-up double.

The rest of the game wasn't nearly as exciting. The Kumquats failed to score Sophie from second, DuPree pitched two innings of admirable, though not stellar, ball, Carleen McLure shut down the Clash for four consecutive innings; but then the catcher hit a base-clearing home run in the bottom of the fifth, and the Clash beat the Kumquats 3 to 1. We were bummed.

Marty and Linda left the stands to introduce themselves to Tommy DuPree, though each of them seemed to have their own reasons for admiring his prowess on the mound, as the Ashes and I rushed down to see Sophie. We waited for her outside the women's locker room. "I'm so proud of you!" I crowed. The three of us wrapped her in a bear hug.

"Sorry I got you all sweaty. And that I didn't score," she said apologetically.

"Not your fault, baby doll," Glenn reminded her. "You gave it everything you had. And I'm proud of you."

After enjoying a rather noisy dinner at one of the local haunts—it seemed like half the campus had descended at once—I parted amicably with the Ashes, and Sophie and I drove back into Manhattan. Sure, we might never entirely "get" each other, but I saw that they had Sophie's best interests at heart, and they realized I was not the Wicked Queen from *Snow White*. I was *very* glad to see the back of Marty and Linda, certain their main objective in showing up was to spy on me to see how I might be getting on with Sophie; assessing the arm of Tommy DuPree was a bonus.

Late one night in November, Sophie and I ran into each other in the kitchen. I'm one of those midnight cereal munchers. Only half jesting, I rationalize it by claiming I'm getting a jump on eating breakfast so I won't have to do it in the morning.

"Ohmigod—you do that, too?" Sophie exclaimed. I almost dropped my bowl. "I've always done this—you know, that 'eat breakfast the night before' thing—and Joy and Glenn never knew where I got that from, because once dinner was over they never raided the kitchen." A light went on inside her head, and with a wondrous sigh she asked me, "Do you think you can inherit something like this? We did the same thing with the salt that first day at brunch, remember?"

I shrugged. "I have no idea. But synchronicity—any time it happens—is pretty mystifying to me."

Sophie finished the last mouthful of her dry cereal and left her spoon and the bowl on the counter. The box of granola was still out as well. "Night, Livy. Don't let the bedbugs . . . and all that."

"Um . . . Soph?" She turned in the doorway. "Who do you think you inherited this from?" I pointed to the dirty dish and spoon. "Do you think the housekeeping staff is going to swoop down and put everything away?" I asked sarcastically. Over the past few weeks that Sophie had been living under my roof, I noticed that she had the tendency to take things out and just leave them somewhere, rather than putting them away again where she found them. "Please put your bowl and your spoon in the dishwasher. And put the granola back on the pantry shelf."

"God—you make it like it's some big crime! Jeez—lighten up."

"Sophie, in the grand scheme of things, taking out a box of cereal and leaving it on the counter after you've finished using it is not the end of the world. But ultimately, it points to a lack of respect. For my stuff, which you are availing yourself of for free—"

"You mean you're going to charge me for eating cereal now? I'm your daughter!"

"You know, Sophie, you pull the daughter card when it's convenient for you; and other times, you want to behave as though I'm some sort of—I don't know, an innkeeper with benefits. You're living under my roof, which means you play by my house rules. And you're not respecting my time by expecting me to pick up after you like you're a little kid. You're too old for that kind of nonsense."

"I don't expect you to pick up after me," Sophie protested hotly.

"Well, then, how do you expect things to get put away? Do you think the dishwasher waddles over to the table to fill itself like something out of a Disney musical?"

"Who knew you could be such a pill? I thought you were cool."

"I think it's possible to be cool and still like a tidy apartment," I argued. "When you live in a crowded city, you learn that you don't want to do anything to encourage roommates of the four- and six-legged variety."

"*Ewww!* Gross!"

"I'm just telling it like it is. But this conversation isn't about roaches, Sophie. It's about respect. I'm your mother, not your maid."

"You're scolding me like I'm a little kid."

"Well, if that's how you feel, maybe it's because you never had this discussion years ago, when your cavalier behavior first became an issue."

"Maybe it never *was* an issue."

I threw my hands in the air. I was in murky waters. I didn't know how much to be a disciplinarian at this stage in Sophie's life—maybe it wasn't my place. Maybe the horse was long gone from the barn by now and it was too late for me to try to grab the reins and retrain it. But I resented the way Sophie was taking it for granted that I'd always pick up after her. She was a grown woman, for Chrissakes. If she wanted to get her own apartment, she could let it become as trashed as she wanted to. But not in my home.

"Sophie, you begged the Ashes to let you live here. And I'm very *happy* you're here. But there are times when I feel like you're taking advantage of my desire to finally get to know you. I didn't say anything about your behavior before because I didn't want to upset the apple cart. I was afraid if I said even one negative thing to you, I'd lose you. So I swallowed a lot of stuff I wanted to say. But if we're ever going to close the circle, we need to be open with each other. Share the not-so-good feelings as well. And frankly, I feel better for having had this discussion instead of stuffing my feelings."

"Well, I feel like shit," Sophie mumbled. "If I'd known that closing the circle would end up being you scolding me over dirty cereal bowls, I wouldn't have moved in."

That hurt. I went over to the kitchen table and sat beside her. "Look," I sighed, "this isn't easy for either of us. And I've been trying to make us behave like blood when we're more like oil and water half the time. We're still strangers to one another . . . and each of us is trying to make the other one more like herself, as if that's the only way to be . . . or at least the right way. A reunion isn't an end cap, Soph; it's a *beginning*—the beginning of a new phase in each of our lives. It's a journey, a process of healing, and we've both got a long way to go in terms of learning about who we are and understanding ourselves as well as each other. So it probably wouldn't kill either of us to try a bit more patience."

Which we did. But did it matter?

⚾

"All rise. Surrogate's Court of the State of New York, County of New York. Justice Salvatore Randazzo presiding."

Sophie and I stood beside Cap Gaines in the oak-paneled courtroom. At the petitioners' table, Marty deMarley, accompanied by Linda, stood next to their ultra-high-powered lawyer, Linda's cousin Sherman Weinstock. Also present were the Cheers' two limited partners with their phalanx of attorneys.

The judge entered and mounted the bench. He was a solidly built man with silver hair, and—to my dismay—a pinky ring.

"What's the matter?" Sophie whispered when she heard my muttered "*uh-oh.*"

"Pinky ring. Whenever you see a character in a movie wearing a pinky ring, it means they're sleazy."

"Please be seated. I have here an Order to Show Cause why the last will and testament of August deMarley should be declared null and void. Mr. Weinstock—you have something to say?"

"Your Honor, I move to have the last will and testament declared invalid because it is my client's contention that August deMarley was incompetent at the time he signed it. Otherwise, there's no rational explanation for the paragraph in which he stipulates that his daughter must 'close the circle' in order to inherit the controlling interest in the Bronx Cheers.

"Additionally, I have located a prior instrument. I offer into evidence a copy of August deMarley's last will and testament dated and duly executed May 4, 1993. In this instrument, he leaves his entire estate to his nephew Marty deMarley."

Marty and Linda grinned triumphantly.

This, alas, was not a surprise to me. The existence of an earlier will, I mean. Only in movies are such things sprung on people. In a real-life lawsuit, if you find a smoking gun, you have to share that information with each of the involved parties.

Mr. Weinstock had produced the two witnesses to the earlier will as well. One of them was a former secretary named Roberta Stivic, who testified that she'd only been working for Cap Gaines for six months at the time she witnessed August deMarley sign his will. It was the only time she'd seen the billionaire and she'd formed no opinion of his character. The other witness was Mr. Gaines's receptionist, Amy Winston, who had been employed in the law firm for eight years at the time she witnessed the decedent's signature.

"He was a nasty man. A *nasty* man," I have to tell you, she testified. "He may have been nice to his ballplayers, but he was an SOB, if you don't mind my saying so, to his own people. There's a paragraph in that will that says that he never liked his nephew—Marty deMarley, that is—but he was so mad at his daughter that he didn't want her to get a thing from him. Not a penny. But then the papers go on to say that Marty was a—he used a Jewish word, which at the time I thought was funny because Mr. deMarley wasn't Jewish—a *putz*, he called his nephew. The will says that he knew he had a granddaughter somewhere out in the world, but that his efforts to find her failed. If you axe me, he didn't look hard enough. So he'd rather leave his worldly goods to his nephew than to some strangers."

The judge mulled this over. "Mr. Weinstock, was this 1993 will ever filed with the court?"

For the first time, the attorney looked a bit sheepish. "Er . . . there does not appear to be a record of that, Your Honor. And we have not been able to locate a copy filed with the clerk's office."

"Then where did you obtain it?"

"From Marty deMarley," Mr. Weinstock told the judge.

"And how do you know that the distribution in that 1993 will was indeed August deMarley's final intention?"

"May I approach the bench, Your Honor?"

Judge Randazzo beckoned him. "Please do, Mr. Gaines. Someone untangle this for me."

"Your Honor, this 1993 instrument was executed and never filed. The decedent felt extremely remorseful after he signed it and requested me to leave it in my office files, and not formally file it with the Surrogate's Court Clerk. August deMarley could have a temper, Your Honor. And this 1993 will is an example of his, well, willfulness. But as time went on, he felt badly that he'd never patched things up with his daughter, and though he was too proud to try to reconnect with her, he didn't really want to cut her out of his will. And he knew that somewhere in America there was another little piece of him running around: a granddaughter. And so the 1993 will was nullified when he made a new will in 2007, which, as is customary, 'revokes all prior wills and codicils.'"

Judge Randazzo frowned. "Mr. Weinstock, if you can offer me no legitimate proof that the 1993 will was filed in court, I can't nullify the 2007 will in favor of a prior one that simply may have languished in Mr. Gaines's file drawer all these years."

"No!" shouted Linda.

"Quiet in my courtroom, please! Mr. Gaines, your office should have destroyed the prior will upon the execution of the later one, but I'm not about to tell a grown man how to keep house," scolded the jurist. "Now, Mr. Weinstock, if you *still* want me to nullify the 2007 will after also nullifying the 1993 instrument, you and your clients are in the on-deck circle without a bat. Because in the absence of a valid will, as counsel knows, the entire estate goes to the decedent's next of kin, which would mean Ms. deMarley gets the whole enchilada."

"Holy sh—!" shouted Marty, just before Linda sharply elbowed him in the ribs.

"And if something had happened to Ms. deMarley somewhere along the line, the estate would be inherited by Ms. Ashe as the decedent's granddaughter." The judge looked from Gaines to Weinstock. He opened a New York Mets desk diary and perused it, making a notation in one of the boxes. "I'm putting the matter over for a week, to give you time to confer with your respective clients and redraft and file a new set of papers with the court. Pax vobiscum, gentlemen. I expect you to clean up this meshuggaas so I can clear the case from my docket."

⚾

A week later, there we all were again. Judge Randazzo's courtroom was beginning to feel like my home away from home. And Sherman Weinstock had altered his tune. But only slightly.

"Your Honor, my clients are no longer seeking to nullify the entire 2007 will. After all, there are a number of philanthropic bequests contained therein that we would be loath to see invalidated. The action has been joined by the two limited partners of the Bronx Cheers and the team's general manager, all of whom are in the courtroom today with their respective counsel. However, in the Amended Order to Show Cause filed with the court three days ago, you will note that the petitioners contest only a specific provisional clause contained within the will, which we believe is vague enough to invalidate that portion of the instrument. That clause specifically applies to the distribution of one of the decedent's key assets—namely the controlling interest in the minor league baseball club known as the Bronx Cheers."

"They've sucked for seasons," the judge observed wryly. "But don't take that as my ruling. Humor, people. Have a sense of humor."

Mr. Weinstock then referred to the "close the circle" wording.

Judge Randazzo leaned forward. "So, Mr. Weinstock, you're claiming the decedent was completely meshuganah when he wrote it. Mr. Gaines, obviously you have something to say about this."

"I most certainly do, Your Honor. "I have a sealed letter written by the decedent which apparently explains what he meant by that phrase. However, that letter was not to be opened until six months after August deMarley's death, which would mean we would not know its contents until February—another two months or so from now."

"So what's the rush?" questioned the judge. "Mr. Weinstock, any way you slice it, your clients are going to get bupkis. Marty deMarley forfeited his rights to the Leroy Neiman painting by contesting the 2007 will in your original Order to Show Cause, so even if the court validates it—the 'close-the-circle' clause notwithstanding—he stands to inherit nothing."

"By February, tryouts for the Cheers will be imminent. I realize that this is highly irregular from a legal standpoint, but I am going to ask Your Honor for a provisional ruling at this time on the meaning of the phrase in question because it is in the interest of *all* parties to have a CEO calling the shots *now*. We have reason to believe that the phrase 'close the circle' refers to the reuniting of my client, the decedent's only child, Olivia deMarley, with her own daughter, Sophie Ashe, whom she gave up for adoption at her birth twenty years ago."

"Objection. Speculation," protested Mr. Weinstock. "How can Mr. Gaines state unequivocally what the phrase means? The wording is open to wide interpretation."

"Would counsel approach the bench?" A sea of dark suits stepped forward. I strained to overhear the sidebar. "Mr. Weinstock, were you acquainted with the decedent?"

"I never met him, Your Honor."

"Mr. Gaines . . . for how many years have you acted as Mr. deMarley's attorney?"

"For thirty-seven years, Your Honor."

"And did you handle many legal matters for him in the scope of your relationship? I'm asking if the two of you had relatively frequent contact with one another."

"I did, sir."

"And were you personally, as well as professionally, acquainted with August deMarley?"

"I was."

"And in *your* opinion, Mr. Gaines, you're quite certain as to the decedent's intention when he wrote the phrase 'close the circle'?"

"It's always been quite clear to me what the phrase means."

"Clear as mud," muttered Mr. Weinstock.

Judge Randazzo peered at my lawyer. "Mr. Gaines?"

"In the last months of his life, August deMarley began to regret that he had not made any effort to reconnect with his daughter. Family meant a lot to him, but he felt that love is something that is earned—that being related by blood doesn't allow you an automatic gimme; and that sometimes people who aren't your family are more of your family than family—if you get my drift."

"Now it's clear as quicksand," quipped Mr. Weinstock.

"The Cheers were a family to Mr. deMarley. But he came to the decision that he had not been as kind to his own kin, and he sought to rectify things. I knew the man very well, Your Honor, and between us guys, he could be a stubborn prick. There was no way he was going to reach out to his daughter after pretending she was dead to him for half her life. But he knew that Olivia deMarley had given up her own daughter for adoption and he sought to effect a reconciliation in the next generation, with the hope that Olivia and her natural child would form a lasting connection."

"That is pure speculation!" argued Mr. Weinstock. "How did August deMarley know his granddaughter would track down her biological mother?"

"He didn't," Cap Gaines admitted. "He was hoping. It's not unusual for a man approaching his final months to become a bit of a softie. Or maybe he had the last laugh and was smarter than any of us, knowing Marty deMarley and his wife all too well. Perhaps he wrote the vaguely worded phrase on purpose because he counted on the will being legally challenged—in which case he knew that his daughter would inherit everything."

"We'll take our chances on what's contained in the sealed letter," said Mr. Weinstock.

"I feel like I'm in Wonderland, here," the judge said. "Mr. Weinstock, I agree with you that the phrase in question is rather vague."

The limited partners low-fived each other under the petitioners' table. Linda and Marty clutched hands.

"However . . . that said . . . pursuant to *respondent's* request, I'm inclined to give a provisional ruling on the meaning of the phrase 'close the circle' based on Mr. Gaines's long-standing knowledge of the decedent's mind and character. I am ordering the sealed letter to be opened in my presence in February; and if the meaning of the phrase is any different from Mr. Gaines's interpretation, we'll deal with it then. However—and this is a big however—as you've opened this can of worms, Mr. Weinstock, I'll mix my metaphors and offer your client a bone here. Ditto of course for the other petitioners in this action—Mr. Fernando, Mr. Argent, and Mr. Weed.

"Mr. Gaines, by the time we reconvene in February, I would like to see some evidence that the circle has in fact been closed, or evidence to the contrary that it has not."

Mr. Weinstock straightened his tie and assumed his most pugnacious stance. "Your Honor, this is highly irregular. How are you going to decide whether Ms. deMarley and her daughter have 'closed the circle.'?"

"They're living together now. That should in and of itself satisfy the will." Cap Gaines argued.

"Not quite, counselor," the judge replied. "I'm looking at this the way an arbitrator might view a Green Card marriage. Cohabitation alone is not sufficient grounds. I'm going to order a continuance, *sua sponte*, which will give the parties time to prepare their respective cases for a February appearance before the bench. At that time, Mr. Gaines, I expect you to put both your client and Ms. Ashe on the stand for cross-examination." The gavel descended with a dull thud. "Case adjourned."

No one spoke a word as we departed the courtroom. Barry Weed coughed and the sound reverberated off the walls. In the elevator Sophie said to Cap Gaines "Did we win?"

"Well . . . we won the chance to win," he replied. "Kind of like getting into the playoffs. The opportunity to win the whole enchilada is there; you just need to seize it. And my advice to the two of you is to spend as much time as you can in each other's company. Find out what makes the other one tick, your likes and dislikes, your hobbies and interests, your favorite flavor of ice cream. Keep diaries. Because Weinstock is going to tear into your personal lives and you need to be prepared to answer his questions."

"I don't see how the judge is going to decide whether or not I get the Cheers based on what we say on the witness stand. Our favorite flavor of ice cream? We could be lying."

"You'll be under oath," Gaines reminded me.

"Oh, yeah. Right. But still—closing the circle is an awfully subjective thing. Frankly, I think Marty and Linda and the rest of them are right in wanting to contest that caveat!"

"_Shhh!_ Don't let anyone hear you say that!" Gaines looked furtively about him even though he and Sophie were the only other people in the elevator.

We stepped out onto the street. "Now go forth and get to know everything about each other. And more than that—_care._" Cap Gaines shook our hands. "Make an appointment with Sheila to come down to the office in three weeks so I can prep you two for the next court appearance." He strode back toward his office while Sophie and I headed for the subway.

By the time we got home, I had a pounding headache. It felt like all the life force had been sucked out of me. I headed straight upstairs to my bedroom and sank onto the mattress. "I don't know why I let myself get into all this," I moaned.

Sophie followed me upstairs with a glass of water and the aspirin bottle. "Because I want you to," she said encouragingly. "Because I want you to inherit the Cheers. Because I care about that team just like Grampa did, and what happens to it is important to me."

"You baseball fans are such fanatics," I muttered, taking the aspirin out of Sophie's hand.

"That's what makes the game so wonderful!" She smiled.

"Nothing is worth having our private lives dragged out into the open."

"The Cheers are," Sophie insisted. "And I won't let you come away from all this with nothing."

I shook my head. "Not nothing. I have you. Getting the chance to know you is worth the weight of all the Bronx Cheers put together." I gave her a hug and the tears began to flow. I was really missing Tom and what we'd had together. I wanted things to be simple again. "I'm sorry to lay all this on you, Soph. I should have just gone back to Colorado after Augie's memorial. This was all too much for both of us."

She offered me a tissue. "Stop it," she soothed. "You know, it's funny. When I first met you, I thought, 'Shit! I've never seen someone with so much self-possession. I wish I had a tenth of her confidence and composure.' And now—" she chuckled, "I've spent the last two months or so realizing that you're a marshmallow under all that tensile steel."

"I'm a mess, you mean."

"Nooo . . . you're just human. The coolest thing that I can say about you, as your daughter, the most amazing thing, is that it's so reassuring to know that you're, well, *normal*."

I hugged her tightly. "I'm afraid you've got my number, kiddo."

"We're going to have a game plan, dude," she said, jumping up from the bed. She rummaged in her desk for a notepad. "You're not the type to relinquish control, Livy. So why let Barry Weed, and the Cheers' limited partners, and dorky cousin Marty and Lady MacdeMarley *win* their lawsuit? You're not a quitter; and if you shrug me off, I won't believe it. I don't want to think that of the woman who bore me."

"Oh Sophie . . ." By now, I was a puddle of tears. What a sweet, sweet kid. It stung all the more that I had missed her childhood.

"You're getting all tangled up in assuming that being a good mother is all about Band-Aids and bake sales. And that if you're becoming my friend it means you've somehow failed at figuring out what it means to be my mother. You can't play catch-up or compete with Joy. That tooth fairy's flown the coop. And Joy will always be my mom, too. Hey—I'm the luckiest kid on the planet! I've got two moms and you couldn't be more different. But what you both have in common is me. And I know you both want the best for me." She reached over and stroked my forehead.

"Okay," she said, trying to stay all business. That child fought her emotions as though they were dragons. "It's all good. You're not a bad person; you just never had to be a mom before. And I don't want that silver-haired judge to have the slightest reason to think you're not up to the job. I saw the way Linda deMarley was looking at you on Parents' Day. When we were walking back from Farina Arena, she was, like, waiting for us to quarrel about something, and for you to trip and fall on your face. And I don't doubt for a minute she would have stepped right on your spine in those stilettos of hers. So," she added, extending her hand, "do we have a deal?"

I shook. "Deal."

But I felt a bit bad about it. What could I do for her in return?

A few days later, Sophie's best friend, Carleen, came to see me in hysterics. As Sophie's "cool mom," and given my life experience, her friends had deemed me an expert on all things related to matters of the heart—and parts farther south; den mother meets Dr. Ruth.

"Ah told Tommy DuPree Ah didn't love him anymore,"

Carleen blubbered, curled into a ball in a corner of my couch. "And he said *okay!*"

"She broke up with him—and he let her!" Sophie explained. "You know all about these things, Livy. What should she do?"

I regarded Carleen's tear-stained face. Sophie spoke for her friend, because the lady ace was too emotionally overwrought to articulate. "Just because Carleen doesn't want to be with Tommy anymore, it still really hurts her that he's cool with that. . . ."

"It shouldn't be so easy," Carleen managed to blurt between sobs. "For Tommy, Ah mean. How much could he ever really have loved me if breaking up didn't seem to matter?"

"But you told me you broke up with him because *you* don't love *him* anymore."

Carleen hugged a box of Kleenex. "Yeah, . . . but still."

I stroked her back reassuringly. "Time and distance is what you need. That'll be a good start. All those clichés—'Time heals all wounds,' 'Out of sight, out of mind'—are truisms as well." For some people, anyway. Tom hadn't been out of my mind once. But a while back, my dear friend Tessa had been the dumpee, and I counseled her to take a much-needed vacation overseas to clear her head. She came back to New York with an adorable Irishman in tow, and now they're married. Still, it would be hard for Carleen to avoid Tommy DuPree; their paths crossed too frequently, unless Carleen really made the effort to avoid running into him.

"Thank Jesus we're not in any of the same classes together this term," Carleen sniffled. "But Ah have so much of his stuff. Ah even have his bathrobe!"

"I'd make a project of boxing it all up and getting it out of your life by asking an impartial third party to deliver it to Tommy." I glanced over at Sophie who gave me such a funny look that I thought better of volunteering her services.

Carleen admitted that my suggestion made sense, but then burst into tears again, throwing herself into my arms and wailing, "Ah never thought something that was my idea could hurt so much!"

"I know, I know," I murmured into her hair. "But that doesn't mean it was a bad idea. Does it really make any sense to keep dating a guy when you no longer feel anything for him emotionally?"

"Then why do Ah feel so duuumb?" she sobbed.

"You're not dumb. What you did was brave, Carleen. And mature. I'm proud of you."

She broke the hug and wiped her nose with her forearm. "Ah think I'd better go home now," she said, rising to her feet. "Sweet Jesus, Ah think Ah need a drink," she mumbled.

"Not in my house, if you're under twenty-one," I said gently.

"Right you are!" Carleen said glumly. "Thank you, Livy. Ah got a lot to think about." She shuffled out of my apartment, still snuffling as she headed toward the elevator.

Sophie didn't move. "Honey, I think Carleen needs you now. Why don't you go up to Clarendon with her tonight, make sure she doesn't do something stupid," I suggested. My girl looked utterly stricken. She glanced away from me to hide her tears. I scooted over to where she was sitting and touched her knee. "Hey, what's up, Soph?"

She turned back to me with a guilty expression. "Livy, I've had a crush on Tommy DuPree since forever. And I could never tell Carleen because it would have been the ultimate betrayal even to mention it. I never did anything about it, though," Sophie added hastily. "As soon as he and Carleen hooked up, sophomore year, I never even thought about him that way anymore. But when she told me she was going to break up with him, all of a sudden, it was, like, having your deepest wish come true maybe, except that it was a secret you had to keep from your best friend. Did that ever happen to you?"

I thought about the day I learned I was pregnant with Sophie. At first I didn't tell anyone because I had no idea what I was going to do about it. Stay, go away, have it, abort it. Rodney was married—though at the time he considered himself separated—at least that's what he always told me. We'd had a fling—not even an *affair*—and even at nineteen I knew enough to realize that becoming the third Mrs. Rodney Peterson was off the table. My roommates didn't know about my pregnancy—not even Tessa. I was too scared, and too embarrassed, to talk about it. The *last* person I could have confided in was my father, and given my circumstances, the most pragmatic course was to have an abortion. A few days later, I had the Planned Parenthood phone number in my hand when Rodney called me—didn't even meet me—to say, "Make it go away, Venus." And that's when I decided to have her. Because the irony was that if I "obeyed" Rodney, I *wouldn't* in fact have had control over my own reproductive system; I'd be taking his orders and making his choice.

I looked Sophie squarely in the eye. "Yes, I've had my share of secrets like that over the years," I said softly.

And then I confessed them.

The other Tommy DuPree cleat dropped just before Sophie's first semester finals.

"I have an ethical question," she said, lifting her nose out of her broadcasting class notebook.

"About FCC stuff? Freedom of speech?"

Sophie laughed. "Why would I ask *you* that?"

"Beats me. Because I have strong opinions on freedom of expression, maybe?"

"Maybe. But no cigar. It's personal." She shut her notebook and gazed at it thoughtfully. "I have a friend . . . who has a friend . . . okay?"

"I guess it's okay," I teased. "Don't roll your eyes, sweetie. Okay, it's okay. Go on."

"And this friend's friend used to be going out with someone, and they broke up a while ago, like a month ago already. And now this friend's friend's ex-boyfriend asked out my friend. Not my *friend's* friend, *my* friend."

"Well then, do you *want* to go out with Tommy DuPree?" I asked Sophie.

"How'd you know?"

This time *I* rolled my eyes. "Because the *friend* beard is one

of the oldest tricks in the book, and because I wasn't born yesterday—and please don't make any snippy quips about it."

"Okay, so Tommy invited me to the Clash's Christmas party, which is always this huge deal with a live band and really
good food and stuff."

And really good booze, too, I imagined. *There had better not be
really good drugs*. Was the current crop of college kids as druggy
as they were back in my day? I wasn't sure I wanted to find
out.

"And it's *sort of* okay if I accept, because Carleen and I are
best friends and she wants me to be happy. But I feel totally
weird about going out with her ex. That's where the sort-of
part comes into play."

"You don't think it will compromise your friendship?"

Sophie mulled it over. "Well, I mean . . . if she says she's
cool with it, then I think she really is. I told her about it right
after Tommy asked me, and she didn't punch me out or pitch
anything at my head."

My poor kid was in such consternation. Her expression, so
often enigmatic, betrayed nothing. It was as though she were
steeling herself against disappointment. Solomon had an easier decision with the baby. I smiled encouragingly at her. "Then
I think you should go to the party."

She let out an excited yelp. "Really?!" followed immediately
by a deeply furrowed brow. "Oh my God, I have nothing to
wear!" She jumped up and strode over to her closet. A bit of
rummaging through the rack produced the skirt I had privately pronounced dowdy when I'd first surveyed her wardrobe
back in September. "I mean, look at this!"

Actually, about a third of Sophie's closet was devoted to my
own clothes. Storage space is always at a premium in a Manhattan apartment. Sophie began to finger the fabrics lovingly.
"For the first time in my life, I wish I had stuff more like *this*."

Her eyes lit upon a custom-made leather minidress that laced up the bodice. I owned over-the-thigh boots to match, with a three-inch heel.

"Why don't you try it on?" I suggested.

"Can I?"

Our figures were totally different. If she stretched out the leather there was probably no way the dress would ever fit me again. Still, such a sacrifice was a no-brainer; my Cinderella would go to the ball in the dress of her dreams, even if it killed me to part with it.

Of course when she asked to drive my vanilla-colored Alfa-Romeo vintage convertible to the party instead of saddling up her Toyota, I almost had a coronary.

"Please-oh-please, I'll be extra careful with it. I won't park near anyone else so it can't get nicked by some drunk on their way home—"

"Excuse me? I know I'd be a naïve dolt to assume that there won't be alcohol at the Clash's bash, even if the coach has banned it—but if I *ever* catch you inebriated, I'll—"

"You'll what?" Sophie demanded.

Come to think of it, I have no idea what I would do. I'd love to think I'd kick her butt over it, or let her wallow in her own vomit until she promises never to get pissing drunk again, but I don't think I'd have it in me to do either one of those things, if push came to shove.

"I don't drink, Livy. Not really. A beer every now and then with Carleen and the Kumquats when we go out after practice sometimes. No one checks IDs."

"Swell," I said sarcastically.

"But you don't have to worry about me. I got through three years of college without you, you know. I can take care of my-self."

Nothing like feeling unneeded when you're trying to be

helpful. Sophie seemed pretty bold in her breeches for someone trying to shoehorn herself into my leather dress.

"Maybe if I give up carbs until the party," she muttered.

Unfortunately, the problem couldn't be solved that easily; she was just broader across the back and thicker through the torso.

"You see why I don't wear dresses," she fretted helplessly.

I found my sewing kit and took out the tape measure. A pal of mine in the garment district owed me a favor. I didn't know what I was going to do about the boots, though.

I made a mental checklist of the other necessary preparations. Small talk wouldn't be a problem for Sophie; at a jock party, she'd be in her element, conversationally. In fact, there'd probably be very little talking, since they'd all go hoarse trying to be heard above the band.

So the next hurdle was the art of makeup application. Sophie's idea. I took her to a Sephora and let her play. Cosmetics aside, you're never too young to develop a good skin-care regimen, I told her. She agreed I looked pretty good for my age. I almost slapped her.

I let her drive the Alfa Romeo up to Westchester, since I wanted to be certain she could handle it safely and competently. "The clutch is a bit wonky," I warned, as she sped past the Cloisters, taking the curves on the Henry Hudson Parkway faster than I thought she should. "And don't pretend you're at a NASCAR rally!"

A mile or so from Clarendon, she pulled over to the curb, killed the engine, and frowned.

"You looked pained, Soph. Is something the matter?"

"I think I might need to stop at a drugstore."

I rested my hand on her forearm. "Sweetie, are you feeling okay?"

"Yeah, I'm fine." Sophie lapsed into a lengthy silence. Those impenetrable eyes were working on something, something that eventually turned her face a lovely shade of burgundy—perfect for the upholstery in an opera house, but not as a skin tone.

"*Ummm* . . . I never told anybody this . . . I mean even Carleen doesn't know. Joy knows, but that was before I started college." Her color deepened even further. "Livy . . . ? I'm still a virgin."

She gave me this woeful look as though I could lift the weight of the world from her shoulders. "And . . . well . . . I thought I should buy some condoms . . . because . . ."

I was a bit stunned by her revelation. "Because you're counting on hopping into bed with a guy you hardly know?"

"That's not true! I've known him since freshman year—just as long as Carleen has."

"Honey, I think you ought to think things through. I mean, I'm happy to suggest which condoms might make the experience more enjoyable, but I'm far from convinced you should just jump—"

Her eyes flashed. Finally, a spark of something! "I never should have said anything to you. I thought you were cool, Livy, which is why I confided in you, but you're just as judgmental as Joy would have been."

"I'm your mother. I get that privilege."

"No, you gave up that privilege twenty years ago!"

"Damn it, Soph, I also gave up my future husband to make it up to you—and it was the second-toughest decision of my life."

Her voice rose. "I never asked you to do that—don't you dare put that shit on me, Livy! Why don't you just leave and go back to him, then?"

"Believe me, kid, there are times when I wish I could do just that. But you're hell-bent on my 'closing the circle.' You don't always make things easy, you know."

"Well, you can be pretty fucking impossible yourself, sometimes, too."

I came this close to smacking her across the mouth. But in a way, she was right, or as right as I was, so I fought to hold my redheaded temper in check. "Get out of the car, Sophie. We're trading places. I'm driving us home."

"Can we still stop at a pharmacy or a convenience store, or something?" she muttered.

"I'll think about it."

In the end, I relented. I pulled up in front of the drugstore right off campus. I figured it would have a higher turnover of product. If Sophie was hell-bent on losing her virginity, despite my attempts to dissuade her from throwing herself at Tommy DuPree, I wanted to at least be relatively certain that the Trojans hadn't been sitting on the shelf since Hector was a baby.

Well, of course she had no idea of the length and girth of Tommy DuPree's equipment, though Carleen had once told her that just because a man wields a Louisville Slugger, it didn't mean he was capable of hitting homers. I took the metaphor to mean that perhaps we should buy a box of "larges," though Sophie wasn't entirely certain Carleen had been referring to Tommy, and in any event, she became so confused over the array of choices—ribbed or not, lubricated or not, flavored or not—that she bought a box of everything (well, I put it on my credit card).

It was hard to suppress a laugh. "Honey, if you're planning on bringing this entire stash to the party, you'll need a much bigger purse!"

⚾

I'm not entirely sure which genius had the idea to schedule the baseball team's holiday bash and intramural batting contest on the night before finals week began. I suppose there was some guy-logic involved, perhaps that people might get the heck out of town as soon as their exams were over, which could severely reduce the guest list. Maybe they figured jocks didn't hit the books nearly as hard as they hit the speed bag, so there wouldn't be too much studying going on, anyway. Sophie's study habits were impeccable, however. Knowing she had a test on the first day of finals week, she holed up in her room, or at the Clarendon library, cramming like crazy so that she would be fully prepared to ace the exam, despite being out late the night before.

Her boots and leather minidress arrived three days before the party. "Oh my God, I can't wait to try these on! You are the most amazing person, Livy!" She launched herself into my arms and nearly tackled me. "Thank you so much! Oh my God, this is so awesome! I have to show Carleen."

She thought better of it, though. Too much like rubbing salt into a wound. Besides, she wanted to make a grand entrance and not spoil it by having a dress rehearsal beforehand. I'd taken her to my stylist for a good haircut, and now her face was framed by subtle layers which enhanced the glossiness and natural lowlights in her dark hair, revealed that she had cheekbones, and softened the line of her strong jaw—though now she worried that her locks might not be long enough to pull into her usual ponytail.

Sophie had been diligently practicing with her new makeup, too, yet she didn't trust herself not to make a mess of it. "Every time I try to do it myself, I come out looking like a clown. Or Joan Collins on _Dynasty_," she fretted. "Would you mind doing my makeup for the party?"

So of course I agreed, though I've never understood how some women can lack the gene for applying cosmetics. I thought we were all born with it, the same way we gals, unlike most straight men, have an instinct for what colors flatter us.

Before she departed for the party, we went back over the basics. "Drive carefully or I will kill you, Soph. Don't drink and drive or *it* will. If you have a drink, have a friend drive you back here. Do not—I repeat, do *not*—give *my* car keys to anyone at that party, regardless of sobriety. Got that, sweetheart?"

"Got it!" I could see that she was jittery. She kept checking herself out in the mirror. "I can't believe it . . . I look so . . . pretty." There were tears in her eyes.

"You *are* pretty, Sophie."

"But not like you."

"Different. Every woman has her own beauty." Oh, boy. Joy Ashe must have missed a spot. Then again, I got a little happy pang thinking that there was still something left for me to cover. Ever since I'd met Sophie, I'd been searching for ways to be useful, helpful, to be a true mom to her.

"Sophie, my girl, you are gorgeous—with and *without* the leather and the makeup." Playfully, I rapped on her freshly coiffed hair. "If you can get that through your skull—and keep it there, you will make both of us very happy."

"But still—this is exactly how I wanted to look! She regarded her reflection one last time. "Tommy DuPree'd better appreciate it," she muttered.

I enfolded her in my arms. "If he doesn't, my darling—remember this—he's toast!" Kissing her cheek, I added, "Have a *wonderful* time, Sophie."

"I will," she beamed, and I thought I caught her wiping away a tear. "Don't wait up for me."

But I knew I would.

⁂

I rode my Vespa up to Larchmont to have dinner with the Ashes. They'd received subpoenas to testify in court on behalf of the petitioners and were understandably nervous about it.

"We've never been sued," Joy said anxiously.

"You're not being sued; I am," I said. I was nervous because Sherman Weinstock had gotten to them before Cap Gaines had. Obviously they'd be cross-examined by my attorney, but they would be there to testify for the other side.

"What are we supposed to say?" Glenn wondered.

Joy frowned. "I'm not afraid to tell you that I don't like this, Livy. Are we supposed to say that you're a bad mom or something?"

"Or that you are closer to Sophie than you really are?" Glenn added.

"You'll be expected to answer their questions truthfully, and to the best of your ability." I was grateful for the cocktail the Ashes offered as they ushered me into the den. "You know, I feel like we're all being asked to take a test that's so subjective it's damn near impossible to pass it," I said, sipping my whiskey. "You guys, I don't know what I'm doing with Sophie half the time. Where do I draw the lines? What are the boundaries? Sometimes I tell her something and I feel like I'm treading on your toes, Joy. I mean, for example—did she pick up after herself when she was growing up?"

The Ashes exchanged a cryptic look and then burst out laughing. "Oh, please!" Joy exclaimed. "I could never get her to clean up!"

Glenn slapped his knee a couple of times. "Yes! We used to bribe her! A new glove if she'd straighten up her room; or a trip to the movies if she actually washed a dish or put her dirty clothes in the hamper. When she went away to college, Joy had to take her on a field trip to the basement and impart to her the arcane mysteries of that big white whirring machine because she'd never done her own laundry in her life."

He'd made me laugh. "You spoiled her!"

"I knowww," Joy confessed guiltily. "But that's what you do with an only child." She sipped her chardonnay and then stared into the glass. "I can't conceive," she said quietly. "Sophie was our blessing. And we didn't mind the consequences if we were a bit indulgent when she was little."

Glenn nodded. "And *not* so little, too. Yeah, we did kind of spoil her rotten, but she didn't grow up so badly. She's a good kid; doesn't drink or do drugs . . . "

"Or listen to music we hate," giggled Joy, more relaxed now that she'd shared her big secret with me. "There's no hidden recipe to bonding with your daughter, you know. I mean, Glenn was always a lot closer to Sophie than I am. They both adore baseball, and after all these years I still can't remember what a balk is! So I don't know how the judge is going to render his decision."

"Loving and listening. Those would be the top two things on my list," said Glenn.

"You see—yes—but beyond, or in addition to that, how do you quantify, or qualify, the other stuff? My lawyer wants us to study each other like lab rats or something, learn each other's little quirks—the favorite ice-cream flavor stuff, as he would put it. But that's like having the sparkly ornaments before you have the Christmas tree. I started out by figuring that it was too late for me to do most of the parental things you do with your daughter. So the best I could do was befriend her. But in some ways, your daughter can't be your friend—not in the way that your friend-friends are. With your friends, you support them no matter how dopey they act, because that's what friends do. But with your kid, you want to do everything in your power to *prevent* them from doing something dopey because the last thing you want is to see them get hurt."

Glenn offered to refill my rocks glass, but I declined. After all, I had to drive home on a motor scooter. His seafood risotto was excellent, and the rest of the evening passed relatively amicably, although the tension between the Ashes and me remained pretty palpable. I could certainly sense that, au fond, they wished Sophie had never found me, but since she had, they would soldier on, chins skyward, and make the best of it.

They walked outside with me and wished me a safe ride home. "Just remember one thing," Joy said, right before I donned my helmet. "You can't be us, and you can't give Sophie what we did."

"What my wife is saying—although I'm sure she didn't mean to put her Aerosole in her mouth—is to just be yourself, Livy. Believe me, I don't want Marty deMarley or Dick Fernando or Peter Argent to end up calling the shots in the Cheers front office. Oh, shit—wait! Can you wait a sec before you take off?" Glenn dashed back inside.

Joy shook her head. "I have no idea what he's up to. I'm sorry. Glenn has a way of doing things like that. Mr. Last Minute, I call him. I hope you didn't think I was being rude just now," she added. "I mean, I'm still . . . we're still . . . not quite used to the fact that you exist—I mean, as a tangible being in our lives—and it hasn't been an easy adjustment to lose Sophie."

"You haven't lost her," I said softly. "She'll always be your daughter, too."

Glenn came running out of the house holding a black canvas backpack. It looked extremely heavy. "In here," he said breathlessly. "Some of Sophie's game tapes. I never quite got to transferring them to DVD. But . . . I thought you might want to watch them."

I beamed. "Thanks!" Glenn helped me shoulder the backpack, and I put-putted out of their cul de sac and headed for the highway.

It was close to midnight by the time I arrived home from the Ashes. Sophie hadn't come back yet from the Clash's team Christmas party. I undressed and slipped on a vintage silk kimono, a gift from a Kyoto businessman who used to frequent one of my nightclubs back in Vegas. Then I fed one of Sophie's game tapes into my VCR and cuddled up with a cup of cocoa—no kidding.

It was 1:47 when she stumbled through the door. Believe me, I'd been watching the clock. With a significant amount of wobbling and weaving, Sophie managed to make it into her bedroom, but not five seconds later, fell to her knees and threw up right in the middle of the carpet. When I flicked on the light, she turned toward me, wincing like Dracula at dawn. Her face was a sickly greenish tint that spelled too-much-to-drink.

With my adrenaline still pumping, my first reaction was not maternal solicitude for her delicate condition; it was rage at her evident flouting of my warning not to drink herself sick or silly. "What were you thinking?" I demanded. "Did you hear a single word I said before you left for the party?" Her hair was a mess, her makeup smeared and streaked. She resembled a nauseous raccoon. What happened to the girl who continually asserted—often to the point of sanctimoniousness—that she wasn't a partier?

"I hate you!" she shouted. "I hate you, I hate you!!"

She tugged at her boots and threw them against the wall, then wriggled out of the eight-hundred-dollar leather dress I'd commissioned for her, and willfully tossed it into the stinking puddle of vomit.

"What—why do you hate me, Soph? What's going on? What the hell happened tonight?" I wanted like anything to hose down the bedroom and disinfect Sophie, the rug, the dress, and everything within smelling distance. I was about to throw up, myself, from the odor. As an old pro at propping up drunk and hung-over girlfriends, I knew from the looks of things (and the smell) that she'd unwisely mixed the grain and the grape, and had then tried to soak it all up and keep it all down with large bites of pizza. *Yuck!*

Sophie burst into hysterical sobs, in between which she managed to tell me that "Everything was great at the party and everyone was totally blown away by how I looked and everything, and I was drinking rum and caffeine-free Coke and then someone handed me a beer, which was really cold, and I guess I sucked it down really fast, but I didn't want anyone to take my cocktail away while I wasn't looking, so I finished that pretty fast, too, I guess; and then after a while Tommy Du-Pree—who thought I looked like a babe—invited me upstairs to talk, he said; and I thought 'what the heck,' so I started kissing him and stuff; and he was pretty wasted—but he's still a good kisser—and then he asked me something like—" and here she lapsed into an imitation of Tommy's voice—"'Hey, Soph, your birth mom's a babe. You think she'd be interested in a three-way?' And then he started going on and on, really drunk, about how gorgeous your legs are, and your hair, and how you had the best tits he'd ever seen on a woman over twenty-five and that you were probably a really great lay; and I wanted to deck him, but I was afraid to; and besides, I liked him sooo much before he said that; and I should really let Carleen have the pleasure of decking him, anyways; and then I went back downstairs and started making drinks from whatever bottle was open on the counter; and no, I don't know how many I had, but there was orange juice in some of them; and then I lost the holiday home run derby; so I snagged a ride home with the Clash's equipment manager because you didn't want me to drink and drive and no one else wanted to leave when I did, which was about the time I realized that I couldn't see straight very well, so no wonder I lost the derby, except everyone else had been drinking too; but if I stayed at the party any longer I was going to do something awful to Tommy DuPree; and the coach put your car in his garage; oh and right before I got to the party, the campus police pulled me over because they said I ran a stop sign and they gave me a sobriety test, but I hadn't had anything to drink yet; and they looked in my purse and found all the condoms I had in there. And they asked me what I planned to do with all of them, and I turned totally red and now the campus police call me the Rubber Maid. And I have a final at 9:00 a.m. and I totally hate my life! And I hate YOU, too, for ruining it!"

"How did I ruin your life, honey?" I sat beside her on the bed and smoothed her hair off her glistening forehead. Come morning, we'd need to have a talk about the dangers of riding in cars with men she barely knew.

Sophie physically pushed me away. "Because you made me beautiful and you made me believe that I was desirable—but it was all a big fucking joke, because all the guys want YOU instead, Mom! No one wants ME. You tried to make me into Cinderella, but I'm just one of the ugly stepsisters!" she wailed.

I tried to hold her, hug her, calm her down, remind myself that it was the booze that was doing most of the talking. She passed out in my arms, just as I'd discovered the one positive that emerged from her in vino veritas. During Sophie's distraught and sadly self-deprecating tirade, for the first time ever—she'd called me *Mom*.

As it was nearing noon, I tiptoed into Sophie's bedroom. She'd somehow managed to make it up to Clarendon for her final, but crashed again as soon as she came home. I'd left her with a cold, wet washcloth over her forehead and eyes, as she moaned that she thought her head was going to explode, adding grimly that she wished it would, so she'd be put out of her misery.

"Feeling any better?" I whispered.

"I'm not dead. Or dehydrated anymore. So I guess it's an improvement," Sophie murmured. She tried to sit up. *"Whoa."* I sat beside her and helped prop up her back against a couple of pillows.

"This isn't going to work," she said finally.

"What isn't, sweetie?"

"Us. This arrangement. I made a mistake. I want to go home."

I felt as though I'd just been sucker punched. "You are home, Soph."

"No. Back to the Ashes, I mean."

I couldn't exactly try to stop her. That would only have made things worse and cemented her decision to bolt.

"B-but what about closing the circle?" I said gently? This

wasn't about earning the Cheers; *that* meant squat to me. I'd lost Tom to gain Sophie. I couldn't bear losing her, too. "Aren't you the one who told me a couple of months ago how disappointed she'd be if I decided to throw in the towel? You said you didn't want to think that you had sprung from the loins of a quitter, if I recall. So I have to tell you, I have no idea why *you* suddenly want to bail."

"It's not suddenly. I told you last night. Because you ruined my life!" She winced in pain. "*Ow,* my head!"

"I'll get you a couple of aspirin. Be back in a minute."

She swallowed the pills with Herculean effort. "You're welcome," I said. I perched on the edge of her bed. "What's really bothering you, sweetheart? You can tell me."

"It's—it's just that you can't make something happen just because you want it to. I don't know what I expected, but I didn't get it."

Whoa.

We took this conversation up to Westchester, where I retrieved my car and the two of us drove over to the Ashes. They welcomed her with open arms, and gave me dirty, questioning looks, as though I had somehow tortured our daughter into fleeing my nest. Joy headed to the kitchen to make a fresh pot of coffee as the rest of us retreated to the den. Glenn had a roaring fire going, and the room was as cozy as a Currier and Ives print.

"I have to say I'm surprised at you, slugger." Glenn had nestled himself into a roomy armchair upholstered in a black-and-white plaid. "I won't use the word *disappointed,* because that's demoralizing. But I'm surprised. You're not a quitter. Your mother and I—" he glanced at me. "Your other mother and I didn't raise you to be a quitter."

"I'm not a quitter," Sophie sullenly replied. "It's just not what I thought it would be."

"And what did you think it would be, Sophie? Did you want to be infantilized with Cream of Wheat for breakfast and cups of cocoa before bed? You couldn't start over with Livy as though you were a newborn for her to raise—birthday parties with silly paper hats and pony rides. You had a great childhood, slugger, if I remember correctly. But you don't get a do-over. You grow up and the nature of your relationship with your parents changes. It has to! Or we'd all be in therapy."

Just then Joy entered with the mugs of coffee on a metal tray embossed with images of kitty cats. *Speaking of infantilizing . . . but, heck, the woman likes kitty cats. So what.*

"Daddy's right, slugger. Both of you have to learn how to love each other for who you are now, as a mother and daughter, but also as adults."

Something about Sophie's little drunken escapade last night came out, and I thought for sure the Ashes would change their minds. They both frowned, then scowled, then regarded each other, regarded Sophie, looked back at each other and remained silent for a least a minute. It was so quiet in their den that I could have sworn I heard the pendulum swinging on the grandfather clock.

"Well, I think we know what's best for Sophie," Glenn said with great finality.

This did not bode well.

"Sophie's a real daddy's girl, so whatever Glenn says, she'll listen," Joy added.

"Good coffee, hon," remarked Glenn.

"Thanks! It's from Trader Joe's."

Another uncomfortable silence settled on the room.

"Slugger . . . what happened last night was a prime example of free will, and what happens to people when they exercise it and do dumb things. No one made you get pie-eyed at that party." He tapped his head with his knuckles. "I just have a hunch, in here, that Livy lectured you about drinking, before you left her house. And about the dangers of drinking and driving. And you sure as heck know that your mother and I have done the same. But you were feeling your oats, and you decided not to listen to anything any of your parents ever told you. Lord knows you're not the first young lady to fall all over herself over some guy who doesn't deserve the time of day from her. But no one made you do it. So I'm not going to condemn Livy for being a bad parent. What really bothers me is that you wanted to immediately cut and run when the going got tough. And I've never let any of my players get away with that kind of behavior. You tough it out, slugger. Life isn't always peaches and cream, a bowl of cherries, and raspberry ices. It was a hard decision you made to look for Livy. Well—you found her. And your mom and I don't want you to break your mother's heart by running out on her and the arrangement you begged for just three months ago."

"Besides that," Joy said, nodding her head in agreement, "there's the Cheers to consider. Now I know that takes a backseat to getting to know Livy, but I've never known you to be so hung up on anything more than you are on that baseball team. Now you have a chance to make a difference—in your life, and Livy's, and in who runs your precious baseball club. It's like—what's that called, honey, when a player has one of those two-for-one things?"

Glenn chuckled affectionately at his wife's cluelessness, even after all these years, about the terminology of the game. "A double play," he said.

"That's it—a double play. Now, we love you, Sophie, and we always will. And this house is always open to you as your home. But we think," Joy said, sharing a look with Glenn, "that right now, your place is with Livy."

Well! You could have knocked me over with one of Sally Rand's feathers.

Wow. The Ashes hadn't disappointed me, but they sure as hell had surprised me.

⚾

"Well, that was Sherman," Linda said, hanging up the phone. "We were *so* close," she muttered angrily. "Sherman has a private detective following Venus and Sophie, and they went up to Larchmont yesterday to the Ashes after some sort of blowup between them."

"How does he know about the blowup?" Marty pictured some guy in a trench coat with his cauliflower ears pressed to keyholes.

"I'm not sure I even want to know these things. The gist of it is that Sophie wanted to call off the arrangement, but the Ashes talked her into staying with Livy. What are those people thinking? If my kid came crawling back to me, I wouldn't kick her to the curb. I can't imagine what was going through their heads."

Linda's hairbrush snarled in Rosebud's topknot. The hapless Yorkshire terrier yelped in pain, which was nothing compared to Linda's agony at remaining one step further removed from one-upping her friends by calling herself the wife of a baseball club owner, even if the team was pathetic. "We need someone on the inside. I don't even care if it's not legal, as long as no one finds out."

Marty looked up from the minor league baseball magazine's scouting report. "So Sophie's still in the duplex. What am I supposed to do? Bribe the doormen?"

"It's not a bad idea." Linda pursed her lips. Men! Was she going to have to take matters into her own hands? High-powered cousin Sherman had lost the decision on a motion to preclude Venus from having anything to do with the team until the case was closed. This meant that the judge was permitting Olivia to have a say in how things would be done during the tryouts for nondrafted players, spring training, and the upcoming season. Tryouts were due to begin shortly, with talent scouted from all across the country, including Marty's favorite prospect, Tommy DuPree. Linda couldn't trust Tommy—a jock with mush for brains—to keep tabs on Ms. Va-Va-Venus and her duckling, and bribing Olivia's doormen was an iffy prospect. Linda needed someone seasoned. Someone who'd given his life to the game and would rather die than see the Cheers helmed by Olivia deMarley, no matter how much of a knockout she was. Someone like . . . Dusty Fredericks.

⑦

"Can I sit in on tryouts?" Sophie asked me.

"Won't you be too busy with softball practice?"

"Practices are held in the evenings, when no one's got classes."

"*Ahh.* Classes. Shouldn't you be at them instead of sitting beside me in Farina Arena?"

"Don't worry about me! My study habits are impeccable," she crowed. "Joy and Glenn were always pretty strict with me about hitting the books. Glenn was always, like, 'no dessert unless you've finished your history assignment.' Probably why I don't really have a sweet tooth."

"Whereas, no one ever encouraged me to do my homework at all, let alone on time. Augie was too busy lecturing me about not becoming a slut, or pulling my own weight, or paying my own freight to focus on anything else I was doing. Do you know what he said to me before I went away to college?" I asked rhetorically. "He said, 'Don't become a mattress.' 'Don't worry, Daddy,' I assured him, 'I'll get on top instead and be a

comforter.' Well it was funny to me at the time," I muttered.
"And my *mom*—well Mom was too busy dying." I blinked
back tears. "I know that sounded cavalier just now, but I really
miss the hell out of her. I think about her every day. Believe me,
there are lots of times, even at my age, where I wish I could
throw myself on the bed and cry, 'I want my Mommy!'"

Sophie handed me a tissue. "She loved your dad, even if
you didn't, and it would have made her proud, I bet, to see
him proud of you, even in the afterlife, assuming there is one.
He wouldn't have given you the team in his will—'closing the
circle' and hoops of fire to jump through or not—if he didn't
think you'd carry on his work with dedication and commitment. Either that or he knows Barry Weed is a slime bucket
and Peter and Dick *are* a peter and a dick. Dusty Fredericks
seems pretty cool, though." I widened my eyes. "Don't look so
surprised, Livy; I've been following the Cheers for years. Did
you know his wife was in a sanatorium someplace?"

"Dusty's?"

"Yeah. She's had cancer on and off for years. Her name's
Rosa. She's very Roman Catholic. The only thing *Dusty* practices is baseball. That's his religion." Sophie tugged at a cardboard box on the shelf of her closet, and lifted it down, plopping
it onto her mattress. Inside the box was a scrapbook bound in
pebbled black cardboard and filled with photos and articles on
the Bronx Cheers. "See, I've been kinda talent-scouting *them*
since I was in Little League. Every time there was an article in
the paper, I'd clip it out—Barry Weed arrested for DWI back
in 1992—Carlos Carlito pitching the team's only shutout in
twelve years—Rosa Fredericks to undergo surgery—" Sophie
flipped through the yellowing pages. "Anything you want
to know about the Cheers: I bet it's in here." She confidently
tapped the cover of the scrapbook.

"Let me see that, please." Sophie handed me the book as

though she were passing me the Gutenberg Bible. I fully expected her to ask me if my hands were clean. I gingerly leafed through the pages; in a way, it was a stirring tribute, not just to her love of this scrappy little minor league ball club, but to the grandfather she never knew.

"Aw, Livy, please don't cry on it." My daughter reached for her treasure just as my teardrop splattered onto the black pressboard. I was wishing she'd call me *Mom* again, which was part of the reason I'd teared up. She had still used the word only once, and that was during a drunken rant.

It was our second day in court. One of those post-snowstorm February days when you wake up and wish you could just go back to sleep instead of slogging through gloopy gray puddles that always seem to be deeper than you'd anticipated; when the taxi drivers and dry cleaners join forces to soak the citizens who've had their winter whites sprayed with pewter-colored slush at forty-five miles an hour.

"I'd like to welcome back the deMarley *mishpacha* and their crazy *meshuggaas*," Judge Randazzo said sarcastically. He was the only Italian American I knew who peppered his speech with Yiddishisms. The judge told me he grew up in a Jewish neighborhood. "Besides, all real New Yorkers speak a little Yiddish. I'll bet you every goy you know uses the word *schlep*."

Cap Gaines opened old Augie's mystery letter in front of the court and handed it to Judge Randazzo, who got out his bifocals and read it aloud.

"To my daughter, Olivia, and my attorney Casper Gaines, and everyone else this concerns: You're right about me; I can be a bit of a bastard most of the time. But I'm also a cranky old man who hasn't quite been prepared to meet his maker. I have a feeling that Saint Peter will send me south instead. 'When was the last time you saw your daughter?' he'll ask me. I've lived a long one, but life is still too short, Olivia. Time sneaks up on you, and you've got liver spots on your hands, and hair on your ears when you still see yourself as wet behind them. I blew my chance to make it up to you because I was a stubborn shit, and have no one else to blame for my lousy behavior but myself. And I've got a granddaughter somewhere out there whom I'll never know because of it. The reasons for the separation between you and I and you and she may be different ones, but the results are the same. Our family circle has been fractured, and I am responsible for it. If I had accepted you twenty-one years ago, Olivia, when you were pregnant out of wedlock, perhaps you would not have chosen the same path and severed the ties to your own child. I broke the circle, but you can close it by finding your daughter. Love her, listen to her, and most of all, try to understand her, even if—and especially if—you disagree about something. Do that and the Bronx Cheers are yours. And may you derive as much joy from them as I have. August deMarley."

Judge Randazzo refolded the letter and placed it in the envelope. "Well, Mr. Gaines, the court congratulates you on your prescience. Shall we proceed?"

No one could have been as relieved as I to learn that the whole damn thing was an anticlimax.

But had that dream been sufficiently achieved? Mr. Weinstock was hell bent on proving to the court that it hadn't.

I was called to the stand as the first witness. Sure enough, Sherman Weinstock actually asked me what Sophie's favorite flavor of ice cream was.

"That's a trick question, sir," I replied. "My daughter's a vegan. She doesn't eat anything containing dairy products." There was laughter from the Ashes, and the judge cautioned them—and the rest of the people present—not to react to the testimony or they'd be asked to leave the courtroom.

"What would you say you have learned the most about your daughter?" Cap Gaines asked me on redirect.

"That she's as stubborn as I am," I said. "And that's a compliment. "She may not know what she wants from one minute to the next sometimes, but whichever way she's swinging, she's one hundred percent committed to it."

Right after the words came out of my mouth, I second-guessed myself and regretted having said them.

When Sophie took the stand, she referred to all the points of synchronicity she'd discovered. "I read this book about birth mothers and the children they give up for adoption. And like, sometimes, it turns out that they're so much like their birth mothers even though they were raised from the get-go by someone else."

"Can you give us an example?" Cap Gaines asked.

"Oh, yeah, sure, dude. Like the first time Livy met my parents—Joy and Glenn—she tossed salt over her shoulder before she took the first bite of her omelet. Now, I've been doing that all my life and I never got that from the Ashes. In fact they always used to get mad at me for spilling salt all over the rug. Well, not *mad*-mad at me—but you know what I mean."

"Objection!" exclaimed Sherman Weinstock.

"Overruled."

"Anything else?" asked Mr. Gaines. "Any other points of synchronicity, as they're called?"

"Oh yeah," Sophie replied. "We both are midnight cereal munchers."

Gaines nodded approvingly. "Would you clarify for the court what you mean by that, Ms. Ashe?"

Sophie did, to which Mr. Weinstock naturally raised another objection.

"Overruled." Judge Randazzo seemed amused.

"See! Livy and I were like bonded to each other always! We even both really need to take a nap at around three o'clock every day."

"Objection!" thundered Sherman Weinstock, jumping out of his seat. "You can't inherit a nap!"

Dusty Fredericks sounded tired and worn, which annoyed Linda deMarley because she expected people to give her their undivided attention when she phoned them. "It's not a good time for me, Mrs. M," he sighed, finally getting a word in edgewise. What was it she and Marty were asking him to do? Spy on Olivia and her kid so he could testify against them in court, opening the door for her idiot husband to gain the controlling interest in the team he'd devoted half his life to managing? He thought about telling her that if she wanted to play cloak-and-dagger games with Secret Decoder rings, she was on her own, but he lacked the stomach for sarcasm at the moment.

"I said it wasn't a good time for me, Linda." He paused, not for dramatic effect, but because he was choking on his tears. "I buried Rosa this morning."

Linda hung up the phone in slow motion. So much for her plan B. She tossed back her head with an "after all, tomorrow is another day" defiance and called into the bedroom, where her husband was watching some moronic television program on extreme bass fishing. She knew they never should have bought that Direct TV package. "Marty!" she practically shouted, "Is your winter suit pressed?"

I never knew Rosa Fredericks, but I thought it was the right thing to do to attend her memorial, since she was a member of the Cheers' extended family. And I wasn't sure whether it was appropriate to send a mass card, since Dusty's religion was baseball, but I took a chance and mailed one anyway. The funeral itself had been a very private affair. "I don't want nothing fancy-shmancy when I check out," Rosa had told Dusty when she'd first learned her lymphatic system had essentially processed a summons from the Pearly Gates. And so Rosa Fredericks had been formally mourned at Our Lady of Mercy by an audience of one.

The more public gathering wasn't much of a memorial; it was more like the Jews do when they sit shivah; everyone came over to Dusty's house on City Island and ate cold cuts, except, as Rosa was a Roman Catholic, the mirrors weren't covered and no one sat on wooden crates.

His home smelled vaguely antiseptic. "Rosa wanted to spend her birthday with me, instead of at the hospice. She knew it was going to be her last." Dusty couldn't look anyone in the eye as he spoke about Rosa. I had a feeling it was his way of preventing himself from breaking down again in front of company. "They . . . uh . . . scrubbed the place the morning after she passed. Fifty-two years she was on this earth. And I'm blessed to have known her for twenty-six of them."

Barry Weed nodded into his glass of scotch. "She was a saint," he said, as though concurring with a sentence Dusty never spoke.

"Jeez, is this Cookie delFlorio's hundredth home-run ball?" Marty asked, running his fingers over a glass dome.

"Give it a rest, Marty," Linda muttered under her breath. "You'd think it was the effing Shroud of Turin! And you're at a memorial for God sakes." She grabbed hold of his black serge sleeve and drew him closer with a sharp tug. "Show some respect. I know you thought Rosa was a stick-in-the mud because she hated to travel with the team, but at least act like you're in mourning. Everybody loved the woman. And everybody loves Dusty. *Sooo,* . . . if you want to get anywhere . . ." she added between her teeth, dropping a not-so-veiled hint to her husband, "you'd better act sadder than Va-Va-Venus, and she didn't even *know* Rosa Fredericks. Haven't you ever heard of King Lear?" she whispered.

"Didn't he pitch for the 1997 Mud Hens?"

Linda snorted in disgust. Marty winked at his wife. *"Snap!"*

"You're such a child, Marty."

There's nothing wrong with my hearing; I caught Linda's every hissed syllable, though I was halfway across the room admiring some hand-painted glassware. It stymied me how they stayed married. If I'd been either of them, I'd have killed the other one years ago.

"You like that, huh?" Dusty was suddenly at my side. I felt badly that I kind of towered over him in my heels. He was probably about five-eight, and his husky build made him appear somewhat shorter.

I nodded. "They're very unusual. Very delicate. Where'd you get them?"

"Oh, Livy, bless your heart for making me laugh today! Get them? I made them!"

"You—"

"Yeah, me." His face crinkled into a smile. "And don't act so surprised that a middle-aged geezer like me paints pretty little birds on water tumblers." His smile evaporated as suddenly as it had appeared, and his gray-blue eyes once again began to mist over. "Rosa. It was my Rosita. She got me into it. She was a birder from way back. Used to get me up at the crack of dawn to go bird-watching with her. And by and by, I kinda got to like it. So one day she's got some catalog in front of her and it's got something kinda like you see here. And she says to me, "Dusty, what do you think of these? I think I'm gonna order a set for the kitchen.'

"'You like 'em that much?'" I asked her. 'Yeah," she says, "I like 'em that much.'

"'How much they want for 'em?' So she looks back at the catalog and she tells me they want $39.99 for a set of four. And that was back in the seventies. So I tell her, 'I'll go down to the hardware store, buy as many tumblers as you like for forty-nine cents apiece. And I'll paint whatever birds you like on 'em.' She thought I was kidding. But the truth is, I never paid much attention in school. I was a doodler. And I guess I got some artistic talent in this old noggin somewheres. You show me most things, I can draw 'em pretty good."

"I'm impressed." I smiled. "My Sophie's like that. She showed me her portfolio from the art classes she took at Clarendon. Perfect—to my eye, anyway—imitations of some of the great masters: Cézanne, Picasso, Manet, Vermeer. I told her she could be an art forger if she never breaks into sports broadcasting."

Dusty shook his head. "I dunno what the market's like for women these days."

"Yeah. I hope she doesn't get her heart broken," I sighed. "You see a few on the field now and again, but you still don't see too many women in the commentators' booth."

"I was talking about art forgery!" Dusty gave me a friendly little poke in the ribs. "*Aww*, you gotta get used to my sense of humor, kiddo."

Kiddo? He couldn't have been more than a dozen years my senior. I gently touched his arm. "I plan to. We're going to be seeing a lot of each other, soon."

He steered me into the kitchen, out of earshot. "Don't take this the wrong way, Livy, but it's a good thing Rosa's dead. Cuz I don't think she would have liked you."

"That wasn't terribly reassuring—or flattering!" I said, appalled.

"Nah," he replied. "Take it as a compliment."

Boy, I wondered what their marriage was *really* like! Dusty wiped his eyes again, trying to hide his tears from me. "Don't get me wrong. I miss the gal. There'll never be another one like her. But I didn't walk through life with blinders on, like the colt I put ten bucks on last Wednesday in the third at Aqueduct. Rosa could be a pain in the patoot."

"Everybody can be," I said reassuringly. "Doesn't mean you love them any less." I thought about my dad and added, *"Most* of the time it doesn't mean anything, anyway."

Dusty cocked his head like an old terrier. "Venus, . . . come take a walk with me. I can call you Venus, can't I?"

"My best friends do," I smiled. "Then again, so do a lot of people who seem to hate my guts."

The back door to his kitchen slapped shut, a metal screen against an old wooden door frame. We stood for a moment on the little cement stoop. A damp March wind blew off the Long Island Sound, bringing with it the unmistakable odors of sea air—salt and brine—an organic smell you could almost taste in the back of your throat.

"A lotta people don't know what to make of you," Dusty said, ambling down the steps.

"Do you have arthritis?" I asked him solicitously. He seemed to be favoring his right hip.

"Naw. Slid into second one afternoon against the Durham

Bulls back in seventy-four. I went in wrong and ended up on my side. Only thing was I didn't have a map to tell me about the rock that was embedded in the base path about a foot from the bag. But . . .," Dusty winced, "I figure I've lived with it for thirty-four years, God or whoever willing, I can live with it for another thirty-four. You ever get hip trouble?"

"Nope. In my profession you gyrate so much you keep the axles pretty well greased." I winked at him, and he chuckled.

"Well don't ever get it. Hip trouble, I mean. And while you're at it, don't ever get old, neither."

"By my math, you're only fifty-three. Old to be playing a little boy's game, maybe, but not 'old' in real life."

Dusty sighed. "They say coaches and managers are people who never wanted to grow up once they hadda give it up. I mean whatever sport they're coaching and managing. I mean, what must it look like to some people—a grown guy with gray hair and a beer gut wearing a little league uniform, basically. A Halloween costume. Only way people take you seriously is when you win. Otherwise, you're just a big fat gray-haired joke."

"And the Cheers haven't had a winning season since 2001. And even then, they didn't make the playoffs."

"I get what you're saying," Dusty said. "Follow me." We'd been walking along the sidewalk behind his house; now we ducked through a hole in some metal fencing that opened on to the back of a boatyard. "You like boats?"

I shrugged. "They're okay."

"How can you not like boats?" Dusty was incredulous. "Rosa hated boats," he added ruefully. "Called 'em stinkpots. And she was always threatening to throw up over the side whenever I brought her onboard."

"I don't *dislike* them. And I don't throw up. Even after too much tequila."

We stopped in front of a red and white outboard; it had been shrink-wrapped for dry-dock storage. Dusty began to peel back some of the plastic, then pointed to a cinderblock resting by the port side of the stern. "Hop in." Dressed in mourning and high heels, I hoisted my sheath dress high enough to enable me to swing my leg over the side and climb aboard. "I do my best thinking in here," Dusty said.

"What's its name?" I asked him.

"*Her* name. A boat is always a she. Don't ask me why. It probably has to do with something sexist from a hundred centuries ago, so don't blame me. Anyways, her name is *RosAmor*. You know, for *Rosa* and *love* in Spanish." Dusty's eyes misted over once again. "So now I don't have Rosa no more, but I'll always have *RosAmor*. Until she sinks, anyways, or until I get canned from the Cheers, which I suppose could happen as early as the end of the year, if we don't get back in the plus column. Which brings me to another thing," he said, lighting up a cigar and leaning back to look up at the gray sky, "Who are you, Venus deMarley? *What* are you? And why the hell should we consider listening to you in the coming season—assuming in the next two months you and Sophie 'close the circle' as far as the judge is concerned?"

"Because I'll be your boss, that's why," I replied smoothly.

"But, with all due respect, you don't know shit about baseball."

"And with all due respect right back at you, you veteran *experts*—yourself, Barry Weed, Peter Argent and Dick Fernando, and my dear departed Daddy—haven't had a winning season in—remind me again—seven years, I believe it is. So, if you don't listen to me, not only will you be insulting the major shareholder of the team—never a very good idea—but you'll no doubt repeat all the same mistakes you've been making since '01. And one thing I learned a hundred years ago in my sophomore stats class is that if you keep doing the same thing over and over, in exactly the same way, odds are—you'll get the same result!" I grinned at him.

Dusty shook his head. He wasn't buying. I batted the air with my hand to chase away the wispy ribbons of brown-blue cigar smoke.

"As far as the guys go, I'll give it to you straight; they're not too crazy about the idea of you owning the team."

I laughed. "Gee. Ya think?" I chuckled. "Amazing how it took two lawsuits for me to get the hint."

"Yeah. I think. In fact I *know*. Even if the judge rules in your favor, they want you to prove yourself before they'll respect you."

"Nice. And how am I expected to prove myself if they won't let me prove myself?"

Dusty exhaled another stinky puff of smoke. "You're starting to sound like Yogi."

I could have teased him further, and made him believe I thought he was talking about some swami guru instead of Yogi Berra, but I bit my tongue. After all, the guy just lost his wife. I couldn't rag on him too much, except to try to lift his spirits. "So, you brought me out here to tell me I'm going to have a tough row to hoe with the Cheers." I gazed at him. "And yet I can't tell whose side you're on exactly. Not yet, anyway. Why'd you do it? Warn me, I mean." Dusty swatted away some of his own smoke. "That stuff'll kill you, you know," I told him.

"Why did I 'warn' you? Because, unlike Weed and Argent and Fernando, I don't entirely dislike you. On the other hand, I know you can't possibly do *my* job, so you're not exactly a threat to the old profession, here." He cracked a wan smile. "Uh-course you could always can my ass halfway through the season if the kids aren't up to snuff this year . . . but I'm hoping you'll remember this conversation and cut me a little slack if things are hairy."

"I can't make any promises, you know." I rested my hand gently on Dusty's shoulder. "Business is business. On my watch no one will be safe at home unless the Cheers are kicking ass." Dusty looked grim. "Hey, you fired a warning shot over my bow, I'm sending a salvo right back atcha," I said, co-opting his cadences.

His cigar had gone out. He pulled the metal tube from his jacket pocket and stashed the stogie. As we walked back toward the house I felt like we were moving in slow motion.

"You know, Rosa always told me, 'Dusty,' she said, 'Dusty, you live and die the Bronx Cheers. You breathe them and eat them and the Lord knows you probably crap them, too'—for a good Catholic, she could have a salty mouth on occasion. And now that Rosa's gone, I'm gonna live and breathe and eat and crap them even more because I won't have anything else in my life, Olivia." The words caught in his throat as he choked back tears. "So, I just want you to know that my jury's out on you as to whether you can fill your father's shoes. I don't have a doubt in my mind that you can strut across a stage and shake your booty," he added, checking out my body, "but can you run a ball club?"

"I wouldn't want to be in your stilettos," Sophie said, when I told her about my conversation with Dusty. "'Sides which I have no idea how you people can walk in heels like that, anyway. I want to help. You never said whether I could watch the tryouts. I'm a good talent scout, I promise! I learned from my dad," she said, referring of course to Glenn Ashe, not to Rodney the Red Sock—though there may be something to be said for biology. "Dad was a major talent scout back in the seventies and eighties—and he was really good at it! When he was only my age, he convinced Bing Devine, the GM of the St. Louis Cardinals, to sign Keith Hernandez for their St. Petersberg A-ball team in seventy-two. Hernandez was a forty-second-round pick—but he went on to win eleven straight Gold Gloves and shared the National League's MVP title in 1979."

"I've always had a crush on him," I sighed.

"Yeah, well, you do seem to have a thing for major league infielders," Sophie observed tartly.

"If I didn't, you wouldn't be here."

"I wouldn't be me, that's for sure," she reluctantly agreed. "So—can I help scout?"

"Isn't the scouting over? Aren't we going to be watching the prospects strut their stuff and then make our decision?"

"Well, I can help you decide when to give a guy the thumbs up and when to feed him to the lions instead. *Please, Mom. Pleeease?*"

She'd called me *Mom* again. I couldn't have refused her the moon.

Days later, Sophie and I trudged across a muddy campus to Farina Arena, where at least someone had had the presence of mind to close up the roof. "Isn't this a great way to spend a Sunday morning?" she crowed. I hadn't seen her so ebullient since I'd told her she could sit in on the Cheers tryouts. At her suggestion we'd Googled every player we expected to see. By the time they took the field, I felt like I knew them already, although after having read their blogs, I questioned the maturity level of some of them—those who behaved more like adolescents than twenty-ish. "Maybe it's just me, and undoubtedly I still have a lot to learn about the business of baseball; but frankly, I'm not so sure I want an avowed devil worshiper on my team, no matter how high his batting average," I told Sophie. "I never hired any Goth girls when I had my own nightclubs in Vegas, no matter how tall they were or how well they could wield a pair of ostrich-feather fans. Unlike stripping, burlesque still retains an almost wholesome sweetness. Like baseball. But without the sordid steroid stuff."

My daughter disagreed. "Not hiring Goth girls! That's religious discrimination, Livy!"

"No, it's called *casting*," I replied. "Religion has nothing to do with it."

Sophie shrugged, unconvinced. "Do you know what Sammy Santiago's nickname is?"

I shook my head and took a guess. "The Sultan of Satan?"

Sophie laughed. "They're not that clever. Besides, you're wrong. They call him 'Grand Slammy.' He's an awesome defensive third baseman, too. Besides, I don't think he's a real devil worshiper. I read his blog, too, and it sounds to me like he just dabbles. That streaming video where he was chanting that stuff about Beelzebub—I think those are actually the words to a rap song."

My cousin Marty greeted us on the field, as though he and his lawyer weren't trying to litigate me out of my legacy. "It's gonna be a great day today, isn't it?" He was rubbing his hands together with such glee you'd think he was going to step up to the plate himself. "Uncle Augie never liked the scouts from the majors to pick his players, so he always ran his own tryouts. Of course, he wasn't the only eccentric in baseball—far from it—but since he had so much money, the folks from the majors pretty much left him alone and let him run the team like his own little fiefdom. Linda's running a little late, by the way. Rosebud's stuck at the groomer's. We watch the tryouts every year. She likes the young blood."

I bet she does, I thought, trying hard not to focus on Marty's spindly legs. Some men should never wear Bermuda shorts.

Something on the ground caught my eye as I was avoiding Marty's legs. "Oh my God, that's so adorable!"

"What's adorable?" Dusty Fredericks wanted to know.

I scuffed my toe against the base. "Home plate. Who knew it was shaped like a little house?! House—home—it's so cute!"

Dick Fernando smacked his forehead with his hands. "She's kidding us all, right?" He exchanged disgusted glances with

Barry Weed and the other limited partner, Peter Argent. "Don't tell me the woman who stands to gain the controlling interest in the Bronx Cheers has never even set foot on a baseball diamond! Yes, sweetheart," he said to me sarcastically, "home plate is shaped like a little house. And _inside_ live Hansel and Gretel and the Wicked Witch of the West."

"_Aww,_ leave her alone," Dusty said.

"Fucking bimbo!" Peter Argent muttered to Dick Fernando. "Oh, lookie, it's a cute little house!" he said in a high voice, which I suppose was intended to mimic my own.

Dusty came between the two limited partners and laid a hand on each of their shoulders. "All right, knock it off, you two. We've got a team to put together here."

We settled into seats behind home plate. Farina Arena seemed a ghost town with only a handful of us in the stands. Sophie sat beside me; Dusty staked out a seat a couple of rows back. Marty stretched his legs in the aisle. Any minute I thought he was going to pull a box of Cracker Jack out of his knapsack.

A pitcher trotted out to the mound. "Now this kid's got something special," Barry Weed said to me.

"Actually, it's not what he's _got;_ it's what he _lacks_ that makes him special," Sophie muttered. I asked her to explain. "Pinky Melk is one of the best southpaws to come out of college baseball in a decade," she said. "Check out his hands. They call him Pinky because he lost the one on his left hand—an accident in wood shop when he was in eighth grade."

I winced. _"Damn."_

"Tell me about it," Sophie concurred. "To this day I can't hear a buzz saw without freaking out, and I don't even know Pinky!" She pointed to the player again. "Even in his Little League career, he was considered a hot prospect, but then he got hurt and switched to throwing right-handed instead. He was good, but his college coach suggested he go back to throwing southpaw, even without the pinky—and as a lefty he's even better. He's got a screwball that nobody can hit."

Well, he struck out Grand Slammy Santiago, who'd been hoping for fastballs. I didn't know if that necessarily made Pinky any good. "After all," Barry Weed told me, "Santiago can only hit high fastballs. But he hits them all the way to Cleveland."

Peter Argent chimed in. "Don't worry about the devil-worshiping . . . thing. He says he doesn't do that anymore. He's into collecting butterflies now." Argent shrugged. "What do I know? Just what the kid tells me." He nudged Dick Fernando. "I thought we were going to see Shoji Suzuki today. Where the hell is he?"

"He's from Japan," Sophie whispered to me.

"Yeah, I guessed that."

Sophie cupped her hand to my ear. "Word on the street is Shoji's a great center fielder. Except that no one can understand a word he says. And vice versa."

"Did you get him a translator?" Barry Weed asked the limited partners. They looked at each other accusingly.

"I thought you were taking care of that," Fernando said to Argent.

"Wonderful. And I thought we agreed that *you* were going to hire the translators. Jicama Flores is practically right off the boat from the DR, and Spot Baldo needs a Croatian interpreter. Is Croatian even a language?"

"*Spot* Baldo?" I asked Sophie. "What kind of first name is Spot?"

"It's a nickname; his real first name is Aleksandar. But he's a Dalmatian," she replied, keeping her eyes on Pinky Melk. "From Brela."

"Isn't 'Spot' kind of un-PC, Soph?"

She laughed. "He picked it! Some of the guys call him Bald Spot, too. He seems to take it in stride."

Her knowledge of the players continued to impress me, including her infield chatter on the two right-handed relievers—Debrett Peerage, and some other guy nicknamed Lefty, as well as the actual lefty, Wayne deBoeuf. "Everyone always shouts 'Where's the Beef?' when the starting pitcher is falling apart," Sophie told me. "He's a terrific closer, but his high school team made the mistake of starting him off as a middle reliever, until they realized his potential to shut down the opposition in the clutch. Essentially, Wayne has no central nervous system," she grinned. "Though if you sign him, you're going to have to give him a little lecture about riding his motorcycle without a helmet. Or boots. Well, any kind of shoes, actually. He says he never uses them in Mississippi."

"Would it be bootless to ask if his hero is Shoeless Joe Jackson?"

Sophie smacked my upper arm with the back of her hand. "*Wow*—you made a baseball joke, Livy."

"We're going to see another right-handed starter in a few minutes," said Barry Weed, stamping out his cigarette butt on the cement steps. "Homegrown, too. A Clarendon kid."

"Do I know him?" I asked.

"I think so. Tommy DuPree."

I looked at Sophie but read nothing in her face except that trademark inscrutability.

Marty was practically levitating out of his sneakers, he was so pumped. "I told you on visiting day, this kid's got a great arm."

"Soph?" I waited for her reaction, and when I got none, I drew her to me so that we were shoulder to shoulder. "He was a prick to you at that Christmas party," I whispered. "Why should I consider rewarding him?"

Sophie shrugged noncommittally. "I'm over it. Moved on. I don't even think about Tommy anymore. But you realize you could end up killing his career forever, just because he can be an asshole from time to time."

"Not just any asshole. He was an asshole to *you*. My *daughter*. I don't forgive as easily as you do, apparently."

"Okay, so, Tommy's a jerk. But, if you want to factor character issues into baseball, so is someone like Pete Rose for allegedly gambling on his own team. Does that erase the fact that he was an incredible player?"

"Yeah, but even if I accept your argument, Soph, didn't your—didn't Glenn mention that Tommy's control of the ball is erratic, and that he doesn't really throw that hard?"

"Well . . . that doesn't mean he won't improve with the right coaching."

"Why do you think Cousin Marty is so keen on him? The other guys—Weed, Fernando, and Argent—don't seem so convinced. I find it hard to believe that you and Marty see eye to eye on something. Especially since he's suing me to get your grandfather's will invalidated."

Sophie shook her head. "It's definitely *not* what Gramps had in mind. Trust me. With Tommy, I bet Marty wants to prove that he can pick a winner, and that old Augie was wrong in never letting him have enough shares in the ball club to have any influence on the way it's run. That's been going on for years, you know. I've got articles on it in my scrapbook. Augie never wanted Marty to have any say in the Cheers. He always thought Marty was a loser. If he'd ever wanted to make him a limited partner, he would have done it years ago. Now, as far as right-handers go, *I* think Tommy's got potential; a diamond in the rough that you could polish into a real gem that's going to yield a major return on your investment." She looked at me earnestly. "I say take the chance on him. I'll stake my entire reputation as a talent scout—albeit an amateur one—on it."

"Move over." Dusty had descended the stairs and wanted to muscle into our row. "I don't think he's as good as they say, Olivia. I think what you see is what you get."

"Sophie's inclined to think otherwise." For a couple more minutes, we watched Tommy DuPree in silence. Then Dusty said, "I been managing in the minors for twenty-five years. I got batting gloves older than your daughter. So, who're you gonna listen to—this crusty old salt or some kid who never managed a team in her life?"

Of course he'd made a couple of excellent points. But if Sophie had become an astute judge of talent, even avocationally, at her adoptive dad's knee, maybe her advice was sounder than that of a man who was so set in his ways that he'd posted several losing seasons in succession rather than change his game plan.

I turned to my daughter. "Sweetheart, I'm very serious about this: are you sure you're okay with the way Tommy Du-Pree treated you? Because I don't care how good he is, I don't want him to so much as set foot inside the team's locker room if it makes you in any way uncomfortable or unhappy."

"I told you, *Mom*, I'm over it," she said unconvincingly. But she also knew she'd just hit my Achilles' heel.

I waved over the Cheers' general manager. "Barry," I said, mustering my best authoritative voice and pointing to Tommy DuPree, "offer the kid a contract."

⚾

As the weeks wore on, and we awaited one more court appearance—after which the judge assured us he would issue his final ruling—I grew increasingly anxious to get on with my life. Now I was hungry to take the Cheers and make something out of their sorry blue-and-white asses. The new additions to the team seemed relatively promising, if spring training was a good indication of future performance on the field. The outfield was looking particularly strong, with a slugger named Anton Anton in left, Ahab Slocum—though he had an ego the size of Milwaukee—out in right, and the enigmatic Shoji Suzuki in center. Shoji was always apologizing for something, at least according to his translator—a dropped fly, a miscalculated position on the field where he'd played either too deep or too shallow, a fumbled bunt attempt—and yet he never seemed to be truly contrite. I'd been listening to Japanese language CDs with the hopes of communicating with him myself one of these days, so I could find out what was truly up with the kid. Maybe reading some Manga would help, too. Shoji always had his nose in one of those books whenever he wasn't immediately required for anything. I also wondered—a maternal thing kicking in—whether I should be worried that his hair was dyed royal blue.

⑦

Marty deMarley stared at his *Minor Leaguer* magazine, forcing his brain to memorize a sheet of stats. Then he slumped back in his recliner, which resembled an enormous baseball mitt. Linda hated it. She'd been trying to train Rosebud to scratch up the upholstery for years. But the dog hated the smell of it. "Why do you think Uncle Augie hated me so much?" Marty moaned.

"He didn't hate you, Marty; he just thought you were a putz."

"But I'm not a putz. I'm a very successful bond trader! Fuck—if I crunched the numbers, did a little creative accounting, I could probably buy my own team, instead of waiting around and hoping to inherit the Cheers and getting shafted by everyone."

Linda's brain lit up like the Empire State Building at dusk. "Then why don't you? What do you need the Cheers for? You could buy a *successful* team. And then you could sell it and make an enormous profit, and we could—"

"Why would I sell it?" Marty was appalled. "Linda, all I've ever wanted, as an adult, anyway, was to own a baseball team." Thinking about his dream some more, he realized that it wasn't about owning a team in theory; it all boiled down to the Cheers. Uncle Augie owed him. It was all about family.

"What did you want as a kid?" Linda realized she didn't know this about her husband. Most of the time, she didn't really care to know things about him that had nothing to do with her. What had she seen in him, beyond a fat paycheck and a cushy lifestyle? What did she see in him now, all crumpled up like a little boy in that heinous chair of his? She thought about having a glass of champagne as she ruminated, but it was only noon, so she opted for coffee instead. *Marty. Marty Marty Marty.* Well, it wasn't all that hard to figure out. Her therapist told her years ago that she was one of those people who is considered a "fixer," the type who looks for someone to "rescue." Marty had presented a project on a grand scale. She imagined it was a bit like coming across an old house, a gingerbread Queen Anne with a crumbling facade, sloping floors, and wonky plumbing, and getting dewy-eyed over its possibilities for renewal. So much potential, Linda had thought at the time she met Marty. She'd never forget the night. It was at an Easthampton cocktail party for the designer Lucky Sixpence; Marty was his broker. Linda saw even more promise in Marty after she signed up a personal trainer and sent him for hair plugs. Unfortunately, Marty couldn't seem to bulk up; destiny and biology had given him the physique of a plucked chicken. And the hair plugs made his scalp break out. But that made for another project to tackle; more things for Linda to fix. She realized that one of the things she adored most about her husband was that she would always be needed to fix something about him.

"I wanted to be a paleontologist," Marty said wistfully.

"How did you feel, Mrs. Ashe, when your daughter decided to find her birth mother?"

Joy hesitated before replying. She didn't want to do anything to hurt Livy's case, because that would hurt Sophie as well, but she'd put her hand on a Bible and sworn to tell the truth. And Joy feared the wrath of God more than that of Judge Randazzo if she committed perjury.

"Mrs. Ashe, the court is anxious for your answer," urged Sherman Weinstock.

"Jealous," she said finally. "I have to say I was just a teensy bit jealous." She glanced nervously at Glenn, seated on the bench behind the petitioners' counsel.

"Only a teensy bit?" said Mr. Weinstock, raising an eyebrow.

"Well . . . maybe a little bit more than that—but I didn't discourage Sophie from trying to find her biological mother."

"I didn't ask you that, Mrs. Ashe. Please confine your responses to the questions I pose. I would like to strike the rest of Mrs. Ashe's reply—after she admitted that she was more than a teensy bit jealous—from the record."

Judge Randazzo turned to the court reporter. "So ordered."

"And how did you feel when you learned that your daughter, Sophie, was successful in locating Ms. deMarley?"

"Jealous," admitted Joy with evident discomfort.

"I have no further questions for this witness," Weinstock said.

"So, you were jealous," Cap Gaines said, picking up the thread on his cross-examination.

"I was afraid it would mean that Sophie would love Glenn and me less, somehow."

"But did that happen?"

"No, Mr. Gaines. It didn't. She's still the same Sophie. Only now she doesn't leave things lying around anymore for other people to pick up. I don't know how Olivia—Livy—did it, because she said she had the same problem with Sophie after Sophie moved in with her. But somehow she managed to make a difference in a way that Glenn and I never could. I mean, it's probably a silly little thing, but still . . ."

"And does that make you jealous, too?"

A little laugh escaped Joy's lips. "Oh no—I'm thrilled!"

Cap Gaines smiled. "That's all, Your Honor."

Glenn Ashe was then called to the stand and sworn in.

"Would you characterize your daughter Sophie as a 'daddy's girl'?" questioned Sherman Weinstock.

Glenn grinned. "Oh, absolutely!"

"And why is that?"

"Well . . . we have so many of the same interests . . . especially baseball and softball. Her mother—Joy—isn't interested in sports."

"Is Olivia deMarley interested in sports, would you say—beyond the outcome of the lawsuit?"

Cap Gaines rose from his chair. "Objection! Speculation. Counsel is calling for the witness to speculate on the respondent's interests."

"Sustained," said the judge.

"I'll rephrase the question, Your Honor. Mr. Ashe, given your contact with Ms. deMarley, would you say that she shares the same passion for baseball and softball that you and Sophie do?"

"She shares the same passion for *Sophie* that *Joy* and I do," said Glenn. "That much is very clear to me. You could give me a stack of Bibles and I wouldn't say any different."

"Move to strike as nonresponsive. Please answer the question I posed, Mr. Ashe."

"I think Livy has a lot to learn about the game of baseball, from a professional standpoint. But I know she enjoys watching her daughter on the field. Livy didn't miss a single game the Clarendon Kumquats played all year. And I know she's watched all of Sophie's game tapes, going back to her days in Little League."

Glenn's testimony frustrated Mr. Weinstock no end; he was clearly intent on letting the judge know what he felt in his heart, even if he strayed from the attorney's questions, which he knew were designed to box him in, in a way that would help the petitioners.

On cross-examination, Cap Gaines asked him, "What do you think is the reason we're all here in court today?"

"To give evidence as to whether Sophie and Livy have 'closed the circle,' according to August deMarley's last will and testament."

"And in your view, Mr. Ashe, does this closing of the circle, specifically, actually have anything to do with the game of baseball itself?"

Glenn thought about it. "*Uhh* . . . not really," he replied. "No. Closing the circle, in my view, and, well, in the letter, too, means demonstrating that there is a genuine mother-daughter connection between Livy and Sophie."

"And in your view, do you believe that connection has been established?"

"I do, sir. And I believe it will only get stronger."

"And why do you believe that?"

Glenn scratched his head. The judge had made him remove his Clarendon Kumquats hat in the courtroom. "Baseball has a way of bringing people closer together. 'There's no *I* in team,' you know—and all that. And fans that may have nothing else in common share a passion for their favorite team, and an unregenerate antipathy to the team's biggest rival. In our case, if Livy gets the controlling interest in the Cheers, it would be a dream come true for our daughter. All her life, she's loved that team like it was the Little Engine That Could, even before she discovered she was related to the owner. Sophie'd talk about August deMarley and his decisions the way Yankee fans discuss George Steinbrenner. Already, Livy has made Sophie ecstatic by respecting her analysis of the players' abilities during tryouts. You should see the two of them with their heads together poring over statistics. Do any of you realize how important it is to a kid's self esteem to have a parent come to *her* for advice? And mean it?"

My lawyer turned to the judge and smiled. "No further questions, Your Honor."

Judge Randazzo looked at his watch. "It's looking like lunch, folks."

"Your Honor, with all due respect, I'm as hungry as anyone in this room, but I'm afraid that if we begin with the last witness after we've all digested, that we'll have to continue the case for at least another day. Judicial delay is justice denied," argued Cap Gaines. "And spring training is about to get under way. The players need to know who their biggest *Cheer*leader is going to be."

The judge cracked a smile. "Stick to law, Mr. Gaines. Punning isn't your forte." He summoned his court clerk with a wave. "Can we get an order from Katz's Deli, do you think?" he whispered to the clerk.

"I don't think they deliver, sir," murmured the clerk.

"*Ahh.*" Judge Randazzo leaned back in his chair. "All right, here's what we're going to do," he said, his accent marking him as a son of Queens. "We're going to take a brief recess so that my clerk, Mr. Higginbottom here, can take everyone's order. And while he grabs a taxi for Katz's Deli, we'll hear the testimony of Mr. deMarley. When the sandwiches arrive, we'll take a break, and then resume after everyone has eaten. Does that satisfy you, counselors?"

The attorneys nodded.

"Fine." The judge beckoned to Marty. "Mr. deMarley, would you please take the stand."

Marty wiped his sweaty palms on his Cheers 0 jersey. He, too, was hatless, as the judge had banned any nonreligious headgear in his courtroom. Otherwise Marty would have been wearing a Cheers baseball cap.

"Put your right hand on the Bible and raise your left hand, sir," said the bailiff. "Now repeat after me: 'I swear to tell the truth, the whole truth, and nothing but the truth, so help me God.'"

Cousin Marty repeated the oath and sat down. I could tell he thought the wooden swivel chair was uncomfortable. Not surprising, since his skinny butt had no padding.

"Mr. deMarley, how long have you held shares in the Cheers organization?" Sherman Weinstock asked him.

"Objection. Irrelevant," said Cap Gaines, rising.

"Sustained. Mr. Weinstock, stick to business."

"I am, Your Honor. I am establishing a pattern here."

"All right," Judge Randazzo sighed. "I'll allow it. But you've been warned, counselor. The witness may answer the question."

"Ever since I was eighteen years old. But Uncle Augie never allowed me to have enough of them to make a difference. I love the Cheers more than Cousin Livy does. And certainly more than Sophie does. I've had stock options since before she was even born! Livy always got whatever she wanted," Marty fretted glumly. "And she never thought about anyone else's feelings," he added accusatorily. When we were growing up, she always got everything and I never got anything."

Funny how I don't remember it that way. Did Cousin Marty reside in an alternate universe? In *my* galaxy I recall Marty's dad, my uncle Alan, being a pretty nice guy who used to take us to places like the natural history museum and the circus. *My* dad was a cold fish who never took me anywhere and disapproved of everything I did.

"I don't understand what any of this has to do with the matter at hand," said the judge.

"Livy's been a thorn in my side since I was nine years old," Marty went on.

Judge Randazzo leaned forward. "The court is not in the mood to hear your life story, Mr. deMarley. And Mr. Weinstock, this had better be going somewhere relevant or I'm going to hold you both in contempt. My stomach's rumbling, and I'm not in the mood to digest anything right now that isn't a hot pastrami on rye."

"I'm establishing that the witness and the respondent have a long history," Sherman Weinstock replied. "And that this long-standing relationship gives Mr. deMarley his bona fides when it comes to his opinion on whether his cousin has closed the circle."

"I've hated her since we were kids, too," Marty muttered.

"You're still under oath," the judge reminded him.

"Well, it's the *truth*."

Marty seemed to have dug in his heels and refused to budge. On cross-examination Cap Gaines asked him what he had against me.

"Yeah—you've told the court that you've hated your cousin since you were both little kids. If you were nine years old when the seeds of this long-standing antipathy were sown, that would have made Ms. deMarley about . . . what? Seven?"

"Uh-huh. If I was nine, Livy would have been seven."

"Do you remember what it was that ticked you off so much? So much that you still bear a rather heavy grudge against Olivia deMarley? Was there a single, seminal event, or did your dislike of her arise from an accumulation of events?"

"Oh, I remember it like it was yesterday!" Marty said. He started to get fidgety, restless. I couldn't see his hands, but I would have bet that he was clenching and unclenching them in his lap the way he used to do when something or someone made him really mad. Like he was itching to deck them, but lacked the heft—and the courage—to actually throw a punch.

"I had a hobby when I was a kid. And you'd be surprised to learn, maybe, that it wasn't baseball."

"It wasn't baseball. *Hmmm.*" Cap Gaines stroked his chin like a tribal elder. "So you haven't really been a fan of the Cheers— or of any baseball team—from early childhood. What was this hobby of yours? This was when you were nine years old, right?" Marty nodded. "Mr. deMarley, the court reporter can't make an official record of body language. Let the record reflect that the witness nodded his head in agreement with my last question. So, sir, can you tell the court what happened that was so terrible—that was so traumatic—that you've despised your cousin with a burning hatred in your heart for all these years?"

I thought about the time when we were teens and Marty

tried to feel me up. I guess all bets are off when it comes to the free will of adolescent male hormones; so a teenage guy can hate someone and still want to cop a feel.

"Why? You have to ask me *why*?" demanded Marty. "*Because she ate my dinosaurs!*"

There was a stunned silence in the courtroom, followed by myriad exclamations of confusion and disbelief.

The judge pounded his gavel and called for order. "W-would you like to tell the court what the hell you're referring to, Mr. deMarley?" He leaned forward and stared at Marty. "I have a feeling this is going to be good."

"Okay. It's not funny, people. This is serious!" His face reddened with ire. "I was really into dinosaurs when I was a kid. I'd built up a really cool collection, and a lot of it came from the 1964 World's Fair we had in Queens."

The judge smiled wistfully. "Ah, yes, I remember it well. My high school buddies and I lived nearby and we used to sneak in after dark."

And you still got to be a judge? I marveled.

"The dinosaur stuff was my dad's, originally, because I wasn't born at the time, but he passed it along to me when he found out what a dino-fanatic I was turning into. My bedroom looked like a dino-shrine with posters and toy dinosaurs—and some real specialty items that my dad had saved from the World's Fair. And one of those things was a box of cookies— you know, like animal crackers, only with different dinosaurs instead of lions and tigers and bears."

Oh my.

"It was the only box I had. And you couldn't get another one. They didn't make them anymore after the World's Fair closed. That was it. And I never opened it because I wanted it to be pristine. I didn't think of it as food. To me, it was a collector's item."

"And what happened to this box?" Cap Gaines asked Marty.

"It was on one of my bookshelves. And one day we went to the natural history museum, and afterward Olivia came over to my house to play before her mom picked her up to take her back to Riverdale. And I was going to show her my dinosaur scrapbooks, which I kept in a suitcase under my bed. She was sitting on my bed, kicking her feet, and then she said to me, '*Eww.* These cookies are stale.'" Marty imitated a little girl voice.

"'Where'd you get cookies?' I asked her. 'These,' she said.

"I crawled out from under my bed so fast that I bumped my head on the bed frame. And then I looked up and she was munching away on my dinosaurs! She ate my dinosaurs! She fucking *ate* my dinosaurs! A completely one-of-a-kind item. She compromised my whole collection!"

I jumped up from my chair. "I was *seven years old* and I was *hungry*—how the hell did I know that box of cookies was sacred?!"

"Ms. deMarley, the court shares your shock and awe, but please take your seat and contain your outbursts."

Cap Gaines approached Cousin Marty. "So let me get this straight—you have held a grudge against Ms. deMarley for all this time because she ate a box of your cookies when she was seven years old?"

"Not just any cookies! She ate my dinosaurs!"

"Marty—I didn't do it on purpose—not maliciously, I mean. I didn't *know.* How could I have known it was such a big deal? And I didn't even *remember* the incident until you brought it up just now! I'm not kidding—I don't even remember eating the cookies."

Judge Randazzo's gavel hit the bench with a crack. "Ms. deMarley, please be seated. I won't warn you again."

Mr. Higginbottom returned, and suddenly the entire court-room smelled like Deli.

"All right, everyone. This is lunch!" the judge announced, and the gavel descended again.

I had no appetite. I sipped a diet cream soda because I hoped the bubbles would calm the butterflies in my stomach. Marty had been the last witness, and his testimony wasn't over yet. "Mind if we step outside for a minute?" I asked my lawyer.

Outside the courtroom I asked Gaines, "So what does Marty's meltdown mean? Can you ask for a mistrial?"

"Why would I? He's the petitioner. If the judge thinks he's a nut job who instigated a lawsuit because he still harbors a boyhood grudge, who are we to argue? Dinosaurs." He shook his head in disbelief.

Back inside the courtroom, the lunch detritus was being cleared away. Five minutes later, there was no trace of the meal, except for the rather pronounced aroma of pastrami that hung in the air and clung to the pewlike benches. Marty was called back to the stand, and the judge asked Cap if he had any further questions for the witness. My counsel declined, and my cousin stepped down.

"All right, I know you all have shpilkis and you can't wait for me to issue a ruling," said the judge. "And given what I've heard today, I see no reason to prolong the suspense by retiring to my chamber and mulling it over for hours when I already know what I'm going to say. The written decision will be available at the court clerk's office in about two weeks. And the *Law Journal* may want to publish this one, too—if only for the comic relief," he muttered.

"I feel like I've spent the past few months on Mr. Toad's Wild Ride with you people. Counsel for the petitioner offered into evidence a prior will that left everything to his client, but with no evidence that the will was ever filed in court. The will that forms the gravamen of the action at bar was most certainly filed, but contained a clause so vague it called into question the decedent's competence at the time the will was signed. Then we had the mysterious letter, which felt more Edgar Allan Poe than Lewis Carroll, and finally, once the phrase was decoded, we had to hash out whether or not it had been fulfilled.

"Mr. Weinstock, you should have known better than to waste the court's time with this fakakta action. Ms. deMarley, Ms. Ashe: as far as this court is concerned, and as far as those who know you long and well are concerned, dinosaur cookies notwithstanding, the two of you are doing at least as well as mothers and daughters who did not part ways at the birth of the latter. It is therefore the opinion of this court that you have 'closed the circle.' Ms. deMarley now has the controlling interest in the Bronx Cheers. Go forth and prosper, Ms. deMarley—and for God's sake, bring home a pennant! Case closed."

⚾

More than three cheers were in order. I was now ready, willing, and about to be legally and legitimately able to take on a team of them!

I received two envelopes from Tom; one contained a cute "Congratulations!" card, wishing me all the best, saying he knew I could do it. Inside the other envelope was a handwritten letter, penned in his usual mélange of printing and cursive, capital and lowercase letters inserted into the words at whim.

"I thought I should tell you I've met someone," the note said, and I felt my throat constrict. "Her name is MaryAnne, she's a vet, and we'll see where it goes."

A vet? Given Tom's unique penmanship, this MaryAnne could have been a horse doctor, or had seen combat in Iraq. Or both, for all I knew. I pictured MaryAnne as tall and horsey-looking, with big horse teeth and a horse laugh. Big hoofy feet, and a hefty rump all out of proportion with her spindly legs. But maybe she's Tom's type, after all. Maybe he just goes for a long mane of hair. Or maybe he just wants to meet a woman to maybe marry him, who didn't inherit a baseball team, and doesn't need to take time to be reunited with the daughter she never knew.

I hate MaryAnne.

My problem is that I don't hate Tom. I love him. And of course he has a right to meet someone new. I just wish he hadn't. I'd still marry him in a heartbeat, if only. Shit! I wanted to be angry with Sophie for showing up and throwing a monkey wrench into my life, and with old Augie for dropping dead and saddling me with a crop of postadolescents wielding baseball bats.

I threw Tom's letter and his card in the trash basket. Silly me for having hoped he wouldn't move on. In my imagination, he'd come to visit me in New York—just because he missed me—arriving with a bouquet of calla lilies and purply-blue anemone; I'd introduce him to Sophie and they'd immediately get along like gangbusters; she'd think he was the coolest man in the world, and that we were perfect together and that it would be totally "awesome" for her to have a place to visit in Colorado; and Tom had realized that it wouldn't be so bad to have a part-time pied-à-terre in Manhattan after all, and admitted that he'd been a total fool to have been so hasty to end things between us, when I was the woman he was meant to spend the rest of his life with.

Not.

MaryAnne, huh?

I had nothing to do now but allow myself a huge crying jag and prepare to become a baseball club owner.

Oh, goody.

The mood in Cap Gaines's conference room was more festive the day old Augie deMarley's will was read. Which isn't saying much.

Surrounded by a sea of glum faces, and one jubilant one, I signed several documents officially giving me the controlling interest in the minor league ball club. Barry Weed and the two limited partners looked homicidal; Marty deMarley looked suicidal; Linda, mechanically stroking Rosebud, looked sedated; and Dusty Fredericks looked like he'd just lost his best friend.

Sophie was all for breaking open the champagne.

It was quite a momentous occasion. Too bad Dad hadn't been around to see it.

After the meeting, Sophie and I took a walk in Battery Park, grabbing lunch from a hot dog vendor and watching the tour boats tootle around the Statue of Liberty. The weather, mild and breezy, couldn't have been more obliging.

"It's a good day for baseball, don't you think?" Sophie said rhetorically, leaning against the park bench and stretching her legs.

"Yup, it certainly is." The magnitude of my new responsibilities began to seep into my consciousness. Although I'd worked my butt off to earn the team, it was rather overwhelming, actually. I laughed and glanced over at Sophie, who'd begun to sun herself. "Yup," I muttered, "world—you're looking at the new owner of the Bronx Cheers!" I turned to Sophie, and with a panic-stricken look, added, "*Now* what?"

"I don't suppose we can do anything about the flight pattern?" It was my first official day on the job. Dusty and I stared skyward at the continual stream of jets that had just taken off from or were approaching the runway out at LaGuardia Airport. "The noise is pretty deafening. How do the fans hear the announcers? How do the announcers hear *themselves*?"

"Can't do nothing about air traffic, Venus. I think you— well, anyone's—gotta have a lot more power than you or me, to be able to change something like that. You're talking about the feds—the FAA, or whatever they call 'em these days. Hell, old Augie was a billionaire, and he couldn't do nothing about them airplanes."

We walked deMarley Field together. The place could definitely use some sprucing up. I could see where Dad's money *hadn't* been spent. The seats in the bleacher section were splintered, the paint cracked and peeling. Damage from City Island's briny air had taken its toll. So had something else. Dusty and I gazed at the sky again, and I said, "I don't suppose there's anything we can do about the seagulls?" That wasn't white paint spattered all over the bleachers.

"We could make 'em our mascot."

"That wasn't the kind of solution I was looking for."

"I was kidding you, Livy. We can't, anyways." Dusty shrugged. "The Brooklyn Cyclones thought of it first."

"Do we have a mascot?" I asked him.

Dusty gave me a sour look. "He looks kind of like Mr. Met, with a giant baseball for a head, but he's dressed up like an aviator, with the leather bomber jacket, goggles, and a white silk scarf with the team logo on it." I knew that the logo was a baseball being dropped, like a bomb, out of a barnstormer, an image that had zero to do with a team called the Bronx Cheers.

"I want to change the mascot," I said decisively. "We need something fresh, something unexpected. The team's got a new owner, we need a whole new look, a whole new—*ethos*."

"A whole new *what*?" Dusty looked perplexed. "Hey, we need a winning ball club here, not window dressing. Who the fuck's going to care what the mascot looks like if no one comes to the park to watch the kids play."

We turned our gaze to the field where the players were limbering up with a calisthenics routine, under the indifferent aegis of the team's assistant hitting coach and part-time spark plug salesman, Mikey Fuller. I found myself pointing to the guys who weren't in shape. "That sort of exercise isn't cutting it, Dusty. Spot Baldo looks fifteen pounds heavier than he did a few weeks ago."

"Aanh, catchers are *supposed* to be sturdy," Dusty countered. "So's a pitch won't knock 'em over into the dirt."

I located the center fielder. "And Suzuki looks like he entered Nathan's Fourth of July hot dog eating contest—and won! What's up with these guys? I thought they worked out every day."

"A lot of them switched their diets. For the season."

"Shouldn't they be *losing* their winter weight? They're

heavier than they were during tryouts. What are they eating? Beer and pizza?"

I walked around the field to home plate and watched the boys continue to go through their paces. "They definitely need to jazz it up a bit," I said to Dusty.

He looked at me quizzically. "What d'you have in mind?"

"Send Mikey to the hardware store for two dozen broomsticks."

"Broomsticks?"

"*Aww*, for the love of Jesus, talk about getting written up in the papers for all the wrong reasons."

"I heard that groan, Barry. But the Cheers' workout was stale. I warned you I would shake things up a little."

The GM brought his hand to his forehead, as if to stave off a killer migraine. "I should have known you'd mean it literally."

"You'll have to excuse me," I grinned. "I've got a routine to teach."

I took a deep breath, and donning my Venus persona, I stowed my shyness and stepped onto the infield. Most of the team looked angry or flummoxed or both, with the exception of the aptly named first baseman, Romeo Hicks—who made Casanova look like a celibate—and the equally aptly named second baseman, Hollis (variously nicknamed Holly or Hollywood or Holly Woodlawn) Golightly.

"Okay! Your girlfriends and dance partners, assuming you go clubbing, are going to thank me for this! I want you to hold your broomstick out in front of you—no, Spot, watch me demonstrate it first—and I want you to roll your hips to the right, and swivel them clockwise all the way around in a circle. Jicama, *va la manera incorrecta. You're* going *counter*clockwise. *Ése* *es contador a la derecha.* We'll go the opposite way in a minute. I want everyone going in the same direction. There is no *I* in *team*, gentlemen."

Jicama Flores beamed and shouted something at me, very excited.

"What does 'ju spee spani' mean?" Barry Weed whispered in my ear.

I rolled my eyes. I'd always thought Weed was a moron, and he'd just confirmed it for me. "Jicama's amazed that I speak Spanish."

"You understood his Spanish just now?"

"No," *you dimwit*, "I understood his *accent*."

After a couple of minutes I had them gyrate their hips to the left. "Looking good, fellas. Let's loosen up those hips. Okay, now, hold onto the broomsticks for balance—we're going to learn to bump and grind."

I was greeted with a collective blush. "This is lame!" exclaimed Ahab Slocum, my right fielder. "You're makin' us do *strip* routines?"

"*Burlesque* routines. If you were stripping, you'd all be shirtless by now." I walked over to him and got right up in his face. "And *you're* going to be *lame* if you sass-mouth the owner of the team, Ahab."

"*Damn . . .* bitch!" I heard him mutter as I walked away.

I wasn't about to let the players get over on me, especially this early in my tenure. It would be a hole I might never be able to dig myself out of.

"Okay, Ahab, I'm fining you for that remark," I shouted, loud enough for everyone on the team to hear. "One week's salary." I leaned over and murmured in Barry Weed's ear, "How much *is* that, exactly?

"You're kidding me!" I said, appalled at the reply, having expected an exponentially higher number. "That wouldn't even buy a week's worth of groceries! Jeez—now I *do* feel like a bitch."

"Ya gotta maintain discipline, though. Or ya lose them," Dusty said, joining the discussion. "Trust me: in the long run, they'll respect you more if you don't take shit from them."

"I feel bad fining Ahab, now that I know how little he makes," I said. "Still, maybe years from now, when he's in the majors, making more money than God, he'll appreciate having learned early on that having an attitude is unacceptable."

Barry Weed laughed so hard he almost choked. "Yeah, tell that to Barry Bonds. Or Albert Belle."

"Or Ted Williams," Dusty guffawed. He scruffed his hand over the top of my head in a gesture that might have been read as mildly affectionate if his attitude hadn't been just slightly patronizing. "Kiddo, you got a lot to learn about baseball."

"Ahab's mother is on public assistance," I said. "I'll send his fine to her, as an anonymous contribution to the family. And if he doesn't get with the program and bump and grind like the rest of them, he'll lose another week's pay."

Little had I known that our conversation had been in earshot of the sports writers. The headline of the next day's *New York Post* read HEAVENLY BODIES; and the entire back cover of the next morning's *Daily News* was a photo of me standing in front of the Cheers and their broomsticks, with the guys in mid-gyration, and the headline: MOUND OF VENUS. Columnist Mike Lupica had interviewed just about everyone on the team and in the front office—except me. Basically, the gist of the article was that no one thought I could cut it, nor did they expect me to survive the season.

"She's a dish I could eat with a spoon," Romeo Hicks had

remarked. "Hell, I'd like to bang her, but I can't say I respect her as an owner. And her setting curfews when we're on road trips, dude? That's too much. I mean, we're not Little Leaguers. And nobody likes the surprise drug tests she springs on us. It's like when you have a crush on your second-grade teacher, but then it all comes true, man. And believe me, dude, the fantasy's not as good as it seems when you're seven."

I made a note to have a word with young Romeo about speaking to the press. Didn't the Cheers have a media relations manager to run interference? And if so, he or she was asleep on the job. I've never failed at anything, as long as I put my mind to it, and I wasn't about to screw up my legacy. I'd make old Augie proud, even if it killed me. But like Ol' Blue Eyes, I was going to do it *my* way.

Opening day was scheduled for a Tuesday night in late June. DeMarley Field was festooned with blue and white buntings for the occasion. The cheap seats in the bleachers—though the choice seats, at fifteen dollars apiece wouldn't break too many banks—had been sanded and repainted. The groundskeepers had also erected metal stanchions topped with owls—a time-honored ploy to scare away the seagulls. However, it quickly became apparent that the gulls were savvy enough not to be gulled into thinking that owls were indigenous to City Island. Bronx bombers of the avian sort, Jonathan Livingston and his less literary brethren continued to do what gulls do, especially after a dinner of local seafood.

I stood in the dugout with Dusty during batting practice. Distracted by a bleacher-hovering seagull with particularly accurate aim, he grumbled, "I wish *DuPree* had such good control. Your cousin Marty loves him, though. You'd think they were related. And he's managed to convert Barry Weed on the subject. But if Tommy's got any better-than-average stuff, I haven't seen any of it yet."

Speaking of related, it had been *Sophie* who'd urged me to take Tommy DuPree. *Barry Weed* couldn't have convinced me to eat ice chips during a heat wave. It was Sophie's insistence that the right-hander was an ace in the rough that clinched my decision to sign him. And I didn't know how to tell her how much I'd begun to second-guess myself, even before Dusty weighed in with his vote of no confidence. I feared it would break her heart—as well as our fragile trust in each other.

I'd like to be able to say that by opening day I had won the hearts and minds of my limited partners, my GM, and my manager, as well as those of the players and the fans.

Hah!

I craved a cocktail to quell the butterflies in my stomach. In the past few weeks since I'd inherited the team, I'd endured an endless battery of snide comments from my own staff. Snarky New York City sportswriters and editors ran headlines like VENUS'S EXERCISE REGIMEN IS FROM MARS, and EXTRATERRESTRIAL EARNS CHEERS. Even *Variety*, whose Las Vegas stringers had occasionally written about my exotic revues, got into the act with CAN HIPS, NIPS, AND LIPS CURE CHEERS' SLIPS, DIPS, AND TRIPS? The emcee of a local news channel's *SportsOn1* show challenged me to prove that a former showgirl could turn the hapless Bronx "Jeers" into a winning club. This was it. Crunch time.

Before the game, first baseman Romeo Hicks posed for pictures with every pretty girl who asked him, dispensing baseball cards with his phone number on them like they were free samples of detergent. The national anthem was sung by a City Island native, a local Bronx girl who'd made it to the final twelve on *American Idol*. My pal, Congresswoman Tessa Craig, threw the ceremonial first pitch.

From there on, it was all downhill.

Though he was expected to mow down the Long Island Sound's righties, Tommy DuPree had utterly fallen apart by the second inning.

"Oh, Christ," Dusty muttered after DuPree walked the first three hitters to load the bases. "An air traffic controller couldn't help that kid find the strike zone!" But Dusty gave Tommy the benefit of the doubt and left him in the game, figuring it was just a case of opening night jitters and that he'd settle down as soon as his nerves did.

By the middle of the fourth inning, we were down, 8 to 1. Our only run had been scored on a high fastball by Grand Slammy Santiago, who attributed it to his newfound born-again beliefs. Evidently, God had visited him in the locker room just before the game and told him to wait for a high fastball.

"Sammy, you *always* wait for high fastballs," a bemused Dusty reminded him. "You never *hit* anything else."

Dusty finally took Tommy out, but Baptista Minola, the right-handed middle reliever, didn't do us any favors. The Sound couldn't have appreciated his pitches any more if he'd delivered them with candy and flowers. Dusty replaced Baptista with Debrett Peerage, but by then the damage had been done. In the bottom of the seventh, though we'd scored again, thanks to some surprisingly stellar base stealing by Jicama Flores and a stand-up double by left fielder Anton Anton, we were down by twelve runs.

"Where's the Beef?!" the fans began to chant, demanding our closer, Wayne deBoeuf. It was a tremendous relief to the management that the reliever did his job, albeit barefoot, shutting down the Sound for the next two innings, but it didn't change the final score: 14 to 2.

I was not a happy camper. In fact, I could feel the heat rising on my body until steam was ready to blow out of my ears.

Storming into the Cheers locker room, I announced, "You guys really need to think about whether you want to keep your day jobs!"

Some of the players made a grab for their towels, shocked and embarrassed that a woman (who was their boss, to boot) had dared to penetrate their masculine sphere. Ahab Slocum tried to duck behind the door to his locker, which was about half his width. Shoji threw his towel over his head. Sammy ran around the benches like a flustered turkey with his butt hanging out. Romeo ostentatiously dropped his towel and stood in front of his locker with one foot on the bench, as if he was daring me to say something. I made a point of ignoring him.

"Many of you have seen me mostly naked," I said, referring to the photos in my now-ancient calendars, most of which somehow ended up on the Internet. "Now we're even."

I stood in the center of the locker room demanding their full attention. Suffice it to say that for some of the guys their attention was fuller than others, but I wasn't interested in the literal extent of their interest in me.

"That was pretty pathetic out there tonight, kids. Is that how you would have played for Augie? Because even if *he* were standing here right now instead of me, as much as he loved this ball club, he would have been brokenhearted by your performance—with very few exceptions—on that field this evening. And so am I. You posing for a life drawing class, Romeo? You guys want to 'punish' me for being your boss—go ahead. But don't be so unfathomably stupid that you punish yourselves by playing the game like it's the first time you've seen the equipment. When you step into a stadium—at home or away—act like you've been there before. Because if you kids continue to play as poorly as you did tonight, you're not dashing *my* dreams; you're pissing on your *own*." I strode toward the door, and turning back to the players, I added, "Think about it."

I felt like hiding in the ladies room and having a good cry. Either that or a stiff drink and a good night's sleep.

The Cheers had been soundly trounced, as the sports pages would no doubt announce in tomorrow's papers, though it didn't dampen Romeo Hicks's determination to celebrate afterward at one of the local bars, surrounded by a bevy of pulchritudinous fans.

I refused to permit Sophie to join them. No way was I going to allow her to get mixed up with a ballplayer, especially one who so clearly enjoyed playing the field. But my daughter wasn't exactly thrilled about my efforts to micromanage her social life, particularly since she was now a college graduate, ostensibly out in the world on her own.

"Damn, even the champagne had an editorial comment," she observed grumpily, opening one of the bottles that had been intended for a victory drink. "It's gone flat."

That night, the *SportsOn1* show led off with, "If you were up at deMarley Field in the Bronx tonight, you got to witness an eclipse of Venus, when her Bronx Cheers were pounded by the Long Island Sound."

Charming.

"I'm looking forward to getting out of town," I said to Sophie. "The New York press corps is merciless."

"*I'm* looking forward to our away games, myself," Sophie sighed. "Are you still mad at me about Tommy DuPree?"

"If he continues to suck as badly as he did tonight, yes I am," I admitted.

"He'll settle down. It's just nerves," she replied authoritatively. "You can't expect to polish a diamond in the rough in just a couple of weeks."

"I'm not so sure about the diamond thing, Soph. Dusty says 'you can't polish a turd.'"

"Well, ol' Crusty Dusty has a way with words, hasn't he?"

She smiled and patted my leg. "Don't worry, Mom, I'm a shrewd judge of talent. You just have to trust me."

Well, I wanted to. And as much as I adored my daughter, I wasn't sure my gut wasn't a better arbiter of baseball talent, at least where Tommy DuPree was concerned. But I was reluctant to have it out with her over Tommy's skills, not just because it was too soon in the season to be certain she'd been wrong about him—but because if I *did* confront her, I was afraid I'd lose her.

⚾

We dropped our first two home games, and then it was time to hit the highway for our first road trip of the season.

"How can you name a team the *Fairies*?" Ahab Slocum wanted to know. He was lounging across the back row of seats in the team bus, eating a peanut butter and beef jerky sandwich. "Yo, Holly! You should be right at home there. Maybe Barry and Venus should trade you!"

"Not the Fairies—the Ferry. They're called the Bridgeport *Ferry*." Hollis Golightly rolled his eyes.

"I don't get it."

"Oh, read a map, for goodness' sakes!" Holly lobbed a road map toward the back of the bus. "It's like a local landmark or something. You have to take a ferry to and from Bridgeport, Connecticut, to get to Long Island."

"Yo, Venus! *Damn* . . . woman can't hear me with them headphones on. Always got her headphones on. What kind of tunes you listenin' to, Venus?"

I wasn't listening to music, actually, and I'd heard every word Ahab had said. The kid drove me crazy, but he was one of our better defensive players, and one of the few who was hitting with any consistency; and unless he said something really offensive again, it was the better part of valor to just ignore his existence. Otherwise I'd be sorely tempted to kick his arrogant butt with my stilettos.

Shoji Suzuki, with a Manga book in his lap, was trying very hard not to let his teammates see him cry, but his shoulders were heaving up and down. I took off my headphones, switched off the CD player, and went and sat beside him.

"What's wrong?" I asked him gently in his native tongue.

"Nothing," he replied reflexively in Japanese.

"There must be something wrong," I replied, hoping I was getting the tenses right. In any event, my maiden effort at Japanese was no better than Suzuki-san's rare attempts at English. "Are you homesick?"

The center fielder gave a barely perceptible nod. "No one talk to me here," he said. He had to repeat himself four times before I could understand him, which embarrassed both of us.

"Hey, I can speak Japanese," Pinky Melk said, rapping his knuckles on the back of my seat. "How's this: Sushi. Teriyaki. Honda. Mitsubishi. See how good I can speak!"

"Asshole clown," Shoji muttered in Japanese. I gave him a befuddled look. He translated his remark by whispering in my ear.

I laughed. "I'll practice your English with you, and you can teach me Japanese. Because the CD I've been listening to isn't very good, I think. How's that for a fair trade?"

Shoji looked stricken. "You . . . *trade* me?" he gasped.

"No—*no*, Shoji. Not trade you. That's not what I meant. I meant an *exchange*. Of knowledge."

His face brightened. He was a sweet kid, if a bit strange. I still wished he didn't have blue hair. "Okay! Good deal."

He nodded to me, a quick bow of the head, and I responded in kind. "*Domo arigato*, Shoji."

"You very welcome, Miss Venus. I want to . . . to good English speak."

"*Ganbare, Shoji!*" I said to him in his own tongue. "*You can do it!*"

Shoji blushed at the encouragement.

My attention was drawn away by a wolf whistle coming from the back of the bus. "Romeo and Sophie sitting in a tree, k-i-s-s-i-n-g." Ahab was chanting the snarky little song we used to sing when we wanted to poke fun at two kids enjoying a puppy-love crush.

"Romeo and—Sophie?" I slid out of the seat next to Shoji and walked toward the back of the bus. She must have sneaked back there while I was trying to cheer up our center fielder. There she was, cuddled up with the sexually peripatetic first baseman, oblivious to Ahab's teasing or to the leers of the other Cheers.

"*Ah-ha-hemm!*" I cleared my throat extravagantly, and Sophie's eyes blinked open. Romeo grinned at me.

"Sophie, come up front and sit with me."

She looked torn. And altogether too comfy.

"Hey, Venus. It was just a little cuddle. No harm, no foul, right?"

"Wrong, Romeo. She's my daughter. And I've got my eye on you," I warned him.

"Mom, I'm a grown woman," Sophie whined.

I grabbed her by the arm and nearly lifted her to her feet. "Honey, I will not let you turn into me," I hissed, as we headed for the front of the bus. "I've been where you just were—more or less—remember? It's how you got here. I know it seems like I'm being harsh, but I'm trying to keep you from making at least some of the mistakes I made."

"But I'm not you, Mom. And I can make my own decisions." She glared at me with such ferocity that I shivered.

It was going to take a lot longer than a bus ride to Bridgeport for us to resolve our differences on this issue. And I couldn't really have it out with her on the bus, or it would embarrass us both and, worse, make us look weak.

I was at war with myself, totally unsure of how much to push or demand or try to control, and how much to step away and let human nature take its course, allowing Sophie the opportunity to screw up, so that she might learn something from the experience, rather than attempt to prevent it, in an effort to shield her heart—and other body parts—from getting taken for a ride. So far, I'd found no easy answers. Would the two of us ever be on the same page?

In our first away games, the Cheers' numbers were no better than the stats they'd posted at home. Facing a bunch of left-handed batters he should have sent straight back to the dug-out, the Melk-man failed to deliver and we lost the first game to the Ferry by a score of 5 to 1. The following night, Tommy DuPree's second start of the season resulted in a shutout. If we hadn't been the team that was shut out, it might have been a cause for celebration. Tommy had taken to grunting each time he released the ball; and it wasn't long before the opposing team decoded the grunts, which, evidently, were slightly dif-ferent for each type of pitch. Whether it was a slider, a sinker, or a fastball, the Ferry heard 'em coming.

It was a glum ride back to New York City. The Cheers were already last in their division, and my daughter wasn't talking to me.

"Move over, kiddo." Dusty sidled into the seat beside me. "Chin up, Venus." He kneaded the knots out of my shoulders with surprisingly expert massage skills. A moan escaped my lips before I could check it. I felt myself blush. "Rosa used to have a saying in times like these. 'Dusty,' she'd say to me, 'things always get worse before they get better.' The woman was a veritable Yogi Berra."

He placed a gentle kiss between my shoulder blades. "Rosa had another saying, too, for times like these, ya know, when you feel like a total fuckup and a failure at just about everything in the game of life. 'Just remember: you're not as bad as you think you are,' she'd tell me."

"I'm not as bad as I think I am, huh?" I sighed, as I relaxed into Dusty's strong hands. "Gee, what a comforting thought."

Next thing I knew, I was dreaming that Dusty and I were riding in his motor boat, but instead of gently undulating waves, the surface beneath us was nothing but frenetically bobbing baseballs.

The Cheers were now in a bona fide slump. We'd hit a horrific heat wave as well. Our team mascot passed out from sunstroke while dancing atop the dugout in his heavy leather bomber jacket and had to be taken off the field on a stretcher, a rather inauspicious hitch, since it occurred on Mascot Bobblehead Day. The un-air-conditioned locker room became so stifling— and stinky—that tempers were testy even before the Cheers took the field. I plugged in a bunch of rotary fans, but all they did was spin the foul air in lazy, fetid circles. Even the most intrepid sports reporters resisted venturing into a low-ceilinged venue smelling of sweat socks and jockstraps. I began to think that if I had to look at those fading blue and white uniforms for one more day, I would go nuts.

Morale was in the toilet. It was time for a shake-up. If I couldn't affect it from the inside out, then I'd have to try the opposite tack. The team needed a major league makeover. A totally new look.

So I did what I'd done back when I was dancing for a living and my performance persona was no longer exciting the customers. I'd used the same strategy with my girls when a revue began to get stale and business started dropping off. In New York City, everything was at my fingertips, and in some cases, right within walking distance. I dug out my sketch pad and colored pencils and strolled up to the garment district for some fabric swatches.

Joy Ashe sounded surprised to receive my phone call. "I've got an idea I'd like to run by you," I told her. "And I need your skills as a calligrapher. It's about the Cheers. I wonder if you can help me with some prototypes."

A few days later I called a meeting of the management, including Marty deMarley, who owned enough shares in the team to warrant his inclusion at the table, if only as a courtesy. Besides, even though I couldn't stand him, he was still Dad's nephew. And I wasn't going to be a sore winner.

We convened on neutral territory, in Cap Gaines's conference room. Citing the Cheers' lackluster performance, and dwindling interest from the fans, who, from my reading of the attendance figures, seemed to have given up on the team by degrees over the past three seasons, I announced that I was establishing a couple of key cosmetic changes.

"For starters, we're going to revamp the Cheers' uniforms."

You should have seen the appalled faces. I might as well have told them I was replacing the players' paychecks with carnival scrip. I reminded them all that professional sports teams redesign their uniforms practically as often as the players change socks. The last time I checked out the San Diego Padres, they no longer wore brown and orange, but were attired in blue and buff, colors more befitting Lord Nelson's navy than their namesake monks who founded Southern California's missions.

I pressed my point. "Not only do totally new uniforms give the team a fresh look, but it's also an excellent marketing tool.

With attendance down, the Cheers have been steadily hemor-rhaging money, and we need to find alternative ways to recapture the funds we're losing at the gate. We redo the uniforms, and everyone will want to buy jerseys and caps in the brand-new colors and styles." Referring to the Cheers' current outfits, I insisted that "blue and white is basic and boring. It's totally generic and says nothing about who we are—what our ethos, our *zeitgeist* is."

Barry Weed looked nervous before I even dropped the other shoe. "She's talking German at me," he muttered to Peter Argent.

I rose to my feet, leaving the rest of them gazing up at me. Dick Fernando's eyes glazed over. He was probably looking up my skirt. "We're the Bronx Cheers, right? Right. So—what's a 'Bronx Cheer'? C'mon folks, think jargon!"

"I get it!" Cousin Marty exclaimed. He stuck his tongue between his lips and blew, fluttering his lower lip with a loud *putt-putt* sound. "A raspberry! Of course!" Then he gave me an utterly stymied look. "Wait—I don't get it. What does a 'Bronx Cheer' have to do with uniforms?"

"I'm changing their color," I said emphatically. "Executive decision." I looked around the table. "Don't even *try* to talk me out of it." I opened my briefcase and took out my sketch pad, on which I'd rendered, in full color, a drawing of the Cheers' new duds.

"*Ohmigod*, they're pink!" Linda deMarley shouted.

"Fucking pink!" echoed Peter Argent. "You want the Cheers to wear fucking pink uniforms!"

"I don't know what shade 'fucking pink' is, exactly," I replied smoothly. "'Shocking pink' would be closer."

"Well, I, for one, am shocked," Dusty muttered, holding his head. "Venus, what the heck do you think you're doing? The kids are gonna look like a bunch of queers in these uniforms."

I ignored his tone-deaf remark. "Don't you get it, folks? They're *raspberry*-colored. The exact same color as raspberry sorbet."

Dick Fernando practically raised his fist at me. "Sorbet, my ass. They're the color of the inside of a vagina, for Chrissakes."

"Only you would think that, Dick." The man thoroughly disgusted me. And if he was going to continue to stare at my tatas, I wished he would have a fatal heart attack in the process. It would serve him right.

"No one's gonna like this, Olivia." Dick turned to the other limited partner. "I knew she'd be a total disaster, Peter, but never in my hairiest nightmares did I think it would be this bad."

"If Uncle Augie saw these, he'd start spinning in his grave," Marty snarled. I could tell he was still mad at me for eating his dinosaur cookies.

Linda smacked his arm. "He doesn't *have* a grave, you putz. He was cremated, remember?"

"It's a *figure of speech*, Linda. Lighten up."

Barry Weed lit another cigarette and began to pace. "People with penises are going to wear these, Livy. They're going to look like fucking fruits!"

"Actually, raspberries *are* a fruit," Linda said helpfully.

"And while we're on the subject," I said, ignoring my detractors' cacophony, "we're going to have a brand-new mascot, too. With a new logo to match." Joy had done a bang-up job with the lettering for the new logo. I turned the page on my sketch pad to reveal a drawing of the revamped, revitalized mascot costume. "Ta-da!"

Dusty looked at me, aghast. "You're kidding me, right? You want to turn the Bronx Cheers' mascot into a giant raspberry? Oh, for the love of Mike, please tell me I'm dreaming. But this is mild—this mascot—this I could maybe wrap my brain around by the end of the century and finally get used to it. And the little grinning raspberry logo I might be able to live with some day, too. It's the rest of the equation that gets my goat and strangles it. Venus, you want to put a bunch of barely postadolescent, testosterone-fueled athletes in pink uniforms!" He glanced at the pampered Yorkie in Linda's lap, who was sporting a fuchsia bow in her topknot. "I mean, this is how Linda dresses her lapdog, for cryin' out loud!"

"You'd better not be insulting my Rosebud!" Linda exclaimed, her face turning as pink as her pooch's hair bow.

"You people have the courage of agoraphobics," I said. "Put your prejudices aside for a minute and really think about this from a marketing standpoint. Let's just discuss the issue of the *mascot* right now. What does a baseball-headed guy in a bomber jacket have to do with a team called the Bronx Cheers? Now, *this* is *perfect*," I said, pointing to my sketch. "It *is* a Bronx Cheer. You can't get any more accurate—or whimsical—for that matter, than a ginormous raspberry. Minor league baseball is supposed to be *fun*! It's *entertainment*—which is something I *do* have a lifetime of experience in."

Marty deMarley lovingly looked down at his ubiquitous blue jersey with its white piping. "Holy crap!" he shouted, as if he'd just sat on a thumbtack. "Does this mean I'll have to wear pink shirts for the rest of my life? Say it ain't so!" he moaned, glancing at his wife for moral support.

Linda gave him a funny look. I wondered what was going on inside the woman's head as she caressed her yapping dust mop.

Linda suppressed a giggle. Olivia's new raspberry-colored uniforms might in fact be one of the best things that ever happened to her marriage. Maybe Marty would finally begin dressing like a grown-up at home, in preference to sporting polyblend shirts in a color that only Elsa Schiaparelli would have appreciated. "I think the new uniforms are wonderful," Linda said, flashing me a professionally whitened smile. "And I fully support your decision to change them. Not only that—I think the new logo is positively adorable, and the mascot is genius. Genius!" She couldn't wait to get home, pop the champagne, and crow to Marty, "Venus has really done it this time!"

I used my controlling interest to railroad my ideas through, implementing them as soon as it was practicable. Prototypes of the sorbet-shaded uniforms, and the Cheers' "Razzie the Raspberry" mascot were rolled out—the latter almost literally—by the end of the week, with the rest of the gear rush-ordered from a factory in rural North Carolina. I'd hoped for a more enthusiastic response from the players, but I suppose I should have predicted their reactions to my promotional campaign to Think Pink. Only our second baseman, Hollis Golightly, had anything positive to say about the new uniforms, pronouncing them "daring." I took it as a compliment.

Once they tried them on, the rest of the team gave the new uniforms a giant raspberry of their own, carping that the new duds made them resemble wads of bubble gum, bottles of Pepto-Bismol, or just plain fruits. Ahab Slocum, whose backside was somewhat generous, and whose thigh muscles were nothing short of impressive, insisted that he looked like one of his mother's baked Virginia hams.

The uniforms were kind of chic, actually, from a fashion standpoint. And certainly, no other baseball team wore anything remotely like them. My press release quoted me as saying, "The players look positively yummy now," and the media ate it up with a spoon.

Unfortunately, they dished it out, too. VENUS DEMARLEY STRIPS CHEERS OF THEIR DIGNITY read one local sports headline, and the following day the same journalist called for the players to TAKE IT OFF! The one-two combination of my stripper-style exercise routine and the rose-colored attire, compounded by the pounding they were taking in the press, sent the guys' misery index spiking as high as the noonday temperature on the field.

Sophie cautioned, "If you don't watch out, you're going to have a mutiny on your hands, Mom. I mean, the Clarendon Kumquats had appallingly awful uniforms; I *hated* those fuzzy olive-colored jerseys and caps, but at least we didn't dress in one of the ultimate girl-colors. Even our *Little League* club didn't wear pink, and we were a bunch of nine year olds in pigtails who took after-school ballet lessons!"

"The mood is temporary," I insisted. "Things like this happen in every company whenever someone initiates a total overhaul of the status quo. It's a classic business model. Until the tides turn in their favor, the visionary is always mistaken for a pariah. I promise you, Soph, it'll blow over as soon as the boys get some wins under their belts. All they need is some confidence."

Sophie sighed in exasperation. "Well, how are they supposed to get it when you've dressed them like desserts?!"

"There's a method to my madness; you just have to trust me. Up until I designed new uniforms and changed the team's logo and mascot, all the Cheers got from the press was a razzing for another season of lackluster performances. The guys got so much grief from the local media, they lost all faith in their capabilities as ballplayers. Now the focus is on something entirely different, which has absolutely nothing to do with their ability to hit and run and field and pitch. The pressure's off because I've deflected the press's collective attention. Now the guys can just settle down and focus on the fundamentals."

Sophie looked at me in utter bemusement. "*Umm . . .* I'm not exactly sure folks'll see you as a baseball visionary," she sighed. "I love you, Mom, but I'm afraid people are just going to think of you as a half-shelled baseball nut."

My heart suddenly began to sing coloratura arias, hitting notes I never knew I had. At that moment, I didn't care *what* people thought of me—my daughter had just said she loved me!

"Do you think we can sue her for running the team straight into the toilet?" Marty deMarley mused between bites of a particularly crunchy cereal. Linda cringed at the sound. "There must be some way around it. Is there a clause in Uncle Augie's will that said what would happen if Venus screwed up?"

Linda sipped her espresso and shook her head. "I'm looking at the photocopy. I haven't come across any loopholes yet. And don't forget, the team defined mediocrity even before Venus inherited it. It only sucks slightly worse now than it did before."

"Are you on her side now?" Marty gasped. Milk dribbled down his chin into the cereal bowl.

"What, are you nuts? I'm just stating the facts, that's all. Technically—if you read the sports pages," Linda added, turning to the back of the morning edition of the *Daily News*—"the Cheers are a better ball club than they've been in several seasons." She glanced at an article about the team's woes and summarized it for her husband as she nibbled a slice of dry toast. "On paper, the Cheers are stronger both defensively and offensively; they have a deeper pitching staff, but they're not performing to expectations. And why? Because they don't respect their new owner. It's okay if they dislike Venus, even if they hate her—because if they fear her, they'll still play well. But without the respect of the players and coaches, Venus'll never be able to turn them around."

"Does the columnist offer her any advice, in case she's reading the paper?" Marty asked curiously.

Linda skimmed to the final paragraph. "Nope; it just says she needs to earn their admiration."

Secretly, Linda commiserated. In fact, she'd surprised herself with the realization that, as a fellow estrogen producer, she even felt sorry for Venus to a certain degree, though she would never admit it to anyone, and certainly not to Marty, who in her view, wouldn't do much better with the Cheers if push really did come to shove and they could legally yank the controlling interest in the team out from under Venus deMarley. Even with Linda's prodding and scheming backing him up, dorky Marty couldn't command anyone's respect, least of all a bunch of macho kids hoping to get called up to the majors.

The realization was an epiphany Linda deMarley was uncomfortable acknowledging. And Linda didn't "do" sympathy. Sympathy sucked up your time and got you too involved in other people's business. Sympathy came back and bit you in the ass, the way it had when she'd told her sister Marilyn what a loser her gambling, gun-toting husband was—and Marilyn had taken the dickhead back with open arms and hadn't spoken to her since.

Was Marty right? *Was* she now on Olivia's side? She'd never even liked the woman. And she still wasn't about to forgive and forget the way Venus had insulted her—even if it happened well over a decade ago. Sort of like Marty's dinosaur cookies—only important. Linda folded the paper and shoved it across the table toward her husband. For some reason, all her thoughts were jumbled this morning, her opinions zinging back and forth between what it must be like to be in Venus's thigh-high boots and Marty's Bally loafers. Maybe it was just the espresso talking. Linda wasn't liking the confusion. She'd never been confused about anything before. Everything was always black or white; why were things suddenly popping up in shades of gray?

"Rosebud and I are going shopping," she said, abruptly hopping up from the breakfast table. "I'm not feeling like myself today."

Marty reached for the *Daily News*. "What's the matter, hon?" he asked solicitously.

"Something's wrong with my insides," Linda said, placing her hand on her well-toned abs. "I'm feeling *nice*."

⟐

I drove out to the City Island marina, with a copy of the morning paper on the front seat beside me, opened to the sports pages. Something their columnist had written was gyrating in my brain, and I wanted to be able to grab hold of the criticism, stop the spinning, and face the music.

Dusty was already at his boat when I arrived, scrubbing the hull with a huge sponge. "Wouldn't it make more sense to do that after our little excursion?"

He shook his head and pointed skyward. "Fucking seagulls. I'm not gonna let them use the *RosAmor* for a toilet."

"Speaking of the crapper," I said, as Dusty wrung out the sponge and tossed it into an empty plastic bucket, "Mike Lupica says the Cheers are sitting there, stinking up the division, because they don't respect me. And it's not just about the new uniforms or the bump-and-grind exercise routine."

"*Aw*, Venus, that's one man's opinion. Don't take it so hard." He held out his hand and helped me step into the motor boat.

"Do you think it's true? Lupica says it's not just the players who have a problem with my owning the team; it's the management, too." I looked Dusty in the eye. "Do *you* have a problem with it?"

"Venus—I think the team is sucking because they're not playing well."

"Sounds like a Yogi-ism," I chuckled. "But, for argument's sake, let's say that's actually true. *Why* aren't they playing well? Statistically, it's supposed to be the strongest team in a decade. So whatever's at play here is something intangible, ephemeral. It's got to do with personalities, not numbers. You're the manager, Dusty," I said, kicking off my sandals. I wiggled my bare toes. "Maybe the problem is *you*."

The poor man looked like he was about to have a heart attack. His face grew pale and his eyes began to mist over. "I love those kids like they were my own flesh and blood. I've given some of the best years of my life—and Rosa's last years—to the Cheers." His shoulders heaved with emotion.

"Oh, shit, I'm sorry." I stepped behind him and slid my arms around his waist, such as it was. "I didn't mean to imply—I guess what I'm suggesting is that the *approach* has to change. You've been managing the team the same way every season for several years now; and every season, the team has performed below par. It's the definition of 'insanity' to do the exact same thing time after time, and expect different results! The kids seem to love you. You're a father figure for many of them. But I think it's time you considered changing the way you manage the team."

"Wait just a New York minute!" Dusty exclaimed, turning around. We were now chest to chest. "You read an article this morning that blamed the Cheers' failures on you, and now you're telling me the team's piss-poor performance this season is *my* fault?! And on my boat!"

"Then tell me why Tommy DuPree, the great white hope of the year, can't win a game!"

"Because he isn't any good! *That's* why!"

Had there been any casual observers of this little contre-temps, it would have looked for all the world like a manager and an ump going toe to toe over a bad call.

I refused to step away, or to back down. "Look, I've been placed in charge of the Cheers by forces from the Great Beyond. Or at least beyond my control. Now, you guys may not like the fact that I'm a woman, but, guess what—I can't change that. In fact, even if I could, I'd never want to. Some of you may not like the fact that I used to be an exotic dancer—well, I can't change that, either. But I just write the checks. It's you and Barry Weed who ultimately put this team together, and you're the one who's responsible for the kids once they get to the ball park. You make the lineup before every game, you work with the hitting and pitching coaches on how to improve performance, and you're the one who determines the strategy, inning by inning. I've got a business degree, Dusty. When I ran nightclubs in Vegas, I figured out how to beat my competition while keeping my employees' morale as high as their pay-checks; and when I inherited the Cheers, I vowed to maintain the same standards. I take my responsibilities to the team, and my father's legacy, very seriously. I told you weeks ago that no one was safe if the team wasn't performing, and I haven't changed my mind."

We were nose to nose. I was sure Dusty could feel my breath on his face. He gave me a funny look, and I leaned back, ever so slightly. I didn't want him to think I wasn't a woman of my word.

"Well, maybe this will make you look at things a little differ-ent." His arm encircled my waist and pulled me back against him. And then his lips were pressed against my surprised, even shocked, open mouth. I kept my eyes open through the kiss, staring at Dusty. I was utterly confused; part of me was angry, yet the rest of me was confounded that I was enjoying it.

"Well . . . that came out of left field!" I exclaimed, sliding out of his embrace. My hands flew to my temples. Suddenly I had a raging headache.

"Sorry about that, Venus." Dusty looked a bit sheepish. "I've . . . I've been wanting to do that for a while, now."

"You're—you're a widower!"

"And you're a looker. Does that make me a heel?"

I didn't know how to answer. I liked the man, in general. Yet I'd certainly never thought of him as a lover. The notion had been entirely off my radar . . . until now. It was an awkward acknowledgment that I simply didn't know how to handle. "I . . . I'm not up for a boat ride now," I said weakly. I stepped out of the *RosAmor* and back onto the dock. "I . . . I need to go home."

I promised to phone Dusty later to discuss revamped management strategies for the Cheers, but I climbed into my car and headed for Chelsea without the slightest idea what to say to the man. He'd just thrown me a curveball that I hadn't a clue how to hit.

⟨⊘⟩

"Dusty *what*?" exclaimed Sophie. The *New York Times* real estate section fell from her hand onto the area rug.

"He kissed me. We were in the middle of an argument over whether his management skills were cutting it, when he kissed me!"

Sophie pretended to realign her dropped jaw. "Was it *good*?"

"That isn't really the point, Soph."

"Well, but it's more than tangential. Old Crusty Dusty— who'd a thunk it? This is so awesome!"

"Awesome-good or awesome-bad? You kids overuse that word so much, I haven't a clue what you mean by it, anymore." Then I remarked that she'd evidently ceased giving me the silent treatment—which began over the Romeo Hicks issue.

"This is too interesting to ignore. So, what are you going to do about it?"

"We're going to look at new ways to turn the Cheers into a winning ball club. And if we can't come up with something that works, I'm going to have to ask Barry Weed to give Dusty the heave-ho. It would break my heart, but it's my responsibility to keep the team afloat. We've got salaries, upkeep of the stadium—"

Sophie rolled her eyes. "I don't mean what are you going to do about the players—I mean what are you going to do about the *kiss*?"

I sat on the floor, hugging my knees to my chest. "It's kind of the same thing. I can't exactly fire a guy who's just kissed me."

"Not unless you're a total bitch. Which you're not. At least not yet. You would be if you kicked old Crusty Dusty to the curb. I bet Linda deMarley wouldn't think twice about it, though. The only sentient being she gives a shit about is her dog."

"Dusty's only part of the problem," I sighed, leaning against the couch and closing my eyes. It helped me remember the taste of his kiss. "He must have had a Spanish omelet for breakfast."

"What?"

"Nothing, honey."

"*Hmmm.*"

"*Hmmm* nothing, Soph. As I was saying—Dusty's only *part* of the problem. The players themselves are the other part. Starting with your diamond in the rough, Tommy DuPree." I told her that my gut was saying it was time to look for another ace right-hander.

Sophie's eyes filled with tears. "You don't trust me," she said in a small voice, looking for all the world as though I'd somehow betrayed her. I knew she needed to be right. To demonstrate to me that she possessed a worthy and useful talent. Yet, the pitcher wasn't performing up to par. I had reached the point where I had to make a decision either to honor my daughter's delicate ego or do what was best for the team.

And I chose Sophie.

⚾

"I bet you guys aren't using sabermetrics," she said later that afternoon, fully aware she'd dodged a bullet. "Wait!" she commanded, with that I-know-something-you-don't-know bravado. She retreated into her bedroom and emerged a minute or so later, clutching a hardcover to her chest as though it were more precious than the Dead Sea Scrolls. "Glenn gave me this for my eighteenth birthday," she said proudly. "He told me that even an amateur talent scout should know about sabermetrics."

I took the book from her hands and leafed through its pages. "Actually, I came across a couple of articles about sabermetrics on the Internet," I told her, "and at the time I thought it made about as much sense as any other methods of baseball analysis, though it took me a while to wrap my brain around all the necessary number crunching. "I even raised the subject with Barry."

"And?" Sophie asked excitedly, pleased that she might be able to make up for the credit she'd lost in going to bat so strongly for Tommy DuPree.

"*And* he just scoffed at it. Barry doesn't believe it's really possible to analyze baseball by using objective evidence. Dusty agreed with him. He says the game is an art, not a science."

"But it's *both*!" Sophie exclaimed, growing more passionate about her opinion with each word she uttered. "Whoever has the most runs wins the game, right? So, on-base percentage is crucial. Drawing a walk is *as* key, if not *more* so, than batting average. For example, if you drill the ball to centerfield, but the outfielder picks it up and throws to first before you get there, you're one base-on-balls less likely to win the game. Tommy DuPree and the others are good players—they just need to be managed differently. Barry Weed is a chain-smoking dinosaur—I don't care if he's only forty-three years old, he's still Paleolithic when it comes to general-managing a ball club. And Crusty Dusty should at least give sabermetrics a try," she insisted. "I'll help! I'll start compiling the stats of each of the Cheers against each of the pitchers they've faced in the Atlantic Coast League, and I'll do the same thing in reverse: write down the stats of each of our club's pitchers against each of the hitters in the league."

"And do what with them?" I asked her. "I totally agree that we have to have a new approach, since the current model is obviously not working. But A-ball has a relatively short season. We don't have time to scratch our tushies and analyze sheet after sheet of figures. We need some momentum. We need some wins!"

"Well, Mom," Sophie replied, standing her ground, "sometimes you have to take a step back if you want to move forward."

So I once more stepped up to the plate, reminding Barry Weed (using Sophie's examples of success) that the Oakland A's general manager had been successfully relying on sabermetric principles for years; and the Boston GM's use of the system has often been credited with helping the Sox win the 2004

World Series. But the Cheers' GM was not sold on the idea. He and Dusty frustrated me no end by insisting on sticking to the status quo. Their decision was supported by the team's two limited partners. Being outvoted by the testosterone brigade made me wonder if I had enough clout, or stock shares, to limit Peter Argent and Dick Fernando's creative input!

I phoned Cap Gaines for advice and told him what was on my mind. "I'm being stalemated at every turn," I said. "They're hampering me from doing the job I was charged with, and I'm tired of being the one getting hammered for it."

I shared a couple of ideas with him and Cap dispensed a bit of professional advice. "You have to look out for your interests, Olivia. If you've got the funds to do what you just proposed to me, I'll put the ball in motion."

So, after several conversations with my accountant and my financial adviser, I called a meeting of the Cheers management. My only regret was that I hadn't done it sooner and saved myself a lot of tears. Once again, we convened in Cap's conference room.

"Well, all I can say to you guys is that Ms. deMarley is proof that you don't need a dick to run a team. All it takes is a pair of balls." The attorney took an official-looking document from his leather folder. "Mr. Fernando, Mr. Argent, this instrument effectively strips you of your limited partnerships. Pursuant to a clause in the ball club's bylaws, Ms. deMarley has purchased your individual interests in the Bronx Cheers and is now the sole owner of the team."

Every man at the table looked utterly shocked. Completely blindsided. They could not have appeared more stunned had I literally emasculated them with a hatchet.

"If she can fire you guys, what else is she capable of?" Barry Weed said nervously. Argent and Fernando remained too shaken for words.

Finally, Peter Argent thumped his fist on the conference table and jumped up from his chair. "We've been with the Cheers since the beginning!" He exchanged a look with Dick Fernando, who sat slumped in his seat as though he'd been clocked in the head with a bat. "We were like nephews to old Augie!"

"I *was* his nephew, and he never offered me as many shares in the Cheers as you two," Marty deMarley grumbled. He turned to me and asked, "Are you going to cut me out, too, Venus?" He looked like he was going to cry.

I shook my head. "I can't do that to family, Marty. Besides, you don't have enough of a legal interest to be able to tell me how to run my ball club. But I will no longer have my business decisions derided by two men who are waiting for me to fail, and who have so little respect for me, and for their mentor, that they insult and belittle his daughter—which in itself challenges the wisdom of Augie's choice and betrays his trust."

I rose to my feet and picked up my portfolio. "Now, if you gentlemen will excuse me, I've got a team to run."

⚾

After Tommy DuPree blew his next two starts for the team, I could no longer rationalize my decision to give Sophie the benefit of the doubt, and even Barry realized that something had to be done about the kid. "We've got to cut the deadwood," he agreed. "It's not the first time, and it certainly won't be the last, that the sparkly nugget we picked out of the stream turned out to be just a piece of a crushed beer can."

I was mightily reassured that Barry was willing to see things my way. My buying out the limited partners must have really shaken him up. But how would I break it to Sophie? How could I explain to my daughter that her judgment—on which I had so heavily relied when I asked Barry Weed to give Tommy a contract—had been, well, *wrong*?

And what would it do to our fragile new relationship? We were still getting to know each other—as family, as grown, independent women—each of us a strong, and rather opinionated, personality. I learned the hard way, from old Augie, that being blood isn't an automatic "gimme" when it comes to love. Or respect. Or trust. Earning those precious commodities couldn't be done overnight Sophie and I were engaged in a delicate dance that was being incrementally choreographed over time, and the thing I feared most was making a misstep.

"It's business, sweetheart," I explained to her a few days later, as we watched a purportedly promising pitcher warm up in deMarley Field. Overhead, a flock of seagulls hovered, ready to share its opinion.

Sophie scowled at me. "You sound like a character from *The Godfather*."

"Kyle Angel was a hot prospect out of Springfield last year," Barry Weed informed me. "But the Batavia Muckdogs dropped his contract."

"I can see why," I replied, unimpressed by the speed, or lack thereof, of Angel's fastball.

Weed lit his fourth cigarette of the tryout, stamping out butt number three in the stands. He retrieved it only after I gave him a prolonged dirty look. "Actually, they dropped him because they were deep enough in right-handers."

"Could have fooled me." I shielded my eyes with my hand and focused even more intently on the young man standing nervously on the mound. "He's a very good-looking kid—I mean if I were scouting models for a Ralph Lauren ad, I'd sign him immediately—but am I missing something here? As a pitcher, he's no great shakes. Certainly not a future major leaguer."

"She learns fast," Dusty said to Barry. He grinned at me, and I didn't quite know how to react. I was tickled that such a veteran of the game was impressed by my increasing astuteness as to its rudiments, but there was more behind the manager's smile. Since The Kiss, we hadn't conversed about anything except baseball. All the unsaid stuff hung in the air like a nasty cloud of Barry's cigarette smoke.

"You're right, Venus, I'm not seeing the love."

"The—huh?" Dusty had caught me off guard.

"Angel doesn't seem *hungry* enough. This is a tough row to hoe. You gotta *want* it. Most minor leaguers don't come out of college, or even high school, or even a *cornfield*, with a million-dollar contract. This is a minimum-wage job. If they want to get the call to the majors, it takes a lot more than raw talent. Ya gotta have grit and guts and drive and determination—"

"You gotta have heart!"

"Exactly, Venus!" Dusty scratched his head, and in all earnestness muttered to himself, "You gotta have heart. That's good! Where've I heard that before?"

His tryout was lackluster; in all good conscience, we couldn't sign young Mr. Angel. When we gave him the news, he looked disappointed, but unsurprised. And for us, it was back to the drawing board to see who else we could dredge up, with the season already under way.

The other shoe dropped at the end of the week, when Barry Weed got a call from Kyle Angel. The GM punched up my number and conferenced me in.

"I told you, kid, it just wasn't going to work out," Barry reiterated. "You just don't have major league stuff." He didn't add that Kyle's pitching was so erratic, it made him regret dumping Tommy DuPree.

"I need to explain something, sir," Kyle said. "You didn't *see* my stuff out there the other day."

"Well, then, whose stuff did I see?" Weed asked sarcastically.

"I . . . I had the stomach flu that day. And it was really bad."

"I'm sorry; I can't give you a second chance, Kyle. There are no do-overs in baseball."

"But it wouldn't be a do-over. You never saw me pitch."

"Excuse me?!" Weed was utterly flummoxed. "If this is some kind of joke, I don't have time for it. I have twenty-four more hours to find a new right-handed starter to complete our pitching roster."

"I'm telling you, I'm your man. You didn't see me pitch. You saw my twin brother—Lyle."

Then the penny dropped, but neither Barry nor I could believe what we were hearing.

"I didn't want to blow you guys off, but there was no way I was gonna make it up to the Bronx that morning. I couldn't even get out of the *bathroom*. So I asked Lyle to pinch-hit—well, pinch-*pitch*—for me, so you wouldn't think I was irresponsible by canceling on you at the last minute or not showing up at all. Or that I was injury-prone by calling in sick. I *swear* I'm telling you the truth. It's not a do-over, and it's not a second chance—it's a first chance. I promise you, Mr. Weed, Ms. deMarley, you won't regret it."

I didn't know what to make of this last-minute switch. But Kyle sounded so desperate, so plaintive, so . . . hungry. Dusty had said you have to be hungry.

"I say let's give him a shot, Barry." My GM knew enough to realize this was not a suggestion: it was a command. I write his paychecks.

"I need you out at deMarley Field at two o'clock this afternoon," Weed told Kyle. "*You*—not your twin brother—assuming you actually have one."

The Kyle we saw on the mound that day was certainly not

the young man we'd seen earlier in the week. He *looked* like the first "Kyle," to be sure, but the second "Kyle" had a ninety-one-mile-an-hour fastball and could have found the strike zone if we'd blindfolded him. In fact, Sophie, who insisted on watching the tryout, had gaily suggested that we impose that particular impediment.

"*Wow*," she murmured, as she gazed at the tall young man with the sun-streaked blond hair unleashing fastball after fastball with pinpoint accuracy. "Fucking *wow*." I wondered if she was admiring his golden good looks as much as his impressive pitches.

The following day, the *Daily News* published an article headlined: CHEERS' SALVATION? AN ANGEL LANDS IN THE BRONX.

Though Sophie clearly appreciated the talents of Kyle Angel, she remained fairly pissed off at me over the Tommy DuPree affair. She was an adult and I had questioned her judgment—though with good reason, as it turned out. Perhaps, deep down, she was coming to grips with the fact that as a pitcher Tommy had disappointed her, too. She was acting unsettled, off-balance.

And after I forbade her to go partying with Romeo Hicks and then caught her cozied up to him on the team bus, she became more circumspect about her personal life. "I don't have to answer to you about where I go, and who I see, and what I do with them," she'd insisted.

Yet she was still living under my roof, and the truth was that she'd grown up a fairly sheltered, moderately indulged suburban girl, who had a lot to learn about the game of life. Glenn and Joy had given me no indication that they'd devoted a lot of time to schooling our daughter in the mating rituals of the postadolescent male. I was fairly certain that for Sophie, up until now the concept of arriving safe at home had had everything to do with scoring runs. Now I wanted to be sure that she walked through the door of my duplex physically and emotionally unscathed. But I didn't know how to let go and let her be an adult, and take her lumps as they came, just like the rest of us do day to day, while still endeavoring to shelter her from the creeps of the world. I was still very new at this mothering thing, often at a loss myself as to how to handle my role. At least three times a day I wished that long-lost adult daughters came with a how-to manual for moms.

⊘

"Do you have any kids?" I asked Dusty. He'd invited me to a postgame picnic, so I hung around the stadium after a particularly exciting home game. Kyle Angel had pitched the first no-hitter of his career.

Sophie went back to Manhattan after the win. "Don't wait up," she'd happily cautioned me. I think she mentioned something about a nightclub. Funny, how I used to dance at some dicey places, but now that I was a mother, I hoped Sophie hadn't gone to one of those caverns on the wild, wild west side of Manhattan near the river, known less for the music (such as it was) than for the sporadic gunfights, stabbings, and stalkings that occurred on and around the premises.

"Yeah, sure, I got kids. Twenty-four of them every year." Dusty gestured at the empty field. "Rosa never wanted them. She said I was enough of a kid as it is. And I was on the road so often that she didn't wanna raise 'em on her own half the time. I couldn't blame her, I guess. Though it would have been nice to have had a kid to toss a ball with, teach 'im how to play the greatest game in the world," he mused, without the slightest trace of irony.

His smile was so sweet, wistful even, that I tucked my arm under his and snuggled against his sturdy warmth as we watched the gulls scanning for something to call dinner. "I'm finally beginning to make my peace with the fact that I need to give Sophie her space," I admitted to him. "I've wanted so much to make up for all the years we've lost, that in my desire to spend as much time as I can with my daughter, I'm realizing that I've been in danger of crowding her."

"It's all about testing," Dusty said. "Baby bird wants to try her wings; Mommy bird knows she needs to let her do it, but all the same, she's afraid to let go. Baby bird doesn't even know if she's ready yet to fly and wants Mommy bird to keep an eye on her. But they both know that flight from the nest is inevitable. And the fact of the matter is, they're both scared of it. I'm sure Joy Ashe went through that, too, when Sophie asked to move in with you. You ready to go to the picnic?"

"Who else is coming along?"

He smiled and squeezed my arm. "Just you. And some lobster rolls, coleslaw, and pickles, courtesy of the Ancient Mariner."

"Would that be you, or the local seafood restaurant you're referring to?"

"Either or," he grinned. He led me back to the locker room and opened the fridge. "I hope rosé's okay," he said, pulling two bottles of wine from a paper bag marked *Property of D. F. Touch this and die.* "I'm not much of a wine drinker, so I never know what's good. But you know they say you should match the wine to the meat—red wine with steak, white wine with fish. And lobster's pink, so I figured, you know, rosé."

I suppressed a laugh because I was afraid he'd think I was insulting him, when the truth was, at that moment I found him utterly endearing. "I think it's perfect," I said, my smile widening. "Especially for two people who run a team that wears pink uniforms. Hey," I added softly, "I think they're beginning to get used to them. Signs are in the air. Did you notice that Shoji's dyed his blue hair fuchsia?"

"How could I not?" Dusty gave a bemused shrug, as if to say, "Kids."

"Where are we having this repast?" I asked him.

He pointed to the outfield. "Bleachers okay?"

"Suits me fine."

Dusty handed me the wicker picnic hamper. It looked like a relic of kinder, simpler days; a bit battered around the edges, but frequently appreciated. Like Dusty. "I'll be ready in just a sec," he said. "We need a little mood lighting. Besides, it cuts down on the electric bill. When I used to leave the lights on at home, Rosa always said to me, 'Hey, buster, we don't got stock in Con Edison!'"

"My father used to say the same thing." I laughed. "Maybe we're related!"

Dusty chuckled. "I sure as hell hope not." When I gave him a funny look, he added, "Take it as a compliment." He retreated into the control room, and I heard him flip a bunch of switches. "Ready?"

We stepped back onto the field. He'd turned off most of the floodlights, leaving the arena illuminated by the full moon. God can be a pretty romantic electrician.

"Wanna howl at it?" Dusty asked me.

"You know something—I do!" I raised my face to the sky. "*Aaaoooooooooh!*"

"Ooh, that was a nice one. Lemme try, now. *Awwwwwwww-wwooooo!*"

"I'm impressed. You've got a good set of pipes on you!" A fleeting thought of organs made me blush, an extremely rare occurrence. I hoped Dusty couldn't see my raspberry-tinted cheeks. After all, everyone thinks I'm the woman who can take everything in stride. *If they only knew the truth.*

So there we stood on the pitcher's mound, arms encircling each other's waists, howling at the full moon over the Bronx. For every yowl I unleashed, Dusty tried to go one better, lon-ger, louder. "You're quite competitive," I observed, amused at this slightly portly, gray-haired middle-aged man releasing his inner child's voice with such unself-conscious gusto. Then again, he dressed like a little kid for a living.

I slipped off my sandals. The grass felt cool and moist under my arches and between my toes. I was still a few inches taller than Dusty, though I think the extra girth around his midsection made him appear shorter than he really was.

A briny summer breeze wafted across the outfield, riffling our hair as we walked toward the bleachers. We climbed the steps and looked around. "This looks like a good spot," Dusty said, pointing to the center of the fourth row. "We can stretch our legs. Well, *you* can, anyways. I don't got as much to stretch."

We sidled into the row and set the picnic hamper on the plank below us. "Excuse me, madam," Dusty said with mock formality, reaching into the hamper for a blue checkered tablecloth. He shook it open with a good degree of fanfare, laying it across the plank and anchoring each end with a bottle of rosé. Gingerly unwrapping two hand-painted wine goblets, he asked me, "You want the cardinal or the oriole?"

"They're both beautiful," I replied, admiring his handiwork. Dusty's delicate hobby still surprised me.

"Take the oriole, then." He handed me the wine goblet, a melamine plate, and a set of flatware rolled into a cloth napkin. "Sorry, you'll have to set your own place. If I reach over you, I might brush accidentally against your—you-know-whats. I don't want you to think I'm being rude." He served me a lobster roll and a helping of coleslaw. "Better rest your foot up there, so it don't all blow away," he cautioned, as he removed one of the wine bottles from its position anchoring the tablecloth. He filled our goblets with a bubbly *glub-glub*, then raised his glass to me. "Cheers."

"Cheers to the Cheers," I responded, clinking my glass

against Dusty's. I took a sip of the rosé. It wasn't half bad, actually. And it was the perfect complement to the lobster roll, which was pretty delicious. I took another bite of the sweet, chewy meat, enjoying the crunch of diced celery and the tangy taste of mayonnaise on my tongue. "Maybe we should sell these at the concession stands, in addition to hot dogs," I suggested. "You think we can turn enough of a profit on them?"

Dusty shook his head. "I like the idea, but they'd probably cost more than a bleacher seat. It don't sit right with me when a fan ends up spending more on food than he does on a ticket. It just ain't right."

"I take your point, but how are you supposed to run a team and maintain a stadium when your top ticket is only fifteen dollars? You've got to make it up somewhere. At cinemas, in arenas, people have gotten used to spending more money on concessions than they do on admission. They factor it into the cost of the entertainment."

Dusty thumped his fist against his chest. "This conversation is giving me heartburn."

"Are you all right?" I asked gently. His face had begun to turn crimson. My nerves took a nosedive. Perhaps I should run back to the locker room and grab the first-aid kit. Or phone 911.

He pounded his chest again and coughed several times. "Forgive me. I tend to get a little worked up over things like this. I don't know if you get it, Venus. Ya see, baseball is sacred. To me, it's not about dollars and cents. It's a beautiful thing—baseball. When you listen to a symphony, do you think about how much the musicians are getting paid, or how much you shelled out for your seat, or whether you can afford a ginger ale at intermission? Nah—you just sit back and enjoy its beauty. Pure and classical. That's baseball. Your father understood that. He didn't care about the bottom line, so long as there was enough chalk on hand to mark the baseline. And if you don't mind my saying so, you're nothing like him."

"Thank God for small favors," I sighed.

"I didn't mean it as a compliment. Don't get me wrong, old Augie could be a pain in my keister more often than he wasn't, but he loved this game, and his team, more than—"

I finished the sentence. "More than he loved his own daughter." I smudged away the beginnings of a tear with the back of my hand. After all, to quote Tom Hanks in *A League of Their Own*, "there's no crying in baseball." I glanced away, blinking back any other tears that might have had thoughts of trickling down my cheeks, and took a big sip of wine.

"I'm damned if I do and damned if I don't, aren't I?" I said to Dusty. "I mean, if I find ways to bring the team into the black for the first time in seven seasons, I'm considered a soulless businesswoman. And if I don't seem to care about turning a profit, I'm a clueless bimbo. Either way, no one thinks I know anything about the game, let alone care about it." I leaned forward and rested my elbows on my knees, chin in my hands. "Come to think of it, they think I'm a bimbo no matter what I do. I'm feeling . . . overwhelmed . . . do you think I don't know that I haven't got their respect?" Dusty refilled my glass and let me vent between bites of lobster roll. "Half the players hate me, and half of them want to fuck me."

"And the other half hate you *and* want to fuck you."

I wondered whether his Yogi Berra–style math was deliberate—an attempt to make me laugh. For his sake, I tried to muster a smile, but it was hard to make light of an issue that had upset me so much. "You know, Jicama Flores has been learning English by listening to pop music. The other day, I overheard him paraphrasing a lyric—singing 'Sophie's mom has got it goin' on.' Then Pinky Melk joined in. No wonder the kids don't respect my authority!"

"None of them have had had the gumption to hit on you though—have they? If anyone's actually said or done something, I wanna know about it, because I'll kick their sorry butts from here to Baltimore. By the way, you're murdering that lobster roll."

"Whoops." I looked down at the scrap of sandwich between my fingers. I guess I had been kind of letting my emotions drive my appetite. "And I don't quite know how to handle Sophie—who's feeling her oats, trying her wings—testing me, like you say. I know that some of the players have put the moves on her. Romeo Hicks, for starters—a couple of times I've come this close to decking him myself. Our first baseman can hit and he can field, and he also goes after anything in a bra. It's another situation where I'm damned if I do and damned if I don't. I've haven't found that delicate balance between smother and mother."

Dusty slipped his arm around my shoulder and gave me an affectionate squeeze. "*Aww*, I think you're being a little bit hard on yourself. For a new mom, I think you're doing a helluva job."

I tried to ignore the fact that he'd touched me, even if it had only been in friendship, but the cuddle felt pretty good. I told myself he was just being kind, and I should gracefully accept it, so I didn't pull away. Maybe if I didn't acknowledge his hug, it would be easier to deal with. "I know she's a grown woman, and I can't force her to behave in a certain way. On the other hand, if I don't step in, Sophie could get very badly hurt. Yet it delights me that my daughter is basking in masculine attention for the first time in her life, it seems. How do *you* do it?" I asked Dusty. "How do you play The Dad so well and not have the guys resent you when you have to come down hard on them?"

He touched my hair and gently guided my head onto his

shoulder. "Years of practice, Venus. How'd you handle your girls when they were dancing for you? I bet you had to be the Mama Bear a lot of the time. They're just people, you know. You can't think of them as showgirls, or minor leaguers." In silence we looked out at the field, where the sprinklers had just come on. The *hss-bzz-fft* sound they made as they rotated was strangely mesmeric. Dusty stroked my hair. The sensation simultaneously relaxed and excited me, so I decided to stay there and just enjoy it. "I got a couple of questions to ask you . . . that is, if you don't mind my asking." His index finger tenderly traced the line of my chin. I smiled into the night. "I'm a little embarrassed to say this, because . . . well, I don't know how you'll take it, but seeing as you're not running for the dugout, I figure I better say something before I lose the nerve."

"Ask away."

"Do you . . . are you . . . do . . . do you have a fella?"

I found myself charmed by his phraseology. "A fella?"

"Yeah. Oh boy," Dusty sighed nervously. "A *boy*friend. A beau. A . . . *aw*, you know."

I thought about Tom. Tom and MaryAnne. "No, Dusty." I was almost whispering. "No. I don't. Have a boyfriend, I mean. Or a beau. Or a fella."

"Then can I ask you my second question?"

My head bounced against his shoulder when I laughed. "Yes. Yes, you can."

He exhaled deeply. "Can I . . . kiss you?"

I tilted my chin to gaze at him. "I would like that."

"You would?" He sounded surprised.

"In fact, I've been thinking about that since the last one you gave me." It was true. I'd debated with myself incessantly over whether it had been a bad idea or not. I was searching for something—love, really—and maybe, though I'd never thought about Dusty in that way, maybe he had, or was, the answer.

A gull swooped perilously close to our picnic. "He can have it," I muttered, dropping the last bite of my lobster roll through the gap in the bleacher planks, where it settled somewhere in the grass. Dusty cupped my face in his hands and brought his lips to mine. They were soft and supple, and just as I began to feel a little embarrassed that I probably tasted like lobster—but then again, so did he—I discovered that Dusty was a man who really knew what to do with his tongue. The thought sent a tingle along the edges of my spine, and I smiled into our kiss, suddenly feeling happier and giddier than I had in weeks.

We awkwardly readjusted our position on the bleachers, straddling the plank so we could face each other. Dusty pulled me toward him into a hug. If felt comforting. Safe. Exhilarating. He looked me squarely in the eye and asked, "Now what would such a captivating woman like you want with an overweight old guy like me?"

I kissed him again, passionately, before replying, "I'd like to find out."

"Really?" He sounded like he just been given a 1941 baseball autographed by Joltin' Joe DiMaggio.

I nodded. "Really."

"Just a sec, then." He tossed the dirty plates into a plastic bag, shoved it into the picnic hamper, and gently laid our wineglasses inside the basket before closing the lid. Then he grabbed the tablecloth, the second bottle of rosé, the corkscrew, and my hand, and said, "Follow me."

"Where are we going? And why am I whispering?"

We both burst out laughing. "Watch your step, honey," Dusty cautioned protectively as we picked our way amid the planks of the bleachers and descended the flight of steps onto the outfield. We stole another kiss at the bottom of the stairs. "C'mon, c'mere," Dusty whispered, taking my hand. Like adventurous little delinquents we ducked behind the giant Cheer

Detergent billboard that covered the length of the fence in front of the bleachers, into the dark labyrinth of green steel girders and beams that supported the stands above us.

I began to laugh. "It's almost like that pop song—_under the boardwalk_"—I sang. We sank to our knees beneath the highest part of the stands.

"Wait—I don't want you to get your white pants all dirty." Dusty helped me to my feet. He sent the tablecloth fluttering into the air, and let it float gently to the grass. Then he pulled me onto the cloth and into his arms.

"I feel like such a teenager!" I giggled. And I'm not a woman who giggles.

"You're nothing like any woman I've ever been with," Dusty observed. He opened the wine and took a slug from the bottle as though it contained a soft drink instead.

"In what way?" I said softly. He handed me the wine and I took a swig before passing it back to him.

"Well, for starters, you're fun. Rosa was . . . don't get me wrong. Rosa was a good woman. And I miss her. But, believe me, this is the first time I'm using the words _Rosa_ and _fun_ in the same sentence."

I touched his hand. "It's too soon. Maybe we shouldn't think about doing this. Not for a while, anyway."

Dusty shook his head. "Venus, when someone you love dies, trust me, you always miss them, no matter how much time goes by. But Rosa and me . . . we didn't act like lovers for a long time before she passed." He grew thoughtful for a moment, and scratching his head, he added, "Truth told, I don't even remember what it feels like to make love . . . so I hope you won't be too critical of my performance. You're a pretty spectacular woman, and I'm well . . . _look_ at me," he said, self-deprecatingly, patting his belly. He took another gulp of rosé and handed me the bottle again. "Most women who look like you take one look at a guy like me and they see a train wreck upholstered in polyester. But I . . . I want you . . . and the only thing that would stop me from doing anything about it tonight is your feelings about whether you want me, too."

I reached for his belt and undid the buckle. "I do." Dusty began the hunt for my pants zipper, which felt quite nice, although he was surprised when I guided his hand to my hip. "It's on the side," I whispered, suppressing another giggle. "But my bra clasp is where you'd expect it to be."

We peeled off our clothes with such excited determination that it was hard not to laugh about it, even as we undressed, falling into each other's arms. For the next several minutes I was treated to a new definition of "splendor in the grass." I was delightfully surprised by how well, how comfortably, our bodies fit together, how wonderful I felt with my bare breasts pressed against his smooth barrel chest as I rode him toward a very mutual ecstasy. For several weeks, as I'd grown to know him, I'd been thinking about what a wonderful man Dusty was—a kind, strong presence, a man of immense integrity and heart—and most decidedly passionate about certain things, baseball being only one of them, evidently.

"Maybe making love is like riding a bicycle: you never altogether forget how to do it, no matter how long ago you last tried." Dusty cradled me in the crook of his arm, and I placed a gentle kiss on his cheek. Catching our breath, we gazed through the underside of the bleachers at the slats of sky above us. I wriggled a bit, and Dusty asked, "You okay?"

"Yeah. My back is feeling a bit wonky—I was trying not to hit my head on the metal when we were—you know. Next time we do this, a bed might be a good idea."

He considered my point. "Yeah, you're probably right. Roll over." He placed his hands along my spine. "Here?" I nodded, and he began to massage away the soreness, kneading my muscles with such dexterity that I became horny again. I should have remembered from that team bus ride back to the Bronx how great his hands were.

"That feels wonderful," I murmured.

"Glad to hear it." Dusty planted a soft, lingering kiss on each of my shoulder blades. "You almost ready for that bed, now?"

I rolled onto my back again and looked at him in amazement. "Are you kidding me?"

"Not a chance." Dusty shook his head.

"Wow." I let it sink in. *Hmm.* Good for him! Good for *me*! "I guess we should . . . then can I invite you down to my place?" Dusty's house was a lot closer—within walking distance, in fact—but I could not imagine sleeping with him in the bed he'd shared with Rosa for so many years. The bed she might even have died in. *Ewww.* Of course, he'd said they hadn't been lovers in years, but still . . .

"You okay, Venus? You look a little . . . I dunno . . . upset about something."

I leveled with him about Rosa. After all, she's only been gone a few months, I said.

"I . . . maybe I really hadn't thought it through," he admitted. "And I can see your point about not coming back to my humble abode. But, if your offer's still open to head down to yours . . . at the very least I could use a snuggle this evening." Dusty took me in his arms and tasted my lips again. "Even if we don't do anything more tonight, I really wanna wake up with you. If that's okay."

I smiled and kissed him softly. "It's okay." As long as you don't mind Sophie knowing about us. She sleeps in my downstairs bedroom. She's probably still out clubbing, but if you want to wake up with me, I'm giving you fair warning that she'll be staggering into the kitchen for some decaf sometime after dawn."

"I think I can handle seeing Sophie," Dusty said, "if she can handle seeing *me*."

We collected the picnic hamper and, giddily dodging the sprinklers, headed to my car. "Motown okay with you?" I asked Dusty.

"You bet."

I slipped a Marvin Gaye CD into the car stereo. Apart from the slinkily seductive music, our drive into Manhattan was quiet, occasionally punctuated by exchanges of enigmatic glances and shy, slightly self-conscious smiles.

Dusty had never seen my duplex. I hoped it looked presentable; I couldn't remember whether I'd made the bed that morning or left dirty dishes in the sink. Oh, well.

I unlocked the door and found a dark apartment. I suppose Sophie hadn't made it home yet.

"Do you hear music?" Dusty asked me. He was right. Faint strains from the same Marvin Gaye CD we'd just been listening to, emanated from somewhere in the apartment. I felt like I'd entered *The Twilight Zone*. Dusty touched my arm. "Do you own two copies of that album, or do I just have that song stuck in my head now?"

"If you do, I do, too." I followed the sound, reflexively opening the door to the guest room and flicking on the lights.

"*Ahhh!*" There was a gasp from an obviously naked Sophie, who yanked the covers over her bright red face, revealing the lower end of an athletically built male, who had been burrowing under the comforter—pleasuring Sophie would have been my best guess.

"Don't you *knock*?!" she shouted in an embarrassed panic.

I stood in the doorway, rooted to the spot, too mortified to move. "Everything okay?" Dusty asked, stepping up beside me. "*Oh, boy*," he said, covering his eyes with his hands.

"I'm so *sorry*, sweetie. I had no idea you were home!" I

glanced at the hairy blond legs sticking out from the end of the bed and added, "I see you have company."

"_Mom!_"

"_Huh_?!" A sweaty, tousled, and equally naked Kyle Angel— or was it Lyle?—emerged from under the comforter. "Oh, uh . . . hello, Ms. deMarley. Excuse my bare feet," he said, utterly thrown for a loop. "Hello, Dust—_oh_, shit!" Nothing like the team's owner _and_ its manager catching you in bed with the owner's daughter. He jumped out of bed and fell to his knees, hunting for something, which turned out to be his underwear. Tighty-whities. I suppressed a smile. How wholesome. I bet he drank milk, too. Straight from the carton.

"Good evening—_Kyle_?" I tested the waters. What if it was Lyle? What if Sophie thought she was going to bed with Kyle, but he'd sent Lyle in his stead, just like he'd done with his pitching audition? Did it matter? Did she care?

Oh God, I think my daughter lost her virginity tonight!

The pitcher threw on his clothes with the speed of light, as Sophie sat bolt upright in bed, clutching the covers to her body. Only her head stuck out above the comforter. "I see you have company, too, Mom. Hey, _Dusty_. Dusty, you have grass stains on your pants."

Dusty glanced up at me, his expression sheepish, yet giddy, like a little boy with a big secret. Then he turned back to Sophie and said, "I . . . uh . . . slid into home."

"Would anyone like some coffee?" I asked breezily, turning to leave the room. Honestly, I hadn't a clue how to handle the situation. A fresh pot of strong-enough-to-stand-a-spoon-in java, seemed like a good busy-making diversion—like boiling water when a woman's about to deliver a baby. What I really wanted was a belt of whiskey.

"No caffeine, remember!" Sophie admonished me.

Kyle, self-consciously tugging on his jeans, tried to be smooth. "Uh . . . yeah, Ms. deMarley, coffee would be great. Got milk?"

Dusty pulled me aside. "I don't think my ticker can handle anything stronger than decaf at this hour, Venus."

Suddenly I was a short-order cook. And when Kyle mentioned that he was "kinda hungry," I found myself making pancakes for everyone—well, everyone except Sophie, who wouldn't eat them because they contained dairy products.

"Just what I love—the whole family gathered around the breakfast table," I quipped. Maintaining a sense of humor was my only hope of getting through these awkward minutes. But I wasn't about to kick Kyle out of the house. After all, I wanted to know what his intentions were toward my daughter.

So did Dusty. He gestured to Kyle and Sophie. "So, is this
. . . a thing?" he asked his pitching ace. "Because if it's *not* a
thing . . . I can't have no bad blood, Kyle. It wrecks the team's
morale."

Kyle reached for Sophie's hand. Their fingers entwined affectionately. Sophie gave Kyle a shy glance. "Don't worry, sir.
It's a *thing*," he told Dusty.

Sophie blushed. "It *better* be, after tonight." She gave Kyle a
playful shot in the arm.

So my supposition about Sophie's First Time had been correct. I
couldn't wait to have that mother-daughter chat with her. But
time seemed to be moving at the speed of refrigerated maple
syrup. "And you *are* Kyle, aren't you?" I asked the young man,
only half kidding. "After all, you've demonstrated a propen-
sity for making undesignated switches."

Now Kyle blushed. "I only did that the one time, Ms.
deMarley—I swear it. I wanted so bad to be a Cheer that I
couldn't let anything stand in my way."

"So, you didn't send a stand-in into my guest room tonight.
I mean *you* aren't a stand-in."

"I'm not Lyle—I promise. Want to see my driver's license?"

"So . . . are *you* two a 'thing'?" Sophie asked me, looking at
Dusty.

"Dusty was just seeing me home this evening."

Sophie narrowed her eyes. "Unh-*huh*. When he lives less
than half a mile from the stadium."

"Maybe we oughta come clean," Dusty said, smiling at me.
"Sophie, I've become quite fond of your mother. As an expert
on the game of baseball, I still think she's got a lot to learn, but
as a woman, I find her pretty remarkable."

"Join the club," Sophie grinned. "My mom's definitely a
pretty awesome lady. But if you hurt her, you're going to have

to answer to me; and I'll kick your butt." At least she was still smiling.

"Don't worry, Sophie. If ever I do the slightest thing to make your mother unhappy—not counting a pitching change or re-arranging the lineup—I'll be kicking myself 'from here to king-dom come,' as Ro—as someone I knew—used to say."

I caught the slip and looked away. There was a fifth person in the room, even now. It didn't make our little coffee klatch any easier.

Kyle chowed down on the pancakes. I inhaled mug after mug of high-octane coffee. It wasn't even midnight yet. Gee, maybe we should all catch a movie.

After his third helping, the pitcher pushed his chair back from the table. Looking at Sophie, he said, "I guess I'd bet-ter be getting on home, now. I, um, I told my brother I'd help him hook up his stereo equipment. He just moved in with me," Kyle said. "Can I give you a ride home, sir?" he asked Dusty.

"Don't you live in Queens?" the manager replied.

"It's not so far to the Bronx from there. It'll be no trouble at all, sir."

Dusty hesitated. I reached under the table and touched his hand, making it clear that he was free to spend the night if he still wanted to. But he leaned over and murmured in my ear, "*Aww*, I think you and Sophie might like to have a little heart-to-heart tonight, and I'll just be two hundred extra pounds of baggage to deal with."

"Sophie, where'd you put the other helmet?" Kyle asked her.

Dusty paled. "Helmet?"

"Yeah, I brought the bike down tonight."

"On second thought . . . I don't think these old bones were meant for riding motorcycles. 'Sides, I might throw you off-balance," Dusty added, patting his gut.

"It's a sturdy machine, sir," Kyle assured him.

The sight of Dusty Fredericks in his pink Cheers uniform and red crash helmet was worth a photo; in fact, Sophie dashed off to find her cell phone so she could take a picture. "I think I'll send this off to the *Daily News*," she teased, showing us the snapshot. "Look how adorable you look, Dusty!"

"Yeah—kind of like Cupid meets Evel Knievel," I said, tickling him in the ribs.

He grabbed my hand and squeezed it, to keep me from going after his midsection again. "I get the hiccups when I get tickled!" he said. He turned to give me a hug, just as Kyle turned to embrace Sophie.

"See you tomorrow!" the men said in tandem, as though they'd been scripted.

Sophie and I looked at each other and tried not to crack up. "Get home safely," we replied in unison.

As soon as we locked the door behind them, we burst into laughter. It felt good to release the tension. A huge relief. Sophie yanked my hand and dragged me over to the living room sofa. "So? Was he good?"

"What?"

"Oh, c'mon, Mom. You and Dusty. You—you did it, didn't you?"

I tried to maintain an aura of mystery. "None of your business," I said coolly, then started to laugh again. "It's not appropriate to talk about it with you, of all people," I told her.

"Gimme a break. Look at you—you're dying to tell someone what happened after the game tonight. And who *better* but me. Who *else*, I mean?"

"I don't kiss and tell."

She scrunched up her face. "Spoilsport."

"Deal with it." But how was I going to bring up the Kyle-virginity thing? "We need to talk, Soph. I think you owe me a . . . " I was floundering. "I don't know how to put it . . . not exactly an explanation, but . . . I mean I know you're an adult, and in some ways it's not my business, but I'm still your mom, and we missed that oh-so-vital birds-and-bees discussion we should have had about a dozen years ago . . . did you at least use protection?"

"Did you?"

I wasn't about to give her an answer. And if we were going to operate on a level playing field, she had the right not to respond to my question.

"I know what I'm doing," Sophie said simply. "You don't have to worry about me."

"Yes, of course," I said, remembering the trip we'd made to the drug store just before Christmas. "You're the Rubber Maid."

Pretending very hard to be angry and mortally insulted, she tossed a throw pillow at me. "Witch!"

⚾

The Cheers had been performing extremely well for the past couple of weeks, which was all to the good, since I had a fundraiser to coordinate. Sophie's softball coach at Clarendon had approached me about doing a little something to help their program. So the Cheers were going to play three innings against the most recent crop of Kumquats before their 8:00 p.m. start against the Albany Filibusters. It was looking very much like the Cheers and the Filibusters were in a head-to-head battle for the wild-card slot in the A-ball playoffs, so the game was sure to be a sellout. And the girls' softball team was going to be the beneficiary of the entire gate.

⚾

There was a holiday mood in the stands on the day of the fundraiser. We had a sell-out crowd on hand. How many of them were there to support the Kumquats, and how many were itching to see the Cheers forestall the Filibusters, was up for debate, but the bottom line was that it didn't make a difference to the bottom line. Clarendon's women's softball team was going to get the whole tasty enchilada. It was a Title IX dream come true.

One of the selling points of the fund-raiser had been the promise of a full demonstration of the Cheers' stripper-style warm-up in front of the crowd before the start of the exhibition game.

"Take it off!" the fans shouted, as the guys gyrated to the strains of "Love Potion No. 9," bumping their hips and grinding their pelvises, crawling and arching their backs like alley cats, and executing standing crunches that showed off their killer pecs and abs. Romeo Hicks in particular, really got into it, adding a few choice moves of his own that could have landed him a job as a Chippendales dancer. My jaw dropped when some of the women in the stands began to toss dollar bills at him. This, of course, encouraged some of the other players to go for the gusto as well, and in a matter of minutes, the Cheers were being showered with greenbacks.

Wait till I tell them that money's going to the girls' softball team as well, I thought.

We had gift bags for every fan, filled with discount coupons from local merchants, a raffle ticket for a set of Dusty's hand-painted drinking glasses, and a baseball cap designed by Joy Ashe just for the occasion, sporting an image of Razzie the Raspberry and Clarendon's Clara the Kumquat holding hands, a match truly made in the produce aisle.

Sophie was suited up and ready to take the field. "How's your arm feel?" she asked me.

I shook it vigorously and swung it around and around, releasing any kinks in my elbow and rust in my rotator cuff.

"Good, I think. Except my guts are in knots. In all the games the Cheers have played, you know I've never tossed out the first pitch."

"Don't 'toss' it—hurl it. Aim for the center of Spot's mitt. Don't take your eyes off that sweet spot. If you look where you throw, you can't miss—most of the time. And don't be nervous. You've danced mostly naked in front of people who were close enough to you to be sprayed by your sweat; throwing a baseball sixty feet should be a piece of cake by comparison. And don't embarrass me," she teased. "Make me proud of you, Mom."

I gave her a huge hug. "Don't forget to adjust your stance against Kyle so you can make contact with his sinker. He's going to play this game for keeps."

"Don't worry, Mom." She gave me a high five. "So am I."

⊘

You know how people always tell you to picture the crowd in their underwear, so performing in front of them won't seem so daunting? In my case, I had to imagine *myself* in my scanties in order to get up the gumption to step onto the field. I swear I needed to pee throughout the entire national anthem, but there was no escape route. And when I took the mound in my game cap and my Cheers uniform—raspberry is a terrible color for redheads; what had I been thinking?—home plate had never looked farther away. Suddenly, I had a renewed appreciation for pitching skills, even the dearly departed Tommy DuPree's. Gripped with fear, I probably took longer to release the ball than Steve Trachsel. And when it bounced off Spot Baldo's mitt and into the dirt in front of the plate, I sighed with relief that at least I'd reached the catcher.

I jogged back to home plate and shook Spot's hand. *"Stretno,"* I said to him. "Good luck! *Vidimo se!* See you later!"

"You are good woman!" he exclaimed, grinning and pumping my hand. "You speak to me in Croatian! Yes!" He kissed me on both cheeks.

Kyle only pitched the first inning, so he could save his arm for the game against the Filibusters. But people had coughed up good money to see our ace, so I couldn't disappoint them. I practically had an orgasm when Sophie got a line drive off him.

"That wasn't a gimme," Dusty observed. "She really hit him."

I clutched his arm. "*Uh-oh.* I mean, I'm ecstatic for Sophie, but I hope that doesn't bode well for Albany."

"We'll be okay," he assured me. "The guys'll play the Kumquats hard enough—but not *that* hard."

"What are you saying? Or not saying?" Carleen McLure successfully laid down a bunt, moving the Kumquats' base runner over to third. "You go, girl!" I shouted.

"I told them to conserve their energy. They'll give the Clarendon fans a good show for their charitable contributions, but they'll leave enough in the bank to forestall the Filibusters. In fact, I told our kids to give Albany the impression that the upstaters'll be able to stomp all over them later. Then we'll ramp it up again and surprise the hell out of 'em."

I knew Dusty was doing the right thing. And it's what I paid him to do. Though I wanted the Kumquats to kick butt, I also wanted to get my A-ball team into the playoffs. Under my aegis, the Cheers would be a laughingstock no more—in spite of their pink uniforms. And when the Kumquats lost, 3–1, the women were universally deemed to have acquitted themselves quite well against the team that was rapidly becoming the Atlantic Coast League's version of the Little Engine That Could.

"I hit him, I hit him!" Sophie kept exclaiming ecstatically after the game. She ran up to Kyle Angel and jumped him, straddling him with her legs and planting a huge kiss on his lips. "I hit you, I hit you!"

"Remind me never to let that happen again," he teased.

"How's your arm?" She dragged her beau into the dugout, sat him down, and began to vigorously knead his shoulders as if she were managing a prize fighter. "Don't forget the Filibusters' dirty tricks," she reminded Kyle. "The second baseman, Tony Travis, is Mr. Melodrama. He always pretends to be nailed by a pitch. He'll hit the dirt, roll over, and practically play dead until the ump awards him first base. And their center fielder—number 34, Corey Sparks—they call him 'the Sparkplug.' He'll try to fake a sprint for second, and you'll end up getting charged with a balk. He does that to pitchers all the time. Wanna shower with me before the game?"

"What?" Kyle looked like he wasn't sure whether to act shocked or excited by Sophie's unusual invitation.

"Well, I certainly want to hit the showers before I watch you guys play the Filibusters. And I thought you might want to freshen up before you have to get all sweaty again. Mom's about to start the 'intermission' show, so we'll have plenty of time." Sophie flashed him a seductive grin.

I couldn't believe what I'd just overheard coming out of my not-too-lately-virginal and socially reticent daughter. I started chuckling; Sophie reminded me so much of myself in that moment that I wondered if maybe there was something to be said for genetics when it came to libidos. The girl was certainly feeling her oats, and a couple of other things, too.

"Uh . . . Soph. People are watching," I whispered in her ear.

She gazed at Kyle, utterly smitten. "Good!" She beamed. "I bet they all wish they were me right now. Did you know that some guy from *Esquire* called Kyle and wants to do an article on him as the sexiest young athlete of the year?"

"Sorry to break up such a touching love scene," Dusty said unapologetically. "Sophie, I need my ace."

"He's yours—until eleven o'clock tonight," Sophie said. She gave Kyle a kiss, followed by a playful swat on the ass. "Now, go put us one game closer to the playoffs, honey!" she commanded him.

I'd drafted some of the girls who used to dance for me to perform between the Kumquat and Filibuster games. And I got our mascot into the act, just to make sure that the fun stayed more or less on the wholesome side. Razzie and the scantily clad showgirls got the fans onto their feet, teaching them a simple strut and a bump-and-grind routine. The men just ate it up, while the female fans learned some titillating moves that their partners would no doubt enjoy for nights to come. In fact, the show was so well received that I decided to put the girls on the payroll and incorporate their act into the seventh-inning stretch from now on. It certainly had a lot more pizzazz than sending the mascot out to shoot T-shirts into the stands with a giant air gun, or having a hokey foot race between the hot dog, mustard, and relish heads.

Surprisingly, the game against Albany turned into a pitchers' duel, with both starters shutting down the opposing team's batters until the top of the seventh, when our right-hander, Lefty Pace, walked Corey Sparks, who then stole second off him. True to Sophie's scouting report, the Filibusters' Tony Travis turned sideways into a pitch, then acted like Lefty had beaned him right in the kidney. None of us in the Cheers' dugout saw any contact whatsoever between the ball and Tony's body, but the second baseman's theatrics were enough to convince the umpire to give him first base and issue a warning to Lefty. Lefty, who had a temper, as well as a rather pronounced notion of justice, aimed for the next batter's head, which earned him a second warning.

Our kids grew increasingly testy as Albany got cockier, and I thanked my stars that no fights broke out, because we couldn't afford to lose any players to the showers.

Dusty and his pitching coach jogged out to the mound and had a little chat with Lefty. Whatever they said worked, because he retired the side, preserving the no-hitter into the seventh-inning stretch. But the war of attrition dragged on into the eleventh. With a man finally in scoring position, the fans rose to their feet, but Hollis Golightly was picked off at second during an ill-timed attempt to steal third. We held our breath as Grand Slammy Santiago stepped up to the plate. Then, inexplicably, he fell to his knees and crossed himself.

I grabbed Dusty's forearm. "What the hell's he doing?"

"Having a one-man revival meeting, maybe." Sammy genuflected toward center field. "Though I'd prefer it if he didn't interrupt the game to express his religious preferences. So would the ump," Dusty added, noting the increasing impatience of the home plate umpire. "Can you believe that kid used to be a devil worshiper?"

Sammy raised his arms. "Praise Jesus!" he shouted, then rose to his feet and settled into his batting stance.

Maybe God really was listening, or maybe Sammy just believed He was, and that was all the proof the born-again slugger needed to knock the next pitch clear over the fence in left field. "The ball was last seen headed for the Canary Islands," as Sophie put it. Sammy's home run ended the game, putting the Cheers just one win away from the wild-card berth in the playoffs.

I was ecstatic. I'd taken the team from the red to the pink; and now that they'd begun to post Ws—and if our Seventh-Inning Strut continued to pack the stands with libidinous baseball fans—the Cheers' financials could be firmly in the black before the season ended.

But my euphoria was short-lived. After all the players but Kyle had gone home, Dusty and Sophie found me sitting in my car, sobbing over the steering wheel.

"Hey, Mom, is everything okay?" Sophie asked me.

"You feeling all right?" Dusty said solicitously. I rummaged through my purse for a tissue. "Need this?" he asked, offering me a pristinely folded hanky. "Rosa never let me leave the house without one," he said sheepishly.

"Mom, we won! Just one more win, and we could end up headed to the postseason! It's the best news the team's had in years." She leaned over the car and reached out to stroke my hair. "Dude—you've taken a train wreck and turned it around. Why're you crying?"

It took me a minute or two to pull myself together, because Sophie's words of encouragement had made me sob even harder. "Why am I crying?" I echoed. "Because I really wish my dad had been here to see it." For months, the sportswriters had inked up the place with their incessant litany that ever since I'd taken control of the Cheers, old Augie was spinning in his grave. Well, if they were right—if he *was* still spiraling his way toward China—tonight I hoped he was whirling with delirium.

The following morning, I knocked on the door to the guest room. "Hey, Soph, want to go out and celebrate? Brunch is on me. No dairy products, meat, or caffeine—which might be a bit difficult," I added, muttering that last part to myself. "But heck, we've proven pretty dauntless in the face of challenges before, right?"

There was no answer. I knew she must be in there; I'd wished her a good night. And I'd learned my lesson about just barging in, so I knocked louder. When there was no response, I opened the door.

No Sophie. The bed had been neatly made. There were no clothes left out. Ever since our little contretemps about picking up after herself, she'd become pretty organized, so that didn't surprise me. Maybe she'd gone running. I looked in the closet. Her Nikes were gone. Okay, I was right, she's gone running, I told myself.

Three hours later, when she hadn't returned, I phoned her mobile. My call went straight into voice mail, so I left her a message. "Hi, Soph, it's me. Not important. Just wondered where you are—that's all. Give me a call when you get this. Love you!"

By the early evening, when she still hadn't returned the call, I grew concerned. I phoned her cell again, and once again I got her voice mail. "Hey, kiddo, where are you? I mean, I know you're an adult and you don't want your mother keeping tabs on you, but I'd just like to know that you're not under a bus or something. And even if you are—call me."

I dug out my contact sheet for the Cheers roster and called Kyle.

Lyle picked up the phone. "I haven't seen my bro, or Sophie, all day," he told me. "Did you try his cell?" He confirmed that I had the right mobile number.

Kyle's cell went right into his voice mail box as well. "Hey, Kyle, it's Livy. Have you seen Sophie? Please call me ASAP. Bye."

I couldn't sleep all night, hoping that at any moment, the phone might ring. Carleen McLure hadn't heard anything from Sophie, either, and volunteered to text her right away. I paced the living room; I climbed the stairs from the guest room to my bedroom so often I wouldn't need to hit the Stairmaster for a week. I watched the evening news to see if there had been any accident or disaster. I tuned my radio to 1010 WINS, figuring that at some point during their "You give us twenty-two minutes—we'll give you the world" broadcast, I might hear the news I most feared. But at least I'd know *something*.

Several times during the day I'd considered calling Glenn and Joy. Maybe Sophie and Kyle had zoomed up to Westchester for the weekend. After all, he'd just pitched a game; he wasn't due to take the mound again for another few days.

Then, of course, I thought that if Kyle and Sophie *hadn't* gone to visit the Ashes, I'd scare them shitless by phoning them to ask if they'd seen our daughter. If she and Kyle had taken his bike . . . and then I was hit with another zigzag of panic—what if they'd been in a motorcycle accident? Every motorcycle owner I'd ever known had been in a crash. Hell, I'd even been knocked off my Vespa by a Fresh Direct truck. No doubt a lot of online grocery shoppers received broken eggs that day.

By two in the morning, I'd become afraid to fall asleep because I was so tired and tense I worried about being too zonked out to hear the phone ring or the key in the door. It was 4:00 a.m. when I called Dusty.

"Jesus, V, is everything okay?" he asked groggily.

"I can't find Sophie," I told him, then burst into tears.

"Oh, baby. Oh, Jesus . . . oh, shit. I . . . I don't know what to say. *Aww*, baby, try to hold it together, if you can," he soothed. "It's never good to think the worst. It'll only make you crazy. I'll be right over. You just sit tight. I'll be there before you can finish your coffee."

"Bet you a dollar you won't!" I sniffled. You're twenty miles away."

"Betcha double I will. Traffic's kinda light coming down from the Bronx at this hour, and I know how you hate to drink coffee when it's too hot. You could nurse a mug for a week."

It was so sweet, the way he was trying to keep me from drowning in my fears, using humor as a buoy. "You're an angel, Dusty. I love you," I added softly.

"You do?" He sounded so touched. Even a bit surprised.

I smiled into the phone, even though my hand was shaking so much I could hardly hold it to my ear. "You're very good to me, Dusty," I whispered.

"All right, V, I'm heading out the door and I'll be on my way in just a minute. Oh—I almost forgot. I love you, too. I'm just so amazed that you love me. Jeez—I meant to say it back when you said it to me just now, but just telling me you love me got me so flustered. Guys like me dream about women like you, but you know, lightning almost never strikes."

"Then I'm glad you adjusted that metal rod atop your base-ball cap," I teased.

"Okay, sweet pea, I'm out the door for real, now." Dusty hung up his land line.

True to his word, he phoned me from the car. "Remind me to visit you more often at this hour; the Cross Bronx Express-way is empty!"

"Are you sure you're awake enough to drive?" I asked him.

"Too late now. Have you heard from her yet?"

I was so punchy I shook my head instead of speaking.

"I can't hear you," Dusty said.

"I said no, except that I did it with body language. Sorry, I'm running on fumes."

"First things first: we locate Sophie. But, you know, as soon as we know she's safe, I like to converse like that with you again. Body language, I mean. We never did make it to that bed." I could almost hear him blush through the phone line. Dusty could be gruff and tough with the players, but when it came to interacting with the so-called fairer sex—or maybe it was just because I was his boss—I found him endearing, al-most shy, with all the grit of a marshmallow.

When Dusty arrived, I fell into his arms. "I don't know what to do—do I call the police? They'll only tell me I have to wait twenty-four hours before I can file a missing persons report. But maybe she's already been gone for that long—I have no way of knowing. All I know is that she wasn't here when I woke up this morning—yesterday morning, by now."

He let me cling to him like he was the only log floating down a raging river. "If it'll make you feel better, let's take a walk over to the precinct. I got a missing persons report I have to file, myself," he added.

"Oh God—who?"

"Kyle Angel, of course," he said grimly. "I didn't want to tell you he missed practice today."

"I—I need to have a cup of coffee before we go. Or I might fall asleep while we're waiting. And those wooden benches are pretty unforgiving." But as I grabbed the coffeepot it slipped from my grasp and shattered as it hit the kitchen floor. Shards of glass stuck up defiantly amid a giant puddle of java.

"I think you're jittery enough as it is," Dusty said gently, stopping me from sinking to the floor to mop up the mess. "I'll get it." He turned my face to his and softly kissed me on the lips. "You sit. I'll clean up." He practically carried me over to the sofa, supporting my weight and gingerly setting me down. Then he bent over and swung my feet onto the cushions. "Lie down," he soothed. "I'll take care of the coffeepot, and then we'll go talk to the police."

"How can you seem so calm?" I asked him, having a hard time accepting his directive to relax.

"I'm not. My insides are like my great-grandmother's butter churn. But I figure one of us has to act that way. Or at least try to. Where do you keep the mop?"

"The tall cabinet next to the fridge," I called to him. "Ever have a kid go AWOL before?"

"It happens more often than you think," Dusty replied. "But never my best pitcher. And never the responsible kids. Kids with attitude—yeah, it happens. If Sammy Santiago had taken a powder and left no forwarding address, or if Ahab Slocum had gone missing, it wouldn't have surprised me much. They're rocky roads. But Kyle Angel—he's about as close to vanilla as you can get and still have a personality." I heard the sound of shattered glass tinkling into the trash. "Almost done here," he called out. A few moments later, I overheard him muttering, "How did I fail him? I teach my kids the importance of personal and team responsibility. How did Kyle Angel miss the message?"

"He wasn't there to hear your lecture on the first day of practice," I groaned, only half kidding. I was thinking the same of Sophie. I couldn't just lie on the couch; I was way too anxious. So I padded back into the kitchen, where I found myself impressed by Dusty's housekeeping skills.

"Rosa," he said sheepishly. "She was sick more often than not for so many months, I had to learn to pick up after myself. Not a bad skill set."

I agreed. "More men should learn it, though preferably not for the same reasons." I wondered what Dusty was like pre-Rosa, or when she was in the bloom of health. And then I worried that Rosa would always be in the room with us no matter where we were or how much time had passed. A look, a gesture, the most insignificant of incidents might trigger a buried memory, or—more awkward for me—one much closer to the surface. Would I ever get used to it? Because if I wanted to make a go of something with a widower, I'd have to. And not only would Dusty have Rosa's ghost around, he'd have old Augie's, too. I loved a man who knew my dad better than I ever did.

Dawn was breaking as we climbed the steps to the police station. The sergeant at the front desk couldn't quite believe why we were there. "You mean you both have missing persons reports you wanna file?"'

"We each do, yes," Dusty said, as my hand gripped his forearm.

The desk sergeant gave us another funny look. "What is this, some kinda club? Is there a full moon or something?"

We filed the reports, though neither of us knew what Sophie or Kyle had been wearing at the time of their disappearance. The cops said they'd try to trace any cell phone calls the kids made from now on, and suggested we do a little detective work on our own. "Scour your daughter's bedroom for clues," I was told. I didn't know Sophie's password, so I couldn't break into her laptop to see if she'd sent any e-mails to anyone that might provide the answer to her whereabouts.

"And I'd also suggest you call Sophie's adoptive parents and bring them in on this. How long have you known your biological daughter, Ms. deMarley?"

I was so emotionally exhausted that I had to count the months on my fingers. "About a year," I admitted.

"Well, the Ashes have known her for over two decades; chances are, they'd be aware of some of Sophie's behavioral patterns that you'd never recognize." The detective addressed Dusty. "And as far as Mr. Angel is concerned, I think you should talk to the other Mr. Angel, and ask him the same questions Ms. deMarley is going to ask the Ashes. And, Ms. deMarley—if Sophie has a best friend, a girlfriend she confides in, I'd bring her up to speed as well. The more information we have to go on, the faster we can find your daughter and her boyfriend."

Dusty and I went back to the duplex and began our round of telephone calls. Everyone was at my apartment within the hour. The Ashes must have been doing eighty on the parkway.

"They didn't take the bike," Lyle Angel told us. "It's still in our driveway with the cover on it."

Well, that was one anxiety I could eliminate. Only about two hundred thousand more to go.

"Ah texted her again, but she hasn't replied yet," Carleen said. It looked like she'd rolled out of bed and straight into her car. She'd thrown on a rumpled green track suit and hadn't bothered to brush her hair.

Joy Ashe's face matched her surname. Her eyes were puffy from crying, and with her red-rimmed lids set into her chalky complexion she resembled my second-grade class's pet bunny rabbit, Snowball. Glenn looked grim, as if he'd already steeled himself to hear the worst when the news finally came.

"Can I trouble you for some coffee?" he asked me, his voice barely more than a whisper.

Dusty and I exchanged a look. "I'll run down to the corner," he said, and began taking orders. "Milk-no-sugar for Glenn; half-caff, no sugar for Joy; 'black like my mood' for Carleen; extra light and sweet for you, Lyle—"

"If you're going down to the Korean deli—the one with all the fresh flowers in front—'extra light and sweet' is the way they make it when you order a 'regular,'" I told Dusty, trying to be helpful.

He refused to take any money from anyone. "It's good for me to have something to do," he said. "Times like these—I need a task."

"I know I should have called you sooner," I told the Ashes after Dusty had departed. "But at first I thought she'd reply to her messages, or be home any minute, or maybe she was actually *with* you guys, so why worry you needlessly? And when I didn't hear from her for so many hours, I became afraid to call you. I . . . I didn't want to be the bearer of bad news. Especially after all that's gone on this year."

Glenn placed his hands on his knees and leaned toward me. "I confess it did go through our minds as we were driving down here that we'd lost Sophie once already—to you. And it hasn't been easy for us to deal with that, Livy. After all, we gave her everything we had for all the years of her life. *You* gave her away."

"Well, that's hardly fair!" I said, feeling my face grow as red as my hair. "You can't compare the circumstances. Don't you think I'm hurting enough—that I've second-guessed my-self enough, in the past twenty-four hours? It did occur to me that perhaps Sophie had decided to go back to you two in Larchmont. Now that she sees how expensive it is to live in Manhattan—and she hasn't even gotten a job yet. She'd love to find her own apartment but the cost has kind of demoralized her. We weren't exactly the most compatible roommates last fall, if you remember. A huge part of me wants to blame myself for Sophie's disappearing act, but wherever—and why ever—she went, she didn't leave in the middle of a fight. Because if you want to, we can all sit here and have a Mexican standoff of finger-pointing, Glenn. Who raised Sophie with the idea that it was okay to be irresponsible enough not to write a note, if she was leaving the house for more than a few hours?"

"All right, y'all, let's not come to blows over this." Carleen rose to her feet with a great sense of purpose. "Lyle, come with me, dude. We're going to search Sophie's bedroom for clues." With one smooth movement, she pulled the tall blond man out of his chair. "Y'all ever have one of those days where you wished you'd washed your hair?" she whispered to me, as she and Lyle headed for Sophie's room.

They were in there quite a while. Finally, they emerged, blushing and slightly disheveled. Carleen was holding Sophie's portable radio/alarm clock. "Ah see she still wakes up to music," Carleen said.

"It's set to go off at four-thirty in the morning," Lyle told us. "Dude, even the most die-hard runner doesn't get up that early."

Dude. Everyone's "dude."

Joy looked hopeful. "So now we need to figure out why she needed to leave the house well before dawn."

"Wait—I've got a text message!" exclaimed Carleen. "Maybe it's Soph!" As she read the screen, her expression went from puzzlement to anger. "It's from her! Oh, mah God! Ah can't

effin'-gee-aitchin' believe it! Ah'm gonna kill her! She promised me!"

"What—what?!" we chorused excitedly. Everyone immediately sprang to their feet, suddenly energized. We were all
yammering so loudly I hardly heard the doorbell. "Be right
there!" I shouted, and let Dusty into the apartment.

He handed me two soggy brown paper bags. "Here—I think
one of them's leaking, maybe both, so watch your clothes. Better put them down in the kitchen—"

"Carleen's just heard from Sophie!" I told him.

"Kyle, too?" he asked anxiously.

"Kyle, too?" I called to Carleen.

"Her and Kyle both!" she yelled back. "Y'all aren't going to
believe where they are—they flew to Las Vegas!"

"They *what*?!" I raced to her side.

Joy looked at Glenn with the same sort of inscrutable expression I'd often seen on Sophie's face. "What are they doing
in Vegas?"

"Couldn't they have waited until the season ended?" Dusty
demanded. "After Tuesday night's game, for all we know the
Cheers may be packing their duffels until next spring. Kyle
could have all the time in the world to take a vacation with his
girlfriend—sorry, Venus, but it's the truth, and you know it as
well as I do. Sophie loves the Cheers just as much as any of us,
and Kyle knows how crucial his performance is to the team. So
what the hell could have been so important?"

"Oh Christ!" I all but smacked my head with my hand.
"They must have *eloped*!" I shouted.

The reaction, both individual and collective—was an explo-
sive and simultaneous tangle of words.

"Holy cats!"

"Oh my God!"

"They *what*?"

"Did you just say what I thought you said?"

"My bro did what?"

"Over mah dead body!" Carleen's hand was shaking so much, she could barely type a return message.

"I can't believe I didn't think of it—it's so obvious. I guess it didn't occur to me because Sophie's life experiences have been so limited." The Ashes glared at me. "I mean—what could she—they—the two of them—have been thinking?! May I?" I asked. Carleen lateraled the phone to me, past Glenn who made a grab for it as it flew by his chest.

Joy's mouth seemed stuck in a permanently shocked O. "Why couldn't she tell us?" she lamented, genuinely hurt. "And we don't even know the boy."

"Hey—watch what you're saying about my twin!" Lyle's fingers curled into fists.

"Kyle Angel's a good kid," Dusty told the Ashes, as if his opinion carried the weight of finality. He looked utterly betrayed. "Now that we know they're both okay—more than okay, apparently—I feel like benching him as soon as I get my mitts on him, just to teach the kid a lesson about skipping practice and skipping town. I'll never understand some of these kids. He thinks he's mature enough to get married, but he's such a baby, he doesn't even ask permission to leave the city. Or consider his commitment to the team."

"You can't bench him—if we win on Tuesday, we're going to need his arm in the playoffs," I said, feeling too angry about Sophie's secrecy and irresponsibility to be happy for her at that moment.

"And if we don't win, he and Sophie can honeymoon on a slow boat to China, for all the time they'll have to do it." He sighed heavily and shook his head.

I sank onto the sofa and buried my face in my hands. "I can't believe she didn't trust me enough, or care enough, to bring me into her confidence." My tears burned my palms. "And I can't believe she contacted you first—before she told any of her parents," I said to Carleen, who immediately began to get her dander up and defend her friendship.

"Ah've known Sophie a lot longer than you have, Livy! And there are some things girls just tell each other."

"Such as, they're getting *married*. Don't worry, sweetie, I'm not mad at you. Just . . . just hurt."

Tears streamed down Carleen's cheeks. "Well, Ah'm hurt she couldn't wait to tie that knot. Since freshman year we promised to be each other's maid of honor."

Joy came and sat beside me, her animosity shelved, I suppose, at least for the moment. "If it makes you feel any better, Sophie didn't share her plans with us, either—obviously. We didn't even know she was seeing anyone, let alone how serious they'd become."

"We didn't raise her to be secretive," Glenn said. "In our household, we always encouraged totally open communication."

I remembered Sophie's lack of confidence around guys, her utter inexperience in the world of dating. I guess there were a lot of things that the Ashes hadn't communicated to our daughter somewhere along the line. But I didn't want to start a war with them over it. At this point, the water was so far under the bridge it had mingled with the mid-Atlantic.

I read the text message Sophie had just sent Carleen. "They're flying back this afternoon."

"Ah think our work here is done, then," said Carleen. "It dud'nt make sense to wait here for her to show up, like we're some sort of posse. When she gits back, lemme know, so I can come over and punch her lights out." She extended her hand to Lyle like she'd suddenly become Blanche Dubois, and turning on the brights, sweetly asked him, "Y'all want to escort me downstairs?"

Lyle rose to his feet. "My pleasure."

"Well then, we'll leave y'all to yourselves. Call me as soon as they get home—Ah don't care how late it is."

"I wonder where they're going to live," Lyle muttered to her as they left my apartment. "We only have a studio."

Glenn drained his coffee cup, slapped his knees, and stood up. "I guess we might as well hit the road, too." Joy took one last sip from her cup, then joined him.

"We should let you get some sleep, now that we know they're all right," she said, standing on her tiptoes to give me a kiss on the cheek. I wrapped my arms around her, hugging her tightly. "I'll phone you when they get here."

"You didn't do anything wrong, Livy," Joy whispered to me. "It's hard to be a mom. All you can do is give it your best shot. Sometimes, you can cook the spaghetti perfectly, and it still doesn't stick to the wall."

Glenn shook my hand. "Hang in there," he said, patting my back like I was one of his high school ballplayers. "Sorry I kind of blew up at you back there. It's been rough on all of us." He put his arm around Joy's shoulder and the two of them headed for the elevator.

I looked at Dusty. "Well, it's just the two of us," I sighed, looking at the front door as if I expected Sophie and Kyle to walk through it at any moment. I slipped my arms around his thick torso and buried my face in his chest. "Don't go . . . please."

"I wasn't going to," he whispered, cupping his hand against the back of my head. "Unless you wanted to kick me out, of course."

I shook my head. "But I need to go to bed. Joy was right; I've got to get some sleep."

"Want company?"

"Yes, please," I nodded. "But I don't think I'm in the mood to—"

"I wasn't going to suggest it," Dusty said softly as we headed up the stairs to my bedroom. "We'll just snuggle. You can fall asleep in my arms."

Being skin to skin and flesh to flesh with Dusty was comforting, his bulk sheltering and shielding me from all harms, real or imagined, as we spooned. And though I was utterly exhausted, after several minutes of resting dreamily in Dusty's embrace, cuddling segued into caressing, which morphed into slow and gentle lovemaking, ending where we started, his bare barrel chest molding into the curves in my back, his arm lazing protectively and proprietarily across my breasts.

We must have slept for hours. The next thing I heard was the sound of a key turning in the lock. Suddenly fully awake, I leaped out of bed and threw on a silk kimono. Running around to Dusty's side of the bed, I shook his shoulders. His skin was warm and soft, and a little moist. My lips grazed the back of his neck. He smelled deliciously male. "Wake up—they're back!"

"Wha-uh?" he said groggily.

"You might want to put on some clothes." I bent down and retrieved a pair of bright blue stretchy briefs from the floor. "Starting with these." I playfully dropped them on his head, which caused him to bolt up onto an elbow with the underwear still clinging to his face.

"What's so funny?" he asked sleepily, tentatively touching the briefs as if he wondered how he'd somehow gotten stuck behind a curtain.

I was laughing so hard I'd given myself the hiccups. "You are! You're adorable. Here, let me help you." I extricated Dusty from the undies and tossed him his slacks. "I'm going downstairs to greet the happy couple. If you hear any broken crockery, don't give it a second thought. You're welcome to join me, of course."

I kissed his nose and dashed down the staircase.

"Welcome home!" I said, standing at the foot of the stairs, my hands planted on my hips. Out came a hiccup. I held my breath and swallowed hard to suppress the next one. "Mr. and Mrs. Angel, I presume."

"*Umm* . . . not. Actually."

"I'm sorry we didn't tell you where we went, Mom," Sophie mumbled, looking about as guilty as a fox caught with a mouthful of feathers. "It was just a spur-of-the-moment decision."

"I asked Soph to marry me right after our victory," Kyle said, looking equally shamefaced. "I guess we should have said something to everyone so you guys wouldn't worry, but—"

"But no one leaves a note when they elope! That's the whole *point* of eloping," Sophie said, finding her voice.

"What do you mean by 'not. Actually.'"

"Well . . . we got there and were all ready to go through with it . . . but we changed our minds."

"Thank God!" I exhaled an enormous sigh of relief.

"It was Carleen's text message that did it, actually. She can get really violent when she thinks she's been betrayed."

"Jesus, Soph—we were all so worried about you!" I said, grabbing her into a hug and holding on for dear life. My tears moistened her hair. "Toto, we're not in Kansas anymore—it's a crazy world out there!" I drew back and held my daughter at arm's length, relieved and grateful that she and Kyle were home in one piece apiece, and delighted that they'd found so much happiness with each other, but still livid that Sophie couldn't, or wouldn't—and didn't—talk to me about her plans, about how serious her relationship with Kyle had become. "Why did you never say anything to me?" I asked her. I gave Kyle a hug and suggested that he might want to have a word with his coach, who had just shuffled down the stairs to greet him.

"I think we need to have a little talk about the concept of responsibility," Dusty said, crooking his finger at his ace, while rubbing the sleep from his eyes with the other hand. He drew Kyle over to the living room couch for a man-to-man chat, while Sophie and I convened in the kitchen.

"I can't believe the two of you flew all the way to Vegas to not get married!"

Sophie gave me a confused look. "Would you rather we had? Because I kinda got a different impression. Maybe it was your 'Thank God!' comment. We just hadn't thought things through," she added, rummaging in the fridge for something that met her strict dietary specifications. "Carleen was right: I did promise she'd be my maid of honor when I eventually married—which at the time, I thought wasn't likely to happen until the twenty-second century. I really didn't want to come home to a split lip and a busted best friendship. And I know you don't think I'm much of a girly girl, but I do kind of want a wedding with the whole nine yards—of tulle, or whatever you call it. Mostly, I guess," she said, settling on a bowl of blueberries, "I realized how much I wanted you to be there, Mom. On my 'special day.' So we canceled our appointment at the Love Shack and came home."

I didn't know what to make of this admission. On the one hand I was genuinely touched. On the other, I felt disappointed, even a bit betrayed by her behavior. "You confided in me about some things—like being a virgin—so why couldn't you share your feelings about Kyle?" I whispered to her. "I'm really hurt that you couldn't talk to me about how things were going, as your mom, or as a friend, or even woman to woman. You didn't even tell Carleen or Joy how far things had progressed did you?"

"Oh, I definitely never could have told Joy," Sophie chuckled. "She's a great mom, but not the hippest person in the world. And I didn't talk much about Kyle to Carleen. I . . . I just wanted to have something of my very own that was so personal and private, it was like having a secret little treasure chest, I guess."

"Yet we *all* knew you and Kyle were a couple. You two never kept that from anyone. In fact the team always ribs you for your frequent PDAs. But your relationship progressed with the speed of Kyle's fastball. That's another thing that concerns me . . . and he's the first man you ever dated. There's a whole world out there, Soph. Okay—jetting off to Vegas might have been romantic and giddy and spontaneous, but you and Kyle almost made a choice that wouldn't have been any fun to reverse if, God forbid, it came to that. Marriage isn't a toy. A wedding, even a Vegas wedding, for people not named Britney, is still a serious thing. It's not a lark, Sophie."

"How would you know?" she mumbled, her words tumbling in the general direction of her sneakers. "You've never done it yourself."

Ouch. "When I took over the Cheers, I didn't know squat about baseball, either," I said, sounding too defensive. Uncomfortably so. I wanted to change the subject. After all, this was about Sophie, not me. Her choices, not mine.

"Even choosing to get married this young—whether it's in Vegas at the Elvis chapel or downtown at City Hall—I just want to be sure you're doing the right thing," I said gently.

Sophie thought about it for a moment. "Do we ever know that, when it comes to love? Or maybe, as long as any decision is guided by love, it's the right one. Maybe that sounds too Dr. Phil-ly, but the only answer I have for you is that I won't change my mind about marrying Kyle. And neither will he. But we do want to do it differently from the original game plan so we could invite our friends, have a barbecue, wear flowers in my hair, hire someone to officiate who doesn't wear a spandex jumpsuit . . . but that's just window dressing, Mom. I'm really, really happy, for the first time in my life."

I smiled and tried not to chuckle. "You mean all those batting titles you won count for nothing? Or discovering that your bio-mom really wanted to welcome you into her life?"

Sophie hugged me. "Okay, so maybe not the *first* time. But it's definitely way up there. Definitely above the batting titles," she grinned. "Oh—before I forget," Sophie added, rummaging through her purse, "even though we didn't go through with it, we brought you a souvenir from the chapel."

She handed me something wrapped in white sparkly tissue paper. An Elvis key chain.

I let the bit of kitsch dangle from my finger as I beheld my daughter's sparkling eyes. "Awesome!" I said quietly.

Sophie had taken to perusing wedding magazines in between innings. The location of her "destination wedding" was a toss-up between the castle in Westchester where the Ashes always took her to celebrate her birthday when she was a little girl, or the pitcher's mound in deMarley Field. She and Kyle were now alternating nights between my duplex and Kyle's cluttered bedroom at Casa Angel out in Queens.

Too bad the Cheers' relationship with the press wasn't enjoying the same coziness as Kyle and Sophie. Sammy Santiago had announced to the local sports writers that "Venus deMarley is the whore of Satan." Naturally, the hacks ran with the story of the power hitter who had begun to answer to a higher power. According to Sammy, "the Cheers' new owner has injected filth into the purity of the game of baseball. Sins of the flesh. Half-naked women shaking their booty in between innings—if I had a family of my own, I'd sooner take them to the gates of hell than to a Cheers game."

"Scantily clad babes gyrating on the sidelines, revving up the fans. God forbid, people should confuse it with football," Dusty muttered sarcastically.

"I've got a raging headache," I said, reaching for the *Daily*

News. "Do we have any old fish we can wrap with this article?"

Exchanging glances with Dusty, Sophie said grimly, "I knew we should have hidden the newspapers from her."

"So, what's he really saying, Dusty? Is he asking to be traded?"

The Cheers' manager scratched his head. "He doesn't come outright and say it, that's for sure. But one thing that's for damn certain, he's cruisin' for a bruisin', as my Uncle Pete used to say. "Kid's hitting .297, which is the highest average of any player on the team at the moment." Dusty placed his hands on my knees and leaned forward to look straight into my eyes. He asked me if I wanted to trade Santiago, said he could get Barry Weed on board with it, put some feelers out as to who might be looking for a slugger as the teams headed for postseason play. It was my choice—was I willing to overlook the kid's attitude in favor of his performance?

"What happens when his performance becomes affected by his attitude?" I asked Dusty.

"My gut says trade him for insulting my mom!" Sophie said emphatically, stirring her coffee with ferocity. "There's a guy I've been reading up on—a more than halfway decent third baseman whose contract was just dropped by the Rochester Contacts. Anyone been following Gabriel Moses's career lately?"

I was still angry with her over the Las Vegas incident. And I still had the bitter taste of the Tommy DuPree debacle. When it came to Sophie's scouting talents, why should I trust her judgment again? I looked at my daughter. "I thought his name was Moses Gabriel."

Sophie looked confused. "Now that you mention it, I'm not sure which way his name goes."

"It's Gabriel Moses," Dusty said. "I got a *pneumonic* for it: G.M. First of all, G comes before M in the alphabet, and second-

off, G.M. stands for General Manager, who in our case is Barry
Weed, and the story of Moses goes that the princess pulled him
forth from the weeds." He looked at us like he wanted a con-
gratulatory pat on the back. "So that's how I remember which
way his name goes."

"Jeez—*I'd* have trouble remembering the mnemonic," Sophie whispered to me.

⚾

Tuesday morning, in the middle of practice, Sammy walked
off the field.

"Where do you think you're going?" I asked him.

"I don't have to listen to you," he replied.

I was dumbstruck. "What?"

"I don't have to listen to you," he repeated.

"Sammy, I own the team." I crooked my finger at Dusty and
Barry Weed. "Houston, we have a problem."

"'I do not permit a woman to teach or to have authority over
a man; she must be silent.' First Epistle to Timothy."

My jaw dropped so far I got dirt on my chin.

"Well, you're going to listen to *me*," Barry Weed said tes-
tily, lighting another Winston with the butt end of the one he'd
been sucking down for the last minute and a half.

"Venus deMarley is a sinful and unnatural woman," Sammy
stated.

Dusty, trying to make light of the situation, gave my body
the once-over, and replied, "It all looks pretty natural to me."

The slugger sure wasn't shy about sharing his views—some
of which were boilerplate evangelical, and others that were
completely twisted b.s., based on some bizarre personal bias.
Sammy condemned me not only for my career as an exotic
dancer but also for having chosen to put Sophie up for adoption. At this point, Sophie couldn't restrain herself. "Would

you rather she'd had an abortion, like my bio-dad wanted her to?" she demanded rhetorically. "Wait a sec—I don't recall my mother's personal life, or mine, being any business of yours."

"The Cheers have been tempted away from redemption by the attractions of the flesh," Sammy insisted.

"Speak for yourself," Sophie argued, citing as her exhibit A, a certain right-handed ace who hadn't lost a game since they'd started dating.

Barry Weed chain-lit another cigarette. "You're all making this about something it's not really about. Sammy, the choice is simple. If you want to be a Cheer, get your ass back out on the field. If you don't, go clean out your locker."

The air was sticky with anticipation as we glanced nervously at each other, wondering which way the penny would fall. Then Sammy hurled his batting helmet at his locker. The reverberation shuddered in a domino effect along the row of metal doors. We watched in silence as he tossed his gear into a large navy blue duffel bag, and without so much as a nod or a handshake, our third baseman strode out of the locker room.

The rest of us remained rooted to the floor.

"Well, that settles that." Barry exhaled a puff of acrid smoke.

"Truth be told, I didn't think he'd do it," Dusty said, lifting his baseball cap and scratching his head.

"The show must go on, kids," I said to the managers. "We've got a game tonight against the Sound that we need to win, or *everyone* empties their lockers come 10:00 p.m. Not only that, it's Death by Chocolate night, so we're expecting a sellout." Another revenue-increasing tack I'd begun to pursue was hosting themed games. We'd had the requisite ethnic heritage nights—Latino, Jewish, Asian, Polish, Irish, Italian—and the Thousand-and-One Arabian Nights truncated into just the one, after which we were accused of anti-Islamic bias.

I discovered that fans ate up the specialty-food-themed games, too, like Burrito and Beach Bag Day, and our popular Ice-Cream Sundays. Stealing a play from other minor league teams, the Cheers also hosted home games with a community awareness theme. In particular, B.S. night—the Britney Spears Baby Safety event, where fans took home a free DVD on the proper way to strap their tot into a car seat—had been a huge success.

"So, since the show must go on, what happens in the next act, boss?" It was the first time Barry Weed had acknowledged my executive status without an astringent tinge in his voice.

I looked at Sophie. "I'll give you one more chance to prove your scouting prowess," I told her, then turned back to address my GM. "Get me Gabriel Moses," I said to Barry Weed. "By tonight."

⊘

Marty deMarley fiddled with the buttons on his raspberry-colored baseball jersey. "I feel like such a fruit in this," he muttered to no one in particular, seeing as how Linda had long stopped listening to this particular gripe. He scrutinized his image in the mirrored medicine chest, noting that since his cousin had taken full control of the Cheers, his hair had gotten quite a bit grayer. How depressing. Pink shirt, thinning hair more salt than pepper . . . he looked like a dentist who'd mistakenly wandered into a women's hair salon. "Well, by the end of the evening, we'll be able to account Venus's tenure a failure or a success." The last word in his sentence nearly choked him. He couldn't bear to imagine his cousin getting the credit for taking his beloved ramshackle team into postseason play. Sure, the Cheers had been in the toilet for the past several years. Then Venus had plunged them even deeper down the drain. But lately, things had really been looking up. The team had come gasping up for air. Marty took out his anger on the toothpaste tube, squeezing it with such ferocity that the white goo exploded into a minty-fresh snake all over the bathroom mirror.

"Are you going to keep Mommy company tonight?" Linda cooed to Rosebud, as she struggled to force the Yorkie's little limbs into a custom canine Cheers jersey, numbered with the dog's age—seventy seven.

"For God's sake, Linda, can't you leave the dog home tonight?" Marty resented how much time he spent resenting his wife's pet. It was evident to everyone that she preferred Rosebud to any human, especially to him, and he was sick of getting ribbed about it by his colleagues on the Street, and by the folks in the Cheers organization.

"It's a big night for the team—their first real do-or-die night. I need her to calm my nerves," insisted Linda, rubbing noses with Rosebud.

Observing this cozy tête-à-tête, Marty rolled his eyes. "One day I wish she'd bite yours off," he muttered. Too busy playing kissy-face with her pooch, Linda couldn't hear a word he said, but it made him feel better that he'd at least had the balls to express his thought.

Linda slipped into her Cheers jersey, a French-cut version that emphasized the gazellelike slimness of her torso. Glancing at herself in the full-length mirror, she decided that pink was her color after all. It took a few years off her age and brought a healthy glow to her cheeks. Maybe Venus *wasn't* such a bimbo.

Upon learning of Sammy Santiago's rather abrupt departure from the organization, the mood among the Cheers ranged from utter shock and disbelief to an attitude of laissez-faire to a vehement sense of good riddance. Yet no matter the re-action, the result was the same. The team seemed incapable of focusing on the task at hand—preparing for the evening's game against the Long Island Sound. And I'd never realized just how lousy our second-string infielders were until Dusty sent them out to third base. Rodolfo Rasmussen got a fleck of dirt in his eye and claimed he'd been too blinded to continue to field the ball—let alone hit it. Googie Marcantonio developed such a case of hay fever within five minutes of suiting up for practice that he needed to dope himself up with antihistamines all afternoon. By 5:00 p.m, he was passed out and snoring on a bench in the bullpen.

And Gabriel Moses was nowhere in sight.

"Where the fuck is our white knight?" Dusty paced the dug-out. He brought his hand to his eyes and looked out toward the bullpen, where Googie was still dozing. "I can't send a groggy infielder out there tonight. Especially a third-rate one. This game's too damn important. *What*?!" The manager turned around to see Barry Weed's funereal expression.

"Gabriel Moses is stuck at the airport in Rochester. There's a rain delay. No flights out until the weather pattern lifts."

"You have no idea how unhappy I am to hear this," Dusty groaned.

Sophie trotted over with the Moses jersey she'd just picked up from the garment center seamstress who'd stitched on his name. "Wassup, you guys?" Scanning our dismal faces, she added, "Hey, who died?"

"The Cheers' postseason hopes, if we don't get a third base-man within the next couple of hours." I said glumly.

"Awesome!"

"Are you on drugs, sweetie?"

Sophie looked positively beatific. "None of the players know what Gabriel Moses looks like, right? I mean, I'm guessing, here, but what they don't know won't hurt 'em, right?"

"Where are you going with this?" Barry Weed wanted to know.

"The clubhouse," Sophie responded ecstatically. "Anybody got any duct tape?"

"You do realize that we could all get our butts canned for this kind of stunt," I reminded Sophie. "It's far beyond the level of the Kyle-Lyle Angel fake-out. That wasn't much more than a prank, but this is probably actionable. If anyone finds out, we'll be fined up the ying-yang, and possibly banned for life from the great sport of baseball."

"Do we have a choice?" she replied emphatically. "Sammy's history. Rasmussen as good as placed himself on the DL after getting a speck of dirt in his eye. And Googie's in dreamland. If he wakes up in time to take the field, he'll spend the entire game blowing his nose into his glove. In addition to which, for all we know, he's so full of diphenhydromine hydrochloride, he'd probably test positive for illegal substances, in case anyone bothers to ask him for a urine sample." She said it with such authority, that it didn't occur to me to question whether diphen-whatever was banned from baseball. "Now help me with the tape."

We'd locked the door to the ladies' room. Barry and Dusty were sworn to secrecy—a no-brainer for them, since their careers were at stake. "You realize this is going to hurt when you pull it off," I reminded Sophie as I bound her breasts with the duct tape.

"It won't hurt as much as forfeiting the game because your third baseman hasn't arrived yet," she said. "*Oww*—not so tight—I can't breathe."

I was the one who shed tears when she took a utility shears to her beautiful brown hair. I remembered how I'd taken her to get a good haircut before the Clarendon Clash's Christmas party, and how delighted she'd been with the result. Now, she was hacking away at her locks. She'd have the ultimate bad hair day if I didn't take over.

"Here, let Mommy finish." I reached for the scissors.

"Your hands are shaking too much," she protested impatiently, as I sobbed between snips. I finally succeeded in giving her a stylish—though boyish—cut, and she ducked into the stall to don the uniform. I really hoped it would fit her.

"Don't forget the cup," I said.

"This thing looks like a hockey mask," she muttered. "Something Jason would wear in *Friday the 13th*." I heard her fussing with the various components of her gear. "Ta-da!" she exclaimed, emerging from the stall. "How do I look?" Standing in front of the mirror, she gave the most girly twirl I'd ever seen.

"God help me for being an accessory to fraud," I said anxiously, to which Sophie teased, "but you always tell me how important it is to accessorize!"

"Well?" she asked me.

"Oh, my baby," I said, throwing my arms around her. "I think pink is your color! Now, go out there and act like a man."

"Don't worry, Mom. I'll grab my crotch a lot."

"Spit, too. They always spit. Even when they don't seem to have anything in their mouths. Which reminds me—if I catch you shoving a chaw of tobacco into yours, I'll disown you."

"You deMarleys have a way of doing that."

"*Ouch.*"

"You deserved it," she said, giving me a playful shot in the arm.

I swatted her butt. "That's enough backtalk out of you—Gabo. And speaking of talking—don't. Try to keep your mouth shut as much as possible."

"But what about the national anthem?"

"Lip-synch it."

I hugged her tightly one more time. How strange it felt to embrace a girl tricked out to be built like a guy. "Now stay there," I cautioned, while I poked my head out of the ladies' room. "Okay! All clear!"

Sophie made a graceful exit, and headed for the dugout with a masculine swagger to her stride. As much as I adored her, I crossed my fingers and prayed to all I held holy that the real Gabriel Moses would show up before those unofficial final words of the "Star-Spangled Banner": *Play ball!*

⚾

But he didn't. Barry Weed received a follow-up phone call from the distraught and apologetic Moses at 7:04, just before the player's plane left the gate in Rochester. No way he'd make it to the stadium for the 8:00 p.m. start against the Sound.

Barry cornered Dusty and me just before the game. "We've got three options," he told us. "Figure out a way to delay the first pitch, forfeit the game, or cross our fingers and send Sophie out there."

"Number two is definitely not an option," I said. "And I'm all out of ideas for how to make option one work." Out of the corner of my eye, I could see Sophie limbering up on the sidelines, swinging two bats at once so that one of them would feel a lot lighter in her hands when she stepped up to the plate. "Do it," I told the guys. "And don't forget to call her Gabo."

Meanwhile, the fans in the stands scarfed down their complimentary chocolate-raspberry Cheers bars and swarmed the food vendors for the specialties of the night—a chocoholic's wet dream of blackout cakes and mocha shakes, mud pies, hand-dipped fruit, and chocolate-filled crepes. A local confectioner, who'd put herself on the map with themed candy molds, had supplied us with thousands of chocolate bats, balls, and mitts.

Apart from ostentatiously scratching her ass while standing on the bag at third, and adjusting her cup more times than I thought was absolutely necessary, the faux Moses began the game by acquitting herself quite admirably against the Long Island Sound, earning a high five from her teammates after drilling the ball into the gap for a base hit in the second inning. Linda deMarley mentioned how cute she thought the new player was. I couldn't help but agree with her. And if the other Cheers realized what was going on—how could they *not*, I thought, unless they were utterly self-absorbed—they played mum and dumb, which wasn't too taxing an assignment for a few of them. My heart was in my mouth every second of play, fearing we'd be outed at any moment, the consequences of which would have been far worse than all the legitimate outs the Cheers could ever have logged during a game.

And then . . . at the top of the fourth inning, Tiny Matthews, the Sound's shortstop, hit a screaming line drive toward third off Pinky Melk—straight into Sophie's glove for the out. Lunging to her right to step onto third base took care of the runner there. The man on second was in the process of madly charging for third, having assumed that Tiny's hit would go into the gap. When he saw that Sophie had the ball, he tried to apply the brakes, but stumbled instead. Sophie strode over to him before he could get to his feet, then triumphantly touched the ball to his shoulder.

The crowd was on its feet. "And Gabriel Moses turns the Cheers' first-ever unassisted triple play!" the announcer shouted into his mic. "Gabo Moses—who just joined the lineup this evening—he's so new to deMarley Field I'd bet he can't even find the men's room—yessiree, bob, Moses's magnificent defensive play may well lead his team to the promised land of the playoffs!" The fans were ecstatic. Not to mention the family.

"Oh my God! Oh my God," shouted Linda deMarley, placing Rosebud's carry bag on the cement landing in front of her seat and jumping up and down with such fervor I thought she'd break off a spiked heel. "Marty, if your uncle Augie could have seen this—he'd be dancing in the streets!" she said, grabbing her husband's arm. "Think Pink! Think Pink! Think Pink!" she began to chant, and the fans beside her took up the rally cry.

When the cheering died down, she nestled back into her seat and bent down to retrieve her beloved Yorkie. "Rose—" she said, a note of panic creeping into her voice, when she noticed that the dog had jumped out of her carry bag. "Marty—have you seen Rosebud?"

"She's where you left her," he replied, his mouth full of chocolate cake. Linda turned away in revulsion at his crumb-coated teeth.

"Excuse me!" Linda sidled into the aisle. "Excuse me, excuse me," she frantically repeated, as she tried to push her way up the stairs. "My dog got away—I have to find her. Excuse me! Excuse me!"

Barry Weed emerged from the locker room, and put his fingers in his mouth to taxi-whistle me down to the dugout. "He's here," Barry whispered in my ear. "He's suiting up right now."

"Tell him he's got a pretty big jersey to fill," I said, my eyes welling with salty tears—ever the proud mother.

Thankfully, most of the fans were still too busy rhapsodizing over the unassisted triple play, or on too much of a sugar high to notice the fourth-inning switcheroo, when the slightly disoriented, but very real, Gabriel Moses showed up in the dugout. The rest of the Cheers—good eggs, all—didn't so much as bat an eye at the substitution. With a tremendous sigh of relief, I thought, *they've made Mama Bear very, very happy.*

"I only hope he's very, very good," I mumbled to myself. It saddened me that I couldn't rush down and congratulate Sophie for such a spectacular performance, even if we hid out in the ladies' room again to share a hug and a big high five. Who knows who might overhear us; it was too risky to chance it. We'd have to save our celebration until after the game. I wished that Glenn and Joy Ashe, as clueless as all the other spectators in the stands, had been able to know about their girl's—my girl's—our girl's triumph. And it did kind of bug me that a guy who wasn't even in the stadium at the time would get the credit for a record-setting play he hadn't made. I'd have to get to poor Gabo Moses and give him the scoop, swearing him to secrecy before he was swamped by the press!

For a moment, it seemed like everyone in the stands had a comment on the game. Linda deMarley's lapdog suddenly appeared on the field, and began to slowly circle home plate. She was gnawing on something dark. Play was halted, while Linda and Dusty and I ran onto the field. Linda threw herself to the ground in hysterics, trying to pry the chocolate baseball from Rosebud's clenched jaws. "Get a vet!" she shouted. "Is there a vet in the house?!"

But it was too late. There was no joy in chocolate mud pieville when the little Yorkie, in her candy-colored Cheers jersey, curled herself into a ball and expired at the foot of the home plate umpire.

Linda pointed a perfectly manicured finger at me, and released a shriek that was undoubtedly heard all the way in Hershey, Pennsylvania. "Assassin!" Her face was the color of her shirt.

"What? What did I do?" I asked her, confused and utterly shocked that she should blame me for her dog's untimely demise.

"Your stupid, fakakta theme night! DEATH BY CHOCOLATE!" she wailed, as if her brittle heart had cracked into a thousand little pieces, each one no larger than a crumb of cookie crunch.

Under the circumstances, I decided to cancel the Seventh-Inning Strut. The mood in the stands had gone from elation to pall in less than sixty seconds. Instead, after Kate Smith's recording of "God Bless America" resounded through the stadium, the announcer called for a collective prayer for our men and women serving overseas and for the soul of the departed Rosebud, who was about to be given a public burial, in a jersey-draped footlocker that, until a few minutes earlier, had been a repository for sports equipment.

"You can't dig up the pitcher's mound!" Barry Weed had reached maximum frustration. "We have to continue the game, Linda." He pointed to the outfield. "What about out there by the fence, just under the Wall of Fame? Or the bullpen."

Linda accepted Marty's handkerchief and loudly blew her nose. "The bullpen might be okay. She always liked to do her business there."

"I remember it well," muttered Pinky Melk. He was not too pleased that his flow had been interrupted. I knew he wanted Dusty to let him pitch the entire game.

Mike Braddock, the Sound's manager, protested the entire event. "You're going to let them get away with burying a dog in the middle of the game?" he shouted to the cluster of umpires who had gathered around the ex-Yorkie. "This is a stunt—the Cheers are down by a run and they'll do anything to delay the resumption of play."

"Is *resumption* a word?" Dusty asked the home plate ump.

"Are you going to let these guys turn you into a clown?" Braddock demanded of the adjudicator. The two men were nose to nose. "Because, just between you and me, allowing a team to stop the game to inter a mutt is just about the most boneheaded decision anyone could ever make."

"One more insult out of you and the word you're going to hear is *ejected*," the ump warned Braddock.

"All we want is a pain delay," Dusty said gravely.

Braddock looked at our manager like he was an utter nutcase. "A what?"

"A pain delay. You have *rain* delays all the time, and no one gets accused of manipulating play. We want a *pain* delay." Dusty pointed to Linda who was keening over Rosebud's body like the heroine of a Greek drama. "Look at her. She's a deMarley—if only by marriage." Dusty's voice was filled with passion, his eyes rimmed with tears. "Anyways—would the sainted Augie deMarley"—and here Dusty crossed himself, "deny the public exposition of grief in his own arena, in deMarley Field? I put it to you this way. And the answer is no, of course he wouldn't. Old Augie could be a pill and a prick, but when push came to shove, as it so often did, he was a dog lover."

Barry Weed nodded in agreement.

"Is your arm getting cold?" Dusty muttered to Pinky. "Go throw on your jacket, if you want to stay in the game after this whole fiasco is sorted out."

Pinky trotted into the dugout for his rose-colored windbreaker.

The ump looked grimly from manager to manager. "Okay, Fredericks," he said finally. "Get out your shovel."

The players from both teams gathered in a corner of the bullpen, respectfully holding their caps over their hearts. I had a feeling it was the only canine burial in history attended by a guy dressed like a giant raspberry.

"This is just like when it happened my dog died, too," Spot Baldo said in broken English.

"You poor boy. What kind did you have?" Linda gently inquired.

"Like me. A Dalmatian. I am feeling sorry for you. You are a phat woman."

Linda drew back appalled. "How dare you!" She placed her hands on her zero-percent-body-fat torso. "See this? Thin—*thin*! Learn English, for Chrissakes!"

"I am learning English. Phat is something very good." He turned to Sophie, who was now wearing a flowered print dress with a straw sun hat covering her boyish haircut. "Please tell Mrs. deMarley that phat is a compliment."

"Not on my planet," Linda muttered angrily. "Maybe on yours, where people eat sausage and drink beer all day."

Sophie placed her hand on Linda's arm. "*Shh!* Shut up already! I think he's spelling phat with a p-h. In which case he's using the word correctly. And it has nothing to do with your weight."

"American slang! Wonderful!" Spot beamed. "And I am still sorry your doggie is no longer."

The P.S. 173 choir, which had performed the national anthem before the game, quickly regrouped, and under the direction of Henrietta Fiddle, their "maestress," as Sophie called the woman, favored the mourners with a soulful medley moderately appropriate to the occasion: "Swing Low, Sweet Chariot," and some song about being carried across the river, ending the set with "Sometimes I Feel Like a Motherless Child," which sent me running, red-eyed, for a box of tissues.

"Marty, you give the eulogy—I'm too upset," Linda sobbed. I handed her a Kleenex.

Marty opened his arms into a bewildered shrug. "What am I going to say? I never really liked the dog." Linda smashed him in the arm with her purse. "*Oww!*" Marty ducked when his wife took a second swing, this time at his head. "Okay, okay. Rosebud was a wonderful dog. She wore clothes beautifully— like her owner. She was high maintenance—like—" Linda's purse connected with her husband's right ear.

"All right, clearly I'm going to have to eulogize Rosebud myself." Linda took a deep breath, then burst into tears again. She was a selfish, self-absorbed woman, but I felt for her, so I went over and put my arm over her shoulder and gave her a little hug.

"You can do it," I encouraged her. "Pull yourself together— for Rosebud's sake. She would have wanted you to be brave."

"Don't you touch me!" Linda flinched as though I carried the plague. "Don't you come anywhere near me! I'll never forgive you for what you did?"

"I'm sorry that you're blaming me for Rosebud's death, Linda, but—"

"I'm not talking about Rosebud. I'm talking about Precious!"

"Precious? What's precious?" The woman had me utterly flummoxed.

"Precious is not a *what*. She was a *who*. Another Yorkie. Precious preceded Rosebud."

"Wait—what did I do to Precious?" I hadn't even realized Linda had had a string of Yorkies; I guess I figured it was all the same dog. Though I suppose that would have made Rosebud a sort of doggie Methuselah.

"What did you do to Precious?!" Linda's expression was livid. "Ohh—don't tell me you don't remember. Because I'll never forget it!"

The woman was losing her marbles and the umpire was becoming exasperated. "All right, Mrs. deMarley; you just tell Ms. deMarley what she did to Precious so we can get on with burying Rosebud." He pointed to the ground. "This one *is* Rosebud, isn't it?" He smacked the side of his head. "I can't believe I'm refereeing an argument between two women over a dead dust mop."

"That was it!" Linda shrieked. "She called Precious a dust mop!"

I shook my head in disbelief. "To be honest, Linda, I don't even remember saying that. But I'm sorry if I unwittingly offended your dog. Wh-when did I say that?"

"Thanksgiving. Fifteen years ago. We called you on the phone to wish you a happy holiday, and you said to me, 'How's your dust mop?'"

Oh, Christ. She'd despised me for years over a remark I truly didn't remember uttering?

"Will you just accept her apology so we can resume the game?" the Sound's manager demanded.

"I'm sorry, Linda. Genuinely sorry." Then I smiled. "Please forgive me so we can close the circle." I had her and she knew it.

"All right," she said finally, tired of playing Atlas holding up the world. She gave me a stiff hug. "After all, we're still family, even if we're not related."

"Now, c'mon, it's time to face the music,' I said gently. She turned around to the makeshift casket, and I rested my hands on her narrow, bony shoulders. "It's okay. I've got your back."

With massive determination, Linda began her eulogy. "Rosebud was the only person who truly understood me—"

"She wasn't a *person*," Marty muttered under his breath. "*I'm* a person. I'm your husband, for crying out loud."

Linda gave him a dirty look. "... who gave me unconditional love ..." Glaring at Marty, she added, "unlike *some* people."

Some people sure are pretty fucking nuts about their pets, I thought. If Linda had been treating Rosebud like a human being—or better—all these years, Marty, as annoying as he was, might be a candidate for martyr.

"Can we wrap this up?" Mike Braddock looked at his watch. "Aren't there rules about how long a break you can take for a seventh-inning stretch?"

The home plate ump looked over at Dusty and Barry Weed. "The man's got a point. Start digging, people. And make it quick."

"Mom, do you think I can call the rest of the game from the booth?" Sophie asked me.

"You really want to play all the parts today, don't you?" I whispered, teasing her.

"I've been practicing on my own all year. If the Cheers lose this game I'll have to wait until next season to get a shot at it. It's not like it's being broadcast over the airwaves or anything. If I totally blow, then only the fans in the ballpark will know about it, and I won't have to go home and slit my wrists."

"That's not remotely funny. Give me until the funeral's over to think about it."

Rosebud was interred without further fanfare. I figured Sophie deserved a reward for her unassisted triple play, so I escorted her up to the booth and had a word with Biff Buck, the Cheers' announcer. Biff seated Sophie, slid the mic in front of her, and the game resumed.

Our bats weren't as strong as they'd been recently, but then again, our best hitter had walked off the team. All we needed was to hold the Sound where they were and score two more runs to win the game. Easier said than done, however. In the bottom of the seventh, Anton Anton led off with a solo home run to tie the score, but then the Sound's reliever struck out the side in order.

In the bottom of the eighth, he loaded the bases with two Cheers out. My gut seized up. I yearned to be accounted at least partially responsible for taking this Little Engine That Could into the playoffs and for turning a profit for the first time in years. It had been a remarkable journey of self-discovery—that I could be the daughter my father had always wanted me to be, and the mother I never knew I could, yet remain true to who I really was.

"Coming to bat now is Cheers' second baseman Shoji Suzuki," Sophie announced. He'd only been hitting .220—not exactly stellar. In fact I was concerned he might commit seppuku over his somewhat pitiful performance at the plate lately.

"And the first pitch is ball one," Sophie said, followed moments later by "that's not a déjà vu, fans, that's ball two. And Shoji is ahead of the count. What do you say, Biff? It's pretty exciting up here, huh? Sorry, folks, Biff can't answer me. He's too busy scarfing down a sundae."

It was the first time I'd ever heard her call a game that wasn't an assignment for her broadcasting classes. Sophie's poise and polish behind the mic impressed the hell out of me. There wasn't a trace of nerves in her voice. In fact, she sounded like she and Biff had been calling games together for years.

Shoji swung at, and spectacularly missed, the next pitch for strike one. His wrists broke the invisible plane on the one after that for strike two, as Shoji tried to check his swing. The reliever's next pitch was way high. Perhaps his arm was tiring.

"Ball three," Sophie called. "And Shoji's facing a full count."

We held our breath. I grabbed Dusty's hand and squeezed

it. The reliever wound up, and with a high leg kick, released the ball. Shoji swung, making contact.

"Unfortunately for the Cheers, it looks like it's gonna be an easy line drive to first base," Sophie said, followed immediately by an excited "Ohmigod!" as Shoji took off for first, running at full tilt. "You guys, this is totally awesome!"

The fans were on their feet, shouting themselves hoarse.

And then—the ball, which should have been scooped up by the Sound's first baseman, rolled between his legs when he stooped to grab it! Jicama Flores, who'd gotten a good jump from third, poured on the speed, and headed for home, beating the tag by a millisecond.

Sophie called the play with such breathlessness that I was afraid she'd hyperventilate. "And the Cheers score the go-ahead run! The Cheers score the go-ahead run!"

I threw my arms around Dusty's neck and planted a huge kiss on his lips. The players were so revved up, they didn't even notice. The stands practically shook with excitement. No one sat down until the eighth inning was over, after Pinky's bunt was easily fielded and flipped to first base.

My heart thumped wildly as I joined the fans in chanting "Where's the Beef?!"

"You've got to bring in Wayne to pitch the ninth," I said to Dusty. "Pinky's tired. And did you see his face when he failed to move the runner over? I thought he was going to cry."

"Let's see what Cheers manager Dusty Fredericks does now," Sophie said. "Pinky Melk has turned in an awesome performance this evening, but he looked like his arm was flagging a bit during the last inning, and their closer Wayne de-Boeuf—the Beef—has posted an awesome record this season in just such do-or-die situations."

Okay, so she needed to work on her *awesomes*.

Dusty gave the nod to his pitching coach, who jogged out to

the bullpen and gave the thumbs-up to Wayne deBoeuf.

Waving at the crowd, Wayne trotted onto the field, barefoot as usual. I noticed he'd painted his toenails a deep shade of pink. Cheers pink.

No one sat down for the entire top of the ninth. The fans turned their caps backward, rally-style, and shouted, "Eat Beef! Eat Beef!" at the opposing players.

To our utter delight, the Beef notched the performance of his career. In a one-two-three inning, he struck out the demoralized Sound. There'd be no bottom of the ninth; the Cheers, with their one-run lead, had won the game.

Sophie screamed into the mic: "Oh God—oh my God—Mom! This is so awesome! I love you, Mom! We did it! You did it—I mean the Cheers did it! The Cheers have beaten the Long Island Sound, 4 to 3, to clinch the wild-card berth in the Atlantic Coast League playoffs!"

"Oh my God, we did it! We did it!" I kissed Dusty passionately as he enveloped me in a bear hug, giving my butt an affectionate squeeze. I hoped no one noticed. I turned around to wave to Sophie; she was being smothered with kisses by Kyle Angel, who had somehow materialized on high. I could have sworn I'd just seen him celebrating on the field with the other players. Oh dear—where was Lyle? Above the roar of the crowd, you could hear smoochy noises over the hot mic.

The clubhouse emptied as we all ran onto the field, throwing our caps in the air. The players piled onto the Beef—a giant Cheers hero.

I took the opportunity to nab Gabriel Moses, coaching him to just act modest when responding to questions about "his" spectacular play. "And when they ask you how it felt—"

"I'll tell them it went by in such a blur, I can't even remember," he interrupted. "I'm just happy to help the team in any way I can," he added, as if regurgitating a rote memorization that might as well have come from the *Bull Durham* screen-play.

"Don't worry ma'am," said our new third baseman. "I won't blow it for you. As long as no one bothers to check the airline's passenger list." Gabo winked at me and touched his cap.

I hoped to God I could trust him.

"Biff, I have to go down and congratulate my mom and stuff," Sophie said over the loudspeaker. She and Kyle left the booth and leaped the cement steps, two by two, down to the staircase that led to the field.

"What a night!" I exclaimed.

Sophie gave me a hug and then dragged me halfway out to first base where no one could overhear us. "Isn't this awesome?! I only wish I could tell people about the—you know."

"The what?" I said, pretending not to get it.

"The—*you* know. *The unassisted triple play*," she hissed into my ear.

"What unassisted triple play? The one Gabo Moses made in the fourth?"

"I'm so totally bummed that I'll never be able to own up to it. Can't we just tell *someone*?"

I shook my head. "But you know. And I know. And Dusty knows. Barry knows. And I'm sure most of the team, at least those who didn't have their heads up their butts this evening, knows it as well. So in the grand scheme of things, does it really matter if the whole world knows it was you? Because that wasn't why you did it in the first place. We both know that you didn't do it for the glory—you just made the play because your head and your heart were in the moment, and in the game."

"Heads up, ladies!" shouted Dusty. Sophie and I turned back to see a phalanx of photographers and sports writers charging toward us. "Okay, kiddo," I smiled, between gritted teeth. "Time to keep a secret."

"I've been known to do that," Sophie grinned.

We jogged a few feet toward the clubhouse before we were mobbed.

"Olivia deMarley—your Cheers have made the playoffs for the first time in the team's history. You must be quite excited."

"That's kind of an understatement," I told the reporter. "And it was a team effort. The players and the management—every member of the Cheers family—should all be very pleased with their contributions this year."

Another reporter, a local TV guy, shouted my name, and when I glanced in his direction, he fired off his question. "It's been quite a season for the Cheers—from the stripper-style workouts to the team's, shall we say, *revamped* look to the somewhat unexpected departures of Tommy DuPree and Sammy Santiago to this evening's fireworks—that spectacular unassisted triple play by the newest Cheer, Gabriel Moses. And now you've taken the team where your father never did. Do you think your dad would have been proud of you, Ms. deMarley? Or, if he were with us today, do you think he'd be a bit envious of your, shall we say, *surprising* success?"

Sophie rolled her eyes, as though she'd never heard a stupider question, but she answered the reporter before I could open my mouth. "You must be kidding her, right?" she said. "Old Augie is up there dancing to 'We Will Rock You' right now. Leaving the Cheers to my Mom was the best decision of his death. But if he weren't doing the heavenly hornpipe, I bet he wouldn't be the only one feeling a little Venus envy at the moment. You're not going to bleep that, are you?"

"It's been quite a journey—on several roads," I said, glancing at Sophie and trying to keep a straight face in light of her remark. After all, this was a serious interview. "I gained a struggling ball club and a grown daughter in the same year, and I can't say which has been more of a handful sometimes.

If you're going to put that in print, make sure you write that I winked at you when I said it. It's all been a wonderful hay-ride, and this isn't the end—we're barely out of the barn. I look forward to trouncing the Jersey Jerseys in the playoffs next week at least as much as I look forward to being a grand-mother."

Sophie turned to me, utterly shocked, a crimson flush creeping into her cheeks. "How did you know?!" she gasped.

"I didn't. You just told me." I lowered my voice and cupped my hand over her ear. "I was speaking to the press in the abstract, figuring that since you'd considered a quickie marriage, you might want kids. Sooner rather than later, actually," I whispered.

Then the delayed reaction hit with all the force of a grand slam. "Oh my God—you are?! _Pregnant?_ Oh, Sophie! Excuse me folks—can you give us a moment alone?"

I put my arm around my daughter's shoulder and we trotted out to the pitcher's mound. "I can't believe I didn't ask you—after you and Kyle returned from Las Vegas—if you were pregnant, I mean. But then you'd told me you knew what you were doing when I asked you about using birth control, so I assumed that meant you _were._ Using it, I mean."

"I've always wanted to be a mom; and I think Kyle will make an awesome dad—don't you? If she's a girl, Kyle agreed we'd name her after you," Sophie said, beaming.

I threw my arms around her. "Oh, congratulations, my baby!" I patted Sophie's flat belly. "And my baby's baby," I blubbered. Funny, how we'd both ended up, at more or less the same age, pregnant by a baseball player, even skipping town for Las Vegas—yet how different our situations were. Sophie was planning to marry and get settled down, sort of—there was still the matter of renting their own apartment—and knew what she wanted out of life. She had a lot of rudders to guide her: Glenn and Joy, me, even Dusty. I'd been a tillerless mess with long legs and half a business degree.

"Here, Mom," Sophie said, handing me a tissue she'd fished from the pocket of her dress. Your mascara's running and you'll be totally homicidal if they take a picture of you that way."

"You'll have to be my mirror," I told her.

"Then let me do it." Sophie moistened a corner of the tissue with a bit of spit and gently wiped my face. It was then that I knew she'd sail smoothly into motherhood. Sophie was a natural.

Arm in arm we strolled back toward the knot of reporters.

The following day, the story was all over the papers about the Cheers' wild-card victory, and their plans for the playoff games. The headline on the back page of the *Daily News*'s sports section read BERTH OF VENUS.

They were right in more ways than one.

And as Sophie would say, "It's all good."

A+

AUTHOR
INSIGHTS,
EXTRAS, &
MORE...

FROM
**LESLIE
CARROLL**
AND
AVON A

Extra Innings

One Week Later . . .

The playoffs! It all didn't seem real, somehow. And in the precious little time we had before we were due to face off against the Jersey Jerseys' hot bats, I couldn't seem to get my head in the game. I knew that several things weren't working for me anymore; it was time to change the lineup—the lineup of my life, that is—the Cheers' batting order would remain the same.

I'd been doing some serious soul searching, and I needed to talk to Dusty. I wanted to talk to Barry Weed, too, but that was a different conversation—one that would have to wait until the playoffs were over.

But Dusty found me before I got to him. We hadn't slept together since that night at my apartment when we were waiting for Sophie to return from her *non*elopement. I discovered I was glad we hadn't. And why I felt that way. I owed it to him to share my feelings.

He stuck his head in the door of the GM's office, where I was seated at Barry's computer, working on a press release. "You wanna go for a coffee?"

"Sure," I nodded.

We strolled side by side through the Bronx neighborhood, with its homey suburban feel; companionable, modest houses; tidy, postage-stamp lawns; a few Christmas decorations left up for so long that the season was about to roll around again in a couple of months. We found a quiet sunlit diner and slipped into a corner booth. They weren't doing much business at that hour; perfect for a heavy conversation. For a while, we each stared out the window. My brain flashed on a long-buried memory: I'd lost my virginity to a lifeguard . . . lots of fumbling in his sleeping bag on the beach . . . and as soon as we had gotten dressed and headed to a local diner for a midnight snack, he broke up with me.

Diners are for dumping, I thought ruefully. I wasn't sure which was harder: being the dumper or the dumpee.

"Think they'll ever finish that construction?" Dusty said. "Rosa used to say to me 'Dusty, you and I will be pushing up the daisies and they'll still be laying that sewer pipe.'" Embarrassed, he looked at his menu and mumbled, "That's what she used to say." He glanced up at me, uncomfortable. "I still think about her all the time, Venus. I guess what I wanted to tell you is that I think you're just about one of the greatest gals in the world, but I'm not ready to move on. I'm still broken in here." He touched his heart with his fist. "We had a lotta years together, and she's still deep inside me. It can't be easy for you that I'm bringing up Rosita right and left, like she's still around, almost."

Though we'd given it a shot, romantically, we were not a good fit, Dusty and I. I knew that. As friends, as buddies, as confidants off the field and colleagues on it—that worked like gangbusters. He'd just given me an out. Very graceful of him. Very gentlemanly.

"You're right. And it's okay. We've both got ghosts," I told him. "A while back I got a letter from Tom, my ex-fiancé, telling me he'd met someone new. And after I ran to the bathroom to throw up, I realized there was my 'permission' to move on, too—and I wanted to. I didn't want to continue to grieve over our busted engagement, wondering whether we'd ever get back together and how long I should hold out hope instead of getting on with my life. I wanted to find something new with someone special, too." I reached for Dusty's hand. "And you are special. But I guess we just met at the wrong time. For each of us."

Outside, the sidewalk began to rumble. I looked out the window at the jackhammers and listened to the din for a couple of moments. "Tom e-mailed me a couple of days ago. He and Mary-Anne didn't work out." I picked at the edge of the menu. "I really want to go back to Colorado to be with him—if it's possible. If he's willing to give our engagement a second chance. I . . . I don't want to spend the rest of my life without him in it," I added, trying to poke a tear back into the corner of my eye. "I made a choice last year—Tom or Sophie. God knows I haven't regretted the decision to get to know her—I couldn't be prouder of her, even though I question her judgment sometimes. But I feel like one of those heroes in a western: my work here is done. Sophie and I have connected, bonded—whatever—and she's about to embark on a life, and a marriage, of her own now." I didn't mention her pregnancy. Sophie and I are a bit superstitious about it. We both thought it would be a good idea to keep it under wraps until she starts to show and we know the fetus is healthy.

"I've satisfied old Augie, too," I said to Dusty. "And I've done something with his team that Dad never did himself: the Cheers made it to the playoffs. I don't need to be a micromanaging owner when I have the best manager in the minor leagues on my payroll."

"*Awww,* shucks. *Now* you're gonna make a grown man cry." Dusty reached into his pants pocket for a hanky.

"I . . . um . . . I've got some ideas . . . I just need a little time to work through them. Your job is safe, by the way. More than safe. The team—and I—we couldn't have gotten to the postseason without you."

Dusty wanted to know whether I'd shared my feelings with Tom. What happened after I received the message from my MaryAnne-less ex? Had I written to him? Called him?

"I wanted to be on the first plane out west, but we were in the middle of the wild-card battle, and, to tell you the truth, I didn't know at that point whether you and I had a future . . . and I didn't want to do anything to mess that up. You see, in the past, I've never loved more than one man at a time. And the more I thought about it, the more I began to realize that I love each of you in very different ways. I did tell Tom I wanted to see him." I chuckled at my own cowardice. "Dusty, I'm scared shitless. I have this awful vision of myself crawling back to him and finding out that maybe he wants nothing to do with me anymore. Or fantasies of surprising him by flying out there only to find he's not home: gone skiing. Or worse—that there's a new woman there. Tom's the kind of guy who needs to be with someone. It's another thing we have in common. We were good that way. "Oh, Christ—I've missed him!"

I wiped away tears with the back of my hand. It was a funny conversation to have with Dusty, who'd so recently been my lover. But there was something about my relationship with *him* that made me feel safe enough to say anything. Maybe we were meant to be pals above all else. And the way he still felt about Rosa—I knew somehow, though it might be a teensy bit awkward or weird for a moment or so between us, that he would understand what I'd just said about Tom.

"You want me to talk to him for you? 'Cause I'll tell him what an amazing woman he let slip through his fingers. He's not gonna find another one like you, Venus, whether it's in Colorado or New York or Timbuktu." He scratched his head. "Is there still a Timbuktu, or is it one of the places that changed its name?"

I shrugged my shoulders. "I don't know. About Timbuktu or Tom. But I do want to see him. Want to marry him."

Dusty took out his cell phone and laid it on the paper placemat, in the center of a drawing demonstrating the proper way to eat a lobster. "Call him."

"Now? Here?"

"'Strike while the iron's still hot,' Rosa used to say."

It would be morning still, in Colorado. Tom was probably at the factory. Or checking up on some of the local emporia that retailed Elliott and Sons ski equipment. The new season was just around the corner. I took the phone outside.

"Hey, can you hold it for a few minutes? I gotta make an important phone call!" I said to one of the construction workers, adopting my best Bronx accent.

"What?" The guy looked me over—my height, my hair, my legs, my waistline, my boobs—then turned off the jackhammer. "You got a lot of guts, lady. What could be so important you got to interrupt an employee of the city of New York in his daily course of duty?"

"I hear you guys have been putting in these new pipes for years. Five more minutes won't kill you. I'm going to call my ex-fiancé and tell him I think we should ex the ex part."

"Hey!" The construction worker shouted to his buddies. "Pipe down for a sec! We gotta romance goin' on here!" He bowed to me, and I burst out laughing. "You go ahead, girl. Make that call."

My fingers didn't seem to want to work. It took me three tries before I got the number dialed correctly. I called Tom's cell, since I figured he'd answer it no matter where he was.

"Hello?" He sounded confused. "Who is this?"

I hadn't said anything yet. But I realized Dusty's phone number probably came up on Tom's screen as an "unlisted" or "unknown" number.

"Don't hang up, Tom!" I shouted. It wasn't a very good connection. It sounded like there was a thresher or something in the background on his end.

"Ollie?"

"Yes! Tom . . ." Oh God, I had no idea how to handle this conversation. My heart was pounding as madly as the jackhammers that had just stopped for True Love.

"Is everything okay?" he asked me through the static.

"I th-think so," I stammered. "I mean I hope so. Tom . . . I've missed the hell out of you. Oh, fuck, I may have been a dancer but I don't know how to dance around this. Tom, I want to marry you. I'll sublet the duplex to Sophie—she's getting married any day now and has no place to live. The mortgage is paid off; she and Kyle will just have to pay the monthly common charges and the real estate taxes . . . maybe you'll fly east just for the wedding, and we can go home together. Home—your home, I mean. I mean, now that there's no MaryAnne. Oh God, there's no Mary-Sue or MaryEllen or MarySomeone else—is there? Mary Me—I mean, *marry* me, Tom. Please. I feel like such an idiot," I added, as I started to cry. "I've never begged for anything in my life."

"You're kind of adorable when you beg, you know." I could hear the smile in Tom's voice, and felt the sense of relief that began in my throat shimmy through my body all the way down to my Fire and Ice–tinted toenails.

"At the risk of sounding corny—"

"*Aw,* go on. Be corny!" I couldn't seem to catch my breath.

"At the risk of sounding like a Hallmark card, I realized that it wasn't going to work with anyone else. You're it, Ollie. I'm not meant to be with the safe MaryAnyones of this world. I'm meant to wed a wild, impetuous woman named Venus. Being married to you will be like snaking through the giant moguls on Devil's Crotch—but that's what I live for."

I burst out laughing so hard I started to cry. "Great! You've just compared me to Devil's Crotch. I'm not quite sure what to make of that."

"*Umm* . . . take it as a compliment. So—yes—let's make this work. I want to, too." Tom waited for my response, but the words wouldn't come. Pretty embarrassing, actually, to be standing in the middle of City Island Avenue on an impossibly sunny day, sobbing so hard I was shaking. "Rats, I can't hear a thing. Ollie, what's that noise?"

"Jackhammers. I could only stop the flow of the New York City sewer system for so long before the civil servants decided to get back to business." I looked down at my naked ring finger. "Ohhh, Tom, I've missed your face, your hair, your scent, your belly scar—your coffee." I missed several other things about him, but shouting them through the phone, especially with a half dozen construction workers watching me, was probably unwise.

"You can be pretty stubborn about what you want, you know."

"So can you," I reminded him. "You might even win the Inflexibility Prize."

We agreed to speak again later in the day. I'm sure the tall redhead practically skipping back into the diner was a pretty amusing sight to the passersby. My heart felt as light as cotton candy.

"I'll just have a salad," I said to Dusty, as I slid into the red pleather banquette. "I have to watch my weight . . . since it looks like I'll be getting married."

"Atta girl!" he exclaimed, leaning over the table to kiss my cheek. "And I hope the two of you are as happy as Rosa and I were." He thought about it for a moment, and frowning, added, "Well . . . maybe not."

Once again, we were gathered in Cap Gaines's office. Barry Weed, Dusty, Sophie, and I. It felt like "old home week."

The Cheers got hammered by the Jersey Jerseys, our pennant hopes dashed.

Sophie took it in stride. "Wait'll next year!" she said confidently. "Our pitching staff is deep—we just need to find a few more sluggers, guys who act like they want to play the game and put their bats where their mouths are. There are actually a couple of kids coming out of Clarendon I want to talk to you about. Good fielders, too. Guys we should keep an eye on."

Barry drummed his fingers on his leather portfolio. He was going nuts without a cigarette. "I'll make a note of it. Just give me their names, Soph."

"Don't bother, Barry," I said. "Sophie, I have a wedding present for you." She looked at me quizzically. "Barry, I'm relieving you of your position. As of today, I'm naming Sophie Ashe the new GM of the Bronx Cheers."

Each of them—Barry and Sophie—looked absolutely gobsmacked.

"You can't fire me!"

"I'm afraid she can," Cap replied smoothly.

"You really trust me that much, Mom? I thought you hated my judgment."

"Everyone's allowed to make a few errors. Just not enough to make the team a loser," I said, looking at Barry Weed. "You came through on Gabriel Moses, Soph. And I'm willing to give you the benefit of the doubt. We'll try it this way for a year and see how it goes. You've got a good eye, astute business acumen, and you love the game."

"You've got heart," Dusty said. "And you gotta have *heart* to be in this game."

"*I* have heart!" Barry said insistently. "I have *plenty* of heart!"

"We need to shake things up in the front office, Barry. It was time for me to get a new broom. Enough with the status quo: it wasn't working."

"But we made it to the playoffs, Olivia!"

"In spite of you," I replied.

"Aren't you going to fire Dusty, then?"

"No," I said, smiling at the manager. "Because the players love him."

"They love me, too!"

"Not," Sophie said.

"Dusty, I'm making you a sort of regent, to consult with and advise Sophie. I'm not nuts enough to think she can go it alone at her age and with her limited experience. But I'm confident that the two of you will bring home the championship trophy next season."

I glanced at my watch and looked around the room. I felt bad for Barry Weed, but not bad enough to give him his job back. Some owner I'd be if I kept clinging to the driftwood, expecting it to keep us afloat indefinitely. "Forgive me for cutting to the chase, people. I've got a plane to catch this afternoon." It was fun to say that, a smart, curt, businesslike remark, even though I felt all warm and gooey and maternal inside.

Sophie jumped up and threw her arms around me. "You are the coolest! I swear I'll make you proud, Mom! Can I call Glenn when I need to?"

"Bring in whatever guns you need to do the job, kiddo." I started to cry. In the moment, I just couldn't manage to sound tough or corporate. "Oh God, is this what it feels like when you know you're going to be a grandma?" I whispered, as my tears moistened Sophie's neck.

Sophie hugged me hard. "I don't know, Mom. Ask me in twenty years."

"Twenty years. Yeah." A sniffle morphed into a chuckle. "That sounds like the right timetable for the women in our family."

Cap Gaines rose and shook Sophie's hand. "You've got a pretty big pair of shoes to fill, young lady. Barry wears an eleven and a half."

"I'm up for the challenge, sir!" she told the lawyer; and looking at me, added, "I might even try it in heels!"

⑦

I secured my tray table and pushed my seat back, stretching my legs as far as they'd go, which meant bumping my toes up against the stowed hand luggage of the passenger in front of me. Outside the window, a spectacularly cinematic vista—spacious skies of Della Robbia blue, amber waves of grain, and the purple mountains' majesty fast on the horizon—filled my soul with hope and happiness. *Here I am, riding—well,* flying—*off into the sunset,* I thought, as my smile broadened into a mile-wide grin. I wanted to get up and dance, but the seat-belt light was illuminated. It *was* "all good," though. Time to press on. To Breckenridge. To Tom. To marriage; a new world to conquer. For Venus deMarley, the final frontier.

Author's Note

In my research for *Choosing Sophie,* I came across a plethora of information on what's called the "adoption triad" of birth mothers (or birth parents), adoptees, and adoptive parents. I tried to get the dynamics right and still remain true to the lighthearted spirit of the novel and its plot. *Choosing Sophie* is not, per se, a book about adoption, but it explores the theme of what the concept of "family" or even the word itself means to different people, and in different circumstances.

Acknowledgments

I owe a tremendous debt of gratitude to MZR—astute mentor, dear friend, and baseball aficionado—who *did* take me out to the ball game multiple times over the years, bought me Cracker Jack, ate my peanuts, and always picked up the phone to answer my baseball questions as I worked on CHOOSING SOPHIE.

Thanks to my two all-stars: my fabulous editor Lucia Macro and agent Irene Goodman for encouraging me to indulge my passion for the game on paper; a fastball down the middle of the plate to Gail Matos, fellow Mets and Cyclones fan, who cheered for me every page of the way; and a walk-off home run to my California Angel of a husband Scott, who brought me to beautiful Breckenridge (even if it was forty-seven degrees in late July) to show me a double rainbow.

Leslie Carroll

Native New Yorker **LESLIE CARROLL** is a multi-published novelist of contemporary women's fiction, and the author of several works of historical fiction under the pen name Amanda Elyot. She is a professional actress as well as a novelist. On stage she has played classical and contemporary virgins, vixens, and villainesses, has appeared in short films, daytime dramas, commercials, voiceovers, and talking books.

1/08 ✓
13.95